Critical Acclaim for Leigh Russell

'A million readers can't be wrong! Clear some time in your day, sit back and enjoy a bloody good read'
– **Howard Linskey**

'Taut and compelling' – **Peter James**

'Leigh Russell is one to watch' – **Lee Child**

'A brilliant talent in the thriller field' – **Jeffery Deaver**

'Brilliant and chilling, Leigh Russell delivers a cracker of a read!' – **Martina Cole**

'Leigh Russell has become one of the most impressively dependable purveyors of the English police procedural'
– ***Times***

'DI Geraldine Steel is one of the most authoritative female coppers in a crowded field' – ***Financial Times***

'The latest police procedural from prolific novelist Leigh Russell is as good and gripping as anything she has published' – ***Times & Sunday Times Crime Club***

'Another corker of a book from Leigh Russell... Russell's talent for writing top-quality crime fiction just keeps on growing...' – ***Euro Crime***

'Good, old-fashioned, heart-hammering police thriller... a no-frills delivery of pure excitement' – ***SAGA Magazine***

'A gritty and totally addictive novel'
Journal of Books

Also by Leigh Russell

Poppy Mystery Tales
Barking Up the Right Tree
Barking Mad

Geraldine Steel Mysteries
Cut Short
Road Closed
Dead End
Death Bed
Stop Dead
Fatal Act
Killer Plan
Murder Ring
Deadly Alibi
Class Murder
Death Rope
Rogue Killer
Deathly Affair
Deadly Revenge
Evil Impulse
Deep Cover
Guilt Edged
Fake Alibi
Final Term
Without Trace

Ian Peterson Murder Investigations
Cold Sacrifice
Race to Death
Blood Axe

Lucy Hall Mysteries
Journey to Death
Girl in Danger
The Wrong Suspect

The Adulterer's Wife
Suspicion

LEIGH RUSSELL

A POPPY MYSTERY TALE

First published in 2023 by
The Crime & Mystery Club Ltd.,
Harpenden, UK

crimeandmysteryclub.co.uk
@CrimeMystClub

A CIP catalogue record for this book is available from the British Library.

ISBN
978-0-85730-568-8 (Paperback)
978-0-85730-569-5 (eBook)

2 4 6 8 10 9 7 5 3 1

Typeset in 11.1 on 14.5pt Sabon
by Avocet Typeset, Bideford, Devon, EX39 2BP
Printed and bound in Great Britain by Clays Ltd, Elcograf S.p.A.

This story is for Poppy.

It is also dedicated to
Michael, Jo, Phillipa, Phil, Rian and Kezia.

1

We were out on our first walk of the day. Poppy trotted along beside me, pausing to sniff the air. It was chilly, but the worst of the cold weather was behind us and everywhere I looked there were signs of spring. The grass that led down towards the river was sparkling with dew. Dotted with daisies and a few wild crocuses that showed purple and yellow against the greensward, it was bordered by bright daffodils that quivered in a slight breeze. From time to time, Poppy launched an attack on some creature invisible to me, or stopped and began digging furiously in the ground. When that happened, I had to pull on her lead, calling to her to walk on; she could be very single-minded when burrowing for worms and beetles. She was so keen to dig up earth that it seemed unkind to thwart her instincts altogether and, as a consequence, she was allowed to dig holes in the grass in my back garden, where it couldn't affect anyone else. My garden was a mess, but Poppy always seemed happy when the white fur around her shiny black nose was speckled with mud.

Returning home from our early morning walk, I saw a removal van turning off the main road some way ahead of us. Even from a distance, its destination was clear. There were only two houses in the lane where I had been living since inheriting a cottage in the picturesque village of Ashton Mead. Still only in my mid-twenties, and on a relatively low income, there was no way I would have been able to put down a deposit on a home of my own. I had been fortunate enough to inherit my beautiful cottage. Yet my ownership of Rosecroft had not been straightforward, but contingent on my taking care of my great aunt's pet. To begin with, I had experienced serious reservations about accepting the bequest, never having owned a dog before. But it hadn't taken Poppy long to convince me that she was exactly what I needed in my life. So the decision to move to the village of Ashton Mead was effectively made for me, by a small brown and white puppy who stole my heart.

Poppy was a Jack Tzu puppy, a cross between a Jack Russell Terrier and a Shih Tzu. Playful and mischievous, she proved to be far more intelligent than I would have believed possible. As well as being clever, she was adorable. Her fur was soft and white, with brown patches on her back, and she had bright black eyes to match her shiny black nose. Sometimes she gazed at me quizzically, her head tilted to one side, as though she was trying to figure out what I was talking about, and it was uncanny how well she seemed to understand everything I said. We had been together now for less than a year, yet I could hardly remember a time before Poppy came to live with me, and I had become as devoted to my unlooked-for companion as she was to me.

Walking along the lane, I watched as a couple of men in blue overalls climbed out of the van, which had pulled up outside my next-door neighbour's house. Laurel Cottage had stood empty over the winter. From time to time I had seen cars draw up, with potential purchasers arriving to view the property, but not until recently had the 'For Sale' notice finally been taken down. It had probably only been a matter of time before someone bought the house, which was on at below the market price, for a quick sale. Even so, I was pleased, and also a little anxious, on seeing it had been sold. I hoped the new owners would be friendly. As a young woman living on her own, thoughts for my own safety flashed through my mind. Rosecroft was located in a quiet lane on the outskirts of Ashton Mead, with only one other property nearby and that stood between my cottage and the road into the village.

I led Poppy across the road, so she wouldn't pester the removal men for attention. Walking on the opposite side of the lane also afforded me a clearer view of what was being taken from the van, but all I managed to see was a wooden table and several chairs moving in next door. With the only other house in Mill Lane unoccupied over the winter, I had been feeling rather isolated, even though I had friends in the village and Ashton Mead had a reputation as a safe place to live, with a very low crime rate, despite there being no permanent police presence. Of course, I had my dog for protection as well as for company. Admittedly, Poppy was more likely to pester strangers to play with her than to attack them, but she had a loud bark for such a small dog, which was likely to scare intruders away. Nevertheless, overall I was pleased that I would no longer be alone in Mill Lane, and hoped to make friends with my new neighbours.

When I left for work the following morning, there was no sign of the people who had moved in next door. They were probably inside familiarising themselves with their new home, or else still on the way to their new house. Wondering who they were, and what they were like, I made my way to the end of the lane and along to the High Street. Poppy trotted happily beside me, stopping every now and then to sniff at a hedge or a lamp post, and pee on it. We passed the grocery store and the owner waved at me as

I went by. I had learned to be circumspect when talking to Maud, who was well-meaning but an inveterate gossip. She was a diminutive woman, with thick grey hair that dwarfed her narrow face. I paused briefly to quiz her about the new residents in the lane.

'What have you heard about them?' I enquired.

Maud prided herself on her detailed knowledge of everyone living in Ashton Mead, and was the main source of gossip in the village. But she knew nothing about my new next-door neighbours, a fact that appeared to gall her even more than it disappointed me. Having promised to share anything I learned about the newcomers with Maud, who was clearly frantic for information, Poppy and I continued on our way. By the time we arrived at the Sunshine Tea Shoppe where I worked, my friend Hannah was already opening up. She owned the café, where she worked in the kitchen, preparing breakfasts and baking all day. Thanks to her skill in the kitchen, the tea shop was popular, and we were kept busy, especially during the summer months when people stopped off as they passed through the village. While it had never been my dream to work as a waitress, I had been pleased to accept the job as a temporary measure when I first arrived in Ashton Mead. That was nearly a year ago, and I was still working in the café. Hannah and I had quickly become firm friends, and besides, the job suited Poppy. Hannah's mother, Jane, was happy to look after her during the day, and when she wasn't available, I was able to leave Poppy in the yard at the back of the tea shop where she could be safely left to wander around a fenced-in grassy plot covered by an old awning.

'Where else will you find a job with a safe outside space for her?' Hannah had asked me.

On my return from work that afternoon, instead of the removal men and their van, I saw a small red Citroën parked on the drive next door. With some trepidation, I approached the front door, clutching a small camellia bush in a blue and white ceramic pot. Feeling slightly nervous, I told Poppy to sit quietly and behave herself. We wanted to create a positive first impression. She lowered herself to the ground and lay there submissively, watching me keenly. Satisfied that she was settled, I rang the bell. The door was opened by a short rotund man with fluffy white hair who looked at me with inquisitive dark eyes that reminded me of my little dog. I knew that wasn't a sensible reason to trust him, but he had a warm smile. Not only that, but Poppy wagged her tail when she saw him. In the year I had known her, time and again she had proved herself to be a good judge of character.

'I live next door and wanted to say hello,' I gabbled, thrusting the plant towards him with what I hoped was a friendly smile.

The man's round face creased in an answering smile. 'Is that a gift for us?'

'Oh yes, yes,' I stammered, still holding out the camellia.

He took it and thanked me, introducing himself as Richard. 'And who is this?' he went on, turning to Poppy. 'Hello. Are we going to be friends as well as neighbours? As long as you don't bark all night then I'm sure we'll get along just fine.'

'She doesn't bark much,' I hastened to assure him, already liking him.

'What's her name?' he asked, seemingly more interested in my dog than in me, which I took as a very positive sign.

He crouched down and held his hand out for Poppy to sniff, before patting the top of her head. At once Poppy rolled over onto her back in a submissive gesture, allowing him to stroke her belly.

'She likes you,' I said. There was no need to add that she was equally friendly to just about everyone she met.

'She's a cutie all right,' Richard said. 'What kind of dog is she?'

'She's a Jack Tzu, a cross between a Jack Russell terrier and a Shih Tzu.'

'We talked about getting a dog,' he said wistfully. 'That is, I've always wanted one, but my wife was never keen. She thought it wouldn't be fair, what with us living in the city, and being out at work all day. But living here, it makes a lot more sense.'

We chatted for a few minutes about the benefits of owning a dog, before moving on to talk about life in the village. Although limited in scope, I told him the shops in the High Street offered almost every daily necessity, and the food in the pub was plain and old fashioned, but good quality and reasonably priced. He didn't invite me in and since there was no sign of the wife he had mentioned, I was happy to be neighbourly without becoming too friendly. But my conclusion as I walked away was that I liked Richard and was pleased to have such a congenial neighbour living next door. I had yet to meet his wife, and hoped she would be just as pleasant.

That evening I met Hannah at the pub. Having worked together throughout the day, we had exhausted most of our usual gossip, so I was pleased to have some news to share with her, for once. She was interested to hear everything I could tell her about my new neighbours. The village was small, and any arrival inevitably caused a flurry of interest behind closed doors and twitching curtains.

'What do you know about him?' she asked me, leaning forward eagerly until her blonde curls were almost touching my unruly red hair.

'He's called Richard, and he's married,' I said.

'That's a pity,' Hannah replied, her plump face twisted in a disappointed grimace.

We both laughed but, even if he had been available, I told her Richard was unlikely to interest her.

'Why?' she asked.

'For a start, he's old enough to be your father.'

'So was my ex-husband.'

'*Ex*-husband,' I repeated, emphasising the 'ex'.

'Our age difference had nothing to do with us splitting up. It had everything to do with him chasing other women.'

She pulled a face, but I knew her divorce had been amicable, and her ex-husband had given her a very generous settlement which had enabled her to buy her café. She harboured no resentment towards him. Her empathy was one of the things I admired about her. I didn't think I would ever forgive my ex-boyfriend. To be fair, he had treated me abominably, whereas Hannah seemed to think her ex-husband genuinely hadn't been able to help himself. But that in itself was a magnanimous attitude.

'What else have you found out about them?' she asked me, still curious about my new next-door neighbours.

I shrugged. 'Nothing, really. I only met him for a few seconds, on his doorstep. And there was no sign of his wife.'

'Well, you're not much use as a sleuth, are you?' she replied.

'He got on well with Poppy,' I added.

'I'd better ask her then,' Hannah said, smiling. 'She's probably a lot more observant than you anyway. You're useless. Well, Poppy,' she looked down at my dog who was dozing at my feet. 'What do you make of your new neighbour?'

Hearing her name, Poppy opened her eyes and wagged her tail. As Hannah and I were laughing together, one of our friends entered the bar and came over to join us.

Brushing his black hair out of his eyes, Toby lowered his lean frame into a chair.

'What are you two nattering about?' he asked, his blue eyes alight with interest.

As soon as he sat down, Poppy trotted around the table to say hello to him. He stroked the curly fur on her head and she immediately rolled over, her paws waving in the air, her tail beating on the ground as it wagged eagerly. Hannah explained that I had been telling her about my new next-door neighbour.

'He seems very nice,' I said.

'Don't worry,' Hannah added. 'He's not about to steal Emily away from you. He's married.'

Muttering that he didn't know what Hannah was talking about, Toby leaned down to tickle Poppy.

2

EARLY THE FOLLOWING MORNING, I took Poppy for her first walk of the day. Having burnt off the early morning mist, the sun shone over an idyllic scene under a clear blue sky. Instead of scampering around on the grass, as she usually did, Poppy started pulling me in the direction of the red brick bridge across the river. I had been warned that Jack Tzus, like all long-eared breeds, were prone to ear infections, and Poppy seemed instinctively averse to submersion in water. She hated it when I bathed her, and would struggle and splash until I was as wet as she was. Given her propensity to dig, this had resulted in quite a few muddy confrontations. But this morning my little dog seemed determined to drag me down to the river.

'No, Poppy, no. You know we don't go down there,' I told her. 'It's dangerous to go too close to the water's edge. It would be all too easy to trip and fall in.'

Instead of listening to reason, she whimpered and continued trying to pull me towards the bridge.

'Poppy, what's wrong with you this morning?'

She began barking, and seemed so agitated, that in the end I let her lead the way down to the river bank. Even when we were standing right at the water's edge, I almost missed it. And then something moved very slowly in the water. I stared at it, unable to believe what was just a few inches away from me, close enough for me to reach out and touch. I shut my eyes tightly, but when I opened them again a woman's body was still there, lying face down in the water. Strands of long dark hair floated on the surface, like fine tendrils of river weed. Bobbing gently on the current, she seemed to be trapped in the weeds by the bank. Now that she had drawn my attention to this unusual phenomenon, Poppy evidently considered she had carried out her duty and it was over to me to deal with the situation. Stretching out on the grass, she closed her eyes and promptly fell asleep in the sun.

My mobile shook in my hand as I phoned the police and reported having discovered a dead body in the river. The woman who took my call asked for my name. In a tremulous voice I told her that a woman had drowned by the bridge over the river in Ashton Mead.

'Wait there, madam,' she said. 'A patrol car will be with you as soon as possible. Is the person in the water breathing?'

'I don't think so,' I stammered. 'I don't know. That is, I don't think she can be, because she's lying face down in the water and she's not moving.'

As I was answering the question, it occurred to me that I should have checked whether the woman was actually dead. I was trying hard not to panic, although I had no idea what to do next. Yelling at Poppy to stay where she was, I lay down and reached out to grasp the back of the woman's shirt. The cold water hurt my fingers but I clung on and tugged, succeeding only in lifting a fistful of sodden fabric up above the surface of the water. Abandoning my efforts to pull the woman out of the water, I grabbed hold of her hair and attempted to at least yank her head up above the surface. It wasn't easy because my fingers were stiff with cold. At last I succeeded in lifting the woman's nose and mouth above the surface, but her hair slithered through my stiff fingers and she fell back in the water with a loud splash. I didn't attempt to pull her head up again. One glimpse of her grey skin and sightless eyes had been enough to convince me that the woman was dead.

Sitting back on my heels on the damp grass, I shuddered to think that I had just stared into the eyes of a corpse. In that moment it made no difference to me that she was a stranger. All that mattered was that she had once been a human being, and now she was dead. I heard a faint sob, and realised I was crying. Poppy came and lay beside me with her head on my leg, as though she understood I was upset. Thrusting my icy fingers into her fur, I was comforted by her warmth. We seemed to be sitting there for a very long time, unable to move, just waiting. I wasn't even aware that a police car had drawn up, until Poppy began barking at a tall woman striding across the grass towards us.

'Are you Emily Wilson?' she called out to me in a deep voice of command.

With a shudder of relief, I clambered to my feet and snapped at Poppy to be quiet. Fussing and grumbling, as if to say she deserved some credit for finding a drowned woman, Poppy lay back down, with her chin on her paws, staring at me. Meanwhile, the policewoman glanced about, before her piercing black eyes came to rest on me again. There was no need for her to ask me where the body was. She spotted it straight away and ran to check whether there was anything that could be done to save the woman. Feeling stunned, I scarcely registered that a man had joined her. Together they pulled the body out of the water and had her lying on her front by the time another officer joined them. One of them began checking the body while the tall woman talked briskly on her phone. By now several police cars had driven up and parked on the road close to the bridge. They were followed by a couple of police vans. Time seemed to speed up and it seemed that within minutes the peaceful riverside was overrun with strangers in white suits. As if they had been rehearsing for this event for months, the grassy area was rapidly cordoned off on both sides of the bridge.

Dazed and shaking, I watched all the bustle around me. Someone put a glistening silver sheet around me murmuring about delayed shock, and a plastic cup of sweetened tea was thrust in my hand. The tall female officer was barking instructions. Overwhelmed, I picked Poppy up and buried the side of my face in her fur. Meanwhile, a small crowd of onlookers began to gather as a large white tent was erected to hide the body from view. I wasn't sorry not to see it any longer. One look had been enough for me. A young policewoman joined me and questioned me gently about how I had found the body. She wanted to know whether I recognised the dead woman, and what I was doing down by the river so early. I explained about taking my dog for a walk.

'We don't usually go down as far as the river bank, but this morning she kept dragging me down here. She knew something was wrong.'

'What could have given your dog that idea?'

'I don't know. Perhaps she picked up the woman's scent.'

I explained how, prompted by the emergency services, I had pulled the woman's head up by her hair, and had seen straight away that she was dead.

'Her lips were dark blue,' I said, shivering at the memory. 'She was just staring without seeing anything. There was nothing I could do so I – I dropped her head back in the water.'

Horror at what I had done overwhelmed me, and I began to cry.

'Is this your dog?'

I nodded and the policewoman smiled. 'She's a beauty. Why don't you take her home now? We have your details and will be in touch if we need to speak to you again.'

Back home, I had just put the kettle on when there was a ring on the bell. Expecting a police officer, I was surprised to see my friend, Hannah, standing on the doorstep, her chubby face contorted with worry.

'I wanted to check you're all right,' she said, gazing at me anxiously.

'How do you know what happened?' I answered, startled that she seemed to know about my discovery of a drowned woman.

Hannah continued to scrutinise me. 'It's all over the village. Everyone knows about it.'

'But – how did they find out?'

She smiled at the question. 'Well, let's see. There's a bloody big white tent down by the river which isn't a circus, the road's closed, and there's a host of police cars parked near the bridge. It doesn't take a rocket scientist to work out something serious has happened. The police don't turn out in force like that for nothing. It's a fatal accident, isn't it?'

I nodded helplessly. 'You'd better come in. I was there, you know,' I told her when we were both seated in my living room. 'That is, I found a body floating in the river, and called the police. I'm sorry about letting you down. I should have called you to say I wasn't coming to work, but it just went out of my head. Tell me, what made you think I had anything to do with what happened?'

'When you didn't turn up for work this morning, and didn't call to let me know, I thought something must be wrong. Then I heard that someone with a dog had found a dead body floating in the river, and I put two and two together and guessed it might be you.'

I was puzzled. 'How did you know the body was found by someone with a dog?'

'Maud told me. Don't ask me how she found out.'

We both smiled. The local shopkeeper seemed to absorb rumour and gossip from the air.

'Well, I'm really sorry. I feel awful. I should have called you. I was going to call...'

'Don't worry about the café. Seriously, it doesn't matter. One day isn't going to make any difference to anything. It's completely understandable you'd be feeling confused after what you've just been through. These are exceptional circumstances. Now,' Hannah went on, with characteristic practicality, 'have you had breakfast? I know you've had a shock, but you still have to eat.'

Poppy jumped up, wagging her tail eagerly. She clearly thought that was an excellent idea. Hannah flatly refused to open the Sunshine Tea Shoppe that day, so there was no question of my going to work, even if I had wanted to. Instead, my friend insisted that I take it easy and do nothing for a few days, until the shock of my horrible discovery had worn off. After staying to supervise my lunch, she finally left, claiming it was a good opportunity to give the café a thorough clean, although I suspected she was going to open up for the afternoon tea trade. Before she left, she promised to call for me that evening so we could go to the village pub together.

'Toby has arranged to meet us there,' she added, with a sly smile.

Hannah knew that I had fallen for our friend Toby. I sometimes glimpsed his piercing blue eyes gazing at me through the dark hair that flopped down over his eyes but, despite Hannah's assurances that he reciprocated my feelings, so far he only appeared to be interested in being friends with me.

'So I'll see you later,' she said. 'And if you sniff out any more stiffs, look the other way,' she added, turning to Poppy. 'One dead body is quite enough for one day.'

Poppy rolled over for Hannah to tickle her and Hannah grinned.

3

THE HOUSE FELT EMPTY after Hannah left, but I refused to dwell on the morbid feelings that had been lurking in the back of my mind ever since I had seen the drowned woman. Taking Poppy for a long walk lifted my spirits. The sun was shining and there was a hint of summer in the air. Instead of following our usual route across the grassy slopes leading down to the river, we walked around the village, passing front gardens displaying clusters of daffodils, crocuses and delicate snowdrops. A few hyacinths were in flower, and I paused to admire a camellia covered in massive crimson blooms, while overhead the sky formed a bright blue backdrop against the pink blossom of a hawthorn tree. We reached our destination, a small green near the bus stop, where Poppy spent a happy half hour exploring the moss and insect life that proliferated in the grass.

Poppy was clearly having a good time and it was difficult to witness her exuberance and remain dejected. I was just beginning to relax and forget all about my disturbing discovery, when I heard someone calling out. A stocky man was heading in our direction. He seemed to be in a hurry, with his sturdy legs working like pistons, and although it was difficult to make out exactly what he was saying, it was clear that he was angry. He was brandishing a walking stick in the air and, as he drew nearer, I realised that he was shouting at me. His large square face was red with exertion or fury, and he was yelling at me to remove my dog from the green. I stood still, doing my best to conceal my fear. If the man had been directing his ire against me, I would most likely have fled, but he was directing his aggression at Poppy, who had done nothing wrong. There was no sign to prohibit dogs from walking on the green, where she had every right to snuffle around freely. If I conceded this once, we might never be able to return to the green. I stood my ground, refusing to be cowed.

Poppy strained at her lead as the man drew near, and her growls gave way to a low-throated barking. I had never heard her sounding quite so aggressive. Had she been twice her size I suspected the angry man might not have dared come so close, even with the stout stick he was now wielding like a weapon. But he came near enough for me to see the spittle on his fleshy lips, and notice how his nostrils flared in his flat nose, while his tiny eyes glared out at me between slits in his baggy eyelids. He reminded me of a picture of an ogre in one of the books I had read as a child. Reaching us, he raised his stick above his bald head and Poppy jumped up eagerly, hoping he was offering to play with her. She retreated, growling, when he bellowed at me.

'Get that brute off this grass!'

'No,' I replied, shaking and very surprised by my own temerity. 'This is common land and anyone is permitted to walk here.'

'We don't want filthy animals soiling the grass,' he replied.

I was on the point of retorting that Poppy wasn't filthy, when she crouched down and deposited a little parcel at my feet. Muttering under my breath, I lunged at it with a dog poop bag, after which I straightened up to confront the dog hater. But my confidence was dented. It was enough. Sensing his advantage, the man waved his stick in the air, repeating that the green was no place for animals.

'If I catch that animal here again, you'll be sorry,' he shouted. 'Now get lost, the pair of you!'

With that, he turned and stalked away, leaving me shaking and relieved to be rid of him. We went straight home from there, as I didn't want to face the questions Maud would inevitably put to me about my discovery of the dead woman if she caught sight of me in the village.

When my doorbell chimed, I was reluctant to open the door until I saw Hannah was outside. She had come to collect me, not trusting that I would go to the pub as we had arranged. I hadn't intended to mention my unpleasant encounter with the angry villager to anyone, but somehow I found myself telling Hannah about it as we walked to the pub.

'We weren't doing anything wrong,' I concluded. 'I mean, Poppy did do a poo on the green, but that was after the man shouted at me for letting her walk on the grass, so that wasn't what set him off. And it's not as if we left her doings there. You know I always carry bags with me. She has to go somewhere.'

Hannah shrugged. 'Was he bald?' she asked. 'And ugly as sin?'

'He was bald,' I replied. 'And he was carrying a thick walking stick which he kept waving at us. I really thought he was going to hit me.'

Hannah nodded. 'That was Silas Strang,' she said. 'Don't take any notice of him. He's like that with everyone. Just ignore him and avoid him when you can. He's a nasty piece of work. And his mother's worse. Don't look so worried. You're not alone. He's made enemies with everyone in the village, for one reason or another.'

If Hannah had intended to comfort me, she hadn't succeeded.

Far from proving a welcome distraction, at the pub that evening the talk was all about the body that had been pulled from the river. A hush fell when Hannah and I walked in; everyone there knew I had discovered the drowned woman floating in the river. Tess, who worked in the pub, usually treated me with a surly taciturnity, her beady black eyes scowling balefully at me. I had learned to ignore her barely veiled hostility, having been assured that she regarded anyone who had not been born in the village as an interloper. On this occasion she actually smiled at me as she handed me a pint, telling me it was on the house. I appreciated her sympathy, but it turned out she had been intent on making her way through the small crowd gathered around me only to ensure she could hear what had happened that morning. Before I could answer any questions, a stranger manoeuvred herself to the front of my audience. She was tall and thin, with piercing black eyes, short black hair and bright red lipstick. She thrust a dictaphone at me expectantly.

'Get away from her,' Tess snapped. 'Who do you think you are, anyway?' She looked around. 'Does anyone recognise this woman?'

The stranger introduced herself as a reporter from *My Swindon News*, and Tess nodded at the landlord. Cliff was a burly man who rarely raised his voice. His powerful physical presence was usually enough to intimidate the most aggressive antagonist.

'Come on now,' he said to the reporter, his florid face nearly the colour of the tufts of ginger hair sticking out on either side of his bald pate. 'Let's give the poor girl some space. She's had a nasty experience, and the last thing she needs right now is strangers hounding her.'

'It's all right,' I said. 'She might as well hear it from me, but there's honestly nothing much to tell.'

The pub was absolutely silent as I described how my dog had insisted on dragging me down to the river. At my feet, I saw Poppy's ears twitch when she heard me mention her name.

'And that's when I saw her,' I said.

'Can you describe what you saw?' the reporter prompted me eagerly.

'There was a body in the water. It was caught in the weeds by the bridge, lying face down and not moving. The police came very quickly and took my statement and that was it, as far as I was concerned. The police sent me home and after that, you know as much as I do. And that's all there is to say. If you want to know anything else, you'll have to ask the police.'

The reporter enquired where I lived, but at that point, Cliff stepped in front of her, blocking my view of her. My friend Toby rose to his feet and joined Cliff.

'Are you going to leave quietly or does my mate here have to throw you out?' Toby asked with uncharacteristic roughness.

'You can see the girl's had a shock and needs time to deal with it,' Cliff said. 'As for where she lives, that's none of your business.'

'She's in the pub,' the reporter retorted. 'She doesn't seem very shocked.'

'She's come to spend some quiet time with her friends,' Toby repeated.

'She's got a lot of friends,' the reporter said, glancing around at the assembled villagers.

'She's a popular girl,' Toby replied tersely.

The reporter sniffed then turned and walked slowly to the door.

Hannah leapt to her feet. 'If you print anything defamatory, we'll make sure your paper is sued and you lose your job,' she called out at the retreating figure. 'The whole village witnessed what my friend told you, and you weren't the only one recording it.' She brandished her phone in the air. 'You can't trust these reporters,' she added, resuming her seat.

'Bloody parasites,' someone else muttered.

'Why did you talk to her?' Hannah asked me irritably.

'It's hardly a secret that I discovered a dead body floating in the river, so thought I might as well tell the whole story. Once they know I've got nothing interesting to say, they'll leave me alone.'

'Let's hope you're right,' Hannah said.

With the reporter gone, other people started chipping in and everyone seemed to voice a different opinion.

'Well, if you ask me,' an old man sitting in the corner piped up, although no one had asked for his opinion, 'that poor woman were murdered.'

Under the table, Poppy growled in her sleep.

'Stands to reason, don't it?' the old man went on, growing expansive as he realised he had an audience. 'There's more'n enough reeds and weeds along there for anyone to pull theirselves out of the water if they want to. It's not like the river flows fast through the village. I sailed enough sticks under the bridge when I were a nipper to know it's a lazy river.' He shook his head. 'It were murder all right.'

'You can drown in a few inches of water,' someone else pointed out and a few more voices joined in.

'Yes, it could have been an accident.'

'She could have fell in and hit her head.'

'Or been pushed.'

'Or hit on the head before she went into the river.'

It was fish and chips night in the pub. Cliff had underestimated the number of locals who would be there that evening. He complained that his freezer was almost empty by the time he closed his kitchen. But he was beaming. At least the discovery of a body in the village had proved good for business at the pub. The main topic of conversation was the identity of the drowned woman. No one seemed to have any inkling who she might be. The consensus arrived at was that she had fallen into the water further along the river and had floated down to Ashton Mead where she had become tangled in the weeds beside the bridge. It was true that she could have fallen in anywhere further upstream.

'If she'd carried on down the river she could have ended up in the Thames,' Cliff said.

'She might not have been discovered until she reached London,' Toby added thoughtfully. 'Being discovered here means the police can narrow the search to Ashton Mead or anywhere further upstream. She might have fallen in anywhere between Wroughton and here.'

Tess scowled. 'You've got to admit it's odd, a corpse turning up here just when newcomers moved into Laurel Cottage.'

I listened, suddenly alert to what was being said. Laurel Cottage was the only other property in the lane where I lived.

'Odd in what way?' Cliff asked her.

'They move in and next day there's a dead body in the river. We've never had a stranger drown in our stretch of the river before.'

'Are you suggesting the two are connected?' Hannah asked.

'I'm just saying it's a coincidence, strangers arriving in the village at the exact time a corpse turns up,' Tess insisted darkly. 'If you ask me, the police should be investigating whoever's moved into Laurel Cottage.'

'There's no evidence the two are connected. No one's even said the woman was murdered,' Toby protested.

'He did,' Tess countered, jerking her head in the direction of the old man in the corner.

'It could have been a suicide,' someone said.

'It were murder,' the old man in the corner repeated in his reedy voice.

'Probably Silas Strang,' someone said, and there was a murmur of agreement.

'Or that mother of his,' another voice chipped in.

'She keeps a shotgun under her bed,' the old man said thoughtfully.

'That's nonsense and you know it,' Tess chided him.

'It's far more likely to have been an accident,' Toby said firmly. 'The woman probably slipped and fell in, and it was just a tragic accident.'

Tess grunted. 'If that's what you want to call it.'

'What makes you suspect she was murdered?' I asked.

Tess glared at me and I looked away uneasily. Remembering that she distrusted anyone who hadn't lived in Ashton Mead all their lives, I wondered what stories she spread about me behind my back. In the meantime, the discussion continued. In the absence of any evidence, there was scope for endless speculation about the drowned woman. Instead of feeling more disturbed than before by this focus on the dead woman I had discovered, I found the conversation curiously comforting. Having gone to the pub to spend time with my friends, in the hopes they would distract me from my earlier shock, I no longer felt alone with my dreadful discovery, even if the general consensus in the pub seemed to be that I was now living next door to a man who had murdered his wife.

4

The next day I went to the rather grandly named Village Emporium, the local grocery store, for fresh milk and bread. The grey-haired shopkeeper, Maud, put down a glossy magazine she was reading and peered at me over her rimless glasses.

'It was you discovered the body, wasn't it?'

She nodded excitedly as she spoke, making her mass of tightly curled grey hair quiver. She was so inquisitive, it surprised me that she had been absent the previous evening, when the news had been discussed at length in the pub.

'It must have been a terrible shock,' she went on, staring at me with a shrewd expression. 'You've heard the poor woman was murdered?'

I had heard nothing of the sort beyond idle speculation, and gave a noncommittal grunt.

'If you ever want to talk, you know where I am,' Maud said kindly. 'Now, what are you looking for today? I've got some lovely Braeburn apples, and nice pears, and pastries fresh in this morning. And how about a few treats for that little dog of yours?' She nodded at me with an encouraging smile.

After thanking her for her recommendations, I walked around the store, selecting my purchases. When I went to pay, Maud leaned forward beside the till and glanced around to check that no one was listening. We were alone in the store.

'You know what I think?' she murmured.

I waited. Clearly she wasn't going to take my basket from me until she had told me what was on her mind.

'You live in Mill Lane,' she said. It sounded like an accusation. 'You've met him, haven't you?'

'Met who?'

Remembering what Tess had said about the apparent coincidence of Richard moving into the lane just before a body turned up, I waited for Maud to speak. Just then the little bell above the door jingled and a young couple entered the shop. I didn't recognise either of them, and guessed they weren't local. Maud immediately grabbed my basket and began to ring up my purchases. Evidently local affairs were not to be discussed in front of outsiders. The other shoppers moved to the back of the shop and Maud beckoned me closer.

'It seems to me, the police should be investigating the newcomers in Laurel Cottage. You take care now,' she added.

About to remonstrate with her, I saw the strangers returning with a basket of provisions for their onward journey: bottles of water, sandwiches and chocolate bars. With a curt nod at Maud, I left, feeling uneasy. Poppy jumped up at me in delight as soon as I walked in. Having greeted her, I shoved my shopping in the fridge and we set off. Jane was out that day but Poppy was perfectly happy scratching around in the back yard of the tea shop, where she could shelter under an awning if it rained. The area was securely fenced off and we kept the gate padlocked, so I no longer had to worry about keeping her tethered. As long as I took her for long walks, she seemed perfectly content to potter around. On a fine day, she liked nothing more than to lie stretched out on a patch of grass, basking in the warmth of the sun.

I told Hannah everything Maud had said.

'So, it was murder after all,' she replied solemnly.

I was surprised that she seemed so ready to believe the shopkeeper's opinion.

'Only according to Maud,' I pointed out. 'Considering what a gossipmonger she is, it's probably just the most sensational story out of a number of possibilities. My money's on it having been an accident. It's tragic, of course, because the woman drowned, but nothing more dramatic than an accident, all the same.'

'Oh, Maud's probably right about this. It's not the kind of thing you'd invent, is it? No, if Maud thinks it was murder, then that's what it most likely was. No one would make that up with something as serious as this. Besides, Maud knows about these things.'

'How does she do it?' I asked

'What?'

'I mean, how would Maud know so much about the case before anyone else?'

'Maud has a nephew in the police. He's a uniformed constable working in Swindon, but he grew up here in the village.'

I took a moment to absorb this information. 'But if he knows about the drowned woman, he wouldn't tell Maud, would he?'

Hannah laughed. 'She has a way of winkling information out of people. And Barry's very nice, but I wouldn't share my secrets with him, even if he is a police officer.'

I wondered if Maud had shared her suspicions of my next-door neighbour, Richard. Maud wasn't the only one to suggest he might be responsible for the woman's death.

Tess had also muttered darkly about someone moving into Mill Lane just as a body was found floating in the river. I wondered if anyone thought I was involved in the crime.

I voiced my concerns to Hannah. 'I don't see why they suspect my next-door neighbour, just because he's new to the village. Does anyone suspect me as well? I'm a relative newcomer, living in Mill Lane next door to The Laurels, and I was the one who discovered the body.'

Hannah laughed. 'Was it you? Don't tell me I've been harbouring a murderer in the Sunshine Tea Shoppe for the past year. Did the gang of killers send you on ahead to spy out the land and report back whether this was a suitable place to commit the murder?'

I didn't share her amusement. 'If I was an accomplice, I wouldn't have revealed the whereabouts of the body, would I? And if there was a murderer living in Mill Lane, they would hardly dump a body in the river less than ten minutes' walk from our front doors.'

Hannah was clearly amused by my indignation, but I felt there was some justice in my reaction. It was outrageous to suspect someone of murder just because they were a newcomer to the village. I felt sorry for Richard, who had struck me as affable and harmless. But when Hannah asked me what his wife was like, I had to admit that I hadn't yet seen her.

'As far as you know,' Hannah replied with a meaningful frown.

'Oh please, he's hardly going to push his own wife in the river so near to his house, in an open place where anyone could have seen them.'

'He might have done it in the dead of night,' she replied.

I wasn't sure if she was joking. On my way home, I recognised the dark-haired reporter coming out of Maud's grocery store and suspected the shopkeeper had been indiscreet. By now the reporter might even know about Maud's nephew, Barry. Clearly it was going to be impossible to keep anything quiet in the village.

That evening, in the pub, Hannah, Toby and I sat in the garden with a pint. Hannah had brought her mother's old dog, Holly, and she and Poppy lay under the table dozing companionably. Before long, the subject of the drowned woman came up. I was adamant that Richard could have nothing to do with the death.

'I mean, why would he be involved, just because he's only recently moved here?' I asked.

'What makes you so sure he's innocent?' Toby replied. 'That is, I'm sure you have your reasons, but it would be interesting to hear them, because at the moment, frankly, I don't know what to think. Nothing like this has ever happened in the village before. My mother seems to think the woman was killed by someone living in The Laurels.'

'That's what the local gossips are saying,' I replied crossly. 'But I've met Richard, and he seems like a very nice guy.'

Although the fact remained that I hadn't yet seen his wife. Hesitantly, I admitted as much to Toby.

'So what happened to her?' Hannah whispered. 'I think Emily might have seen her,' she went on, glancing around to make sure no one could overhear our conversation. 'Don't you think she might be the woman who drowned? It would explain why she seems to have disappeared. No one's seen her, as far as I know. I'm sure Maud hasn't or she wouldn't be convinced Richard was guilty. And that means the police haven't been able to find her, because Maud would know.'

Everything seemed to be pointing to Richard, but I just didn't believe the friendly man I had chatted with on the doorstep was a cold-blooded murderer, and I said so. 'No one said anything about this being a "cold-blooded" murder,' Hannah pointed out. 'If it was a domestic, it could have been a crime of passion.'

Toby nodded, looking sombre. We had all been following the story in the local news, but the police claimed not to have a name for the dead woman. Since they had questioned everyone in the village, it seemed unlikely that the woman was related to Richard. A reconstructed image of her face was published, but still no one came forward to identify the body. If the police knew where she had entered the water, they hadn't made that information public. It was time to go to the local shop and speak to Maud and find out exactly what she knew about Richard's missing wife. If it turned out to be true that I was living next door to a murderer, I wanted to know about it so that I could stay on my guard until the police figured out what had happened.

5

THE FOLLOWING MORNING I hurried round the corner to call in at the shop before going to work. Maud was busy with a delivery and I couldn't wait around as I had to return home to collect Poppy and get to the café where Hannah would be opening up. It was clear that she was bursting to talk to me, but the café was busy and we didn't have time to chat until after lunch. When we finally sat down together for a coffee, Hannah came straight out with a plan she had been dreaming up.

'You met the man who's moved into the lane, didn't you?' she asked me. I nodded cautiously, wondering where this was going. 'And you saw the woman in the river before they pulled her out?'

Again, I nodded.

'So you had a clear view of her?'

'I saw the back of her head, and I called the police straight away.'

'Of course. But before they arrived you must have seen what she looked like.'

'Not really. She was floating on her front, and what little I managed to see of her face was – well, it didn't look like a normal face. I'd say she would probably have been unrecognisable, even to someone who knew her. All I can remember is a quick glimpse of glassy eyes, and her lips were blue.' I shuddered at the memory.

'Well, anyway, we've all seen the reconstruction of her face that was printed in the papers and posted online,' Hannah went on. I had the impression she hadn't really been listening to me. 'But you saw her actual face, which means you're the perfect person to investigate what happened.' Her eyes were shining with excitement.

'Investigate? Hannah, what are you talking about?'

'You're neighbours, aren't you? So you could easily find an excuse to enter The Laurels. Offer to lend him some sugar or something.'

'Why would I do that?'

'So you can get into his house, of course,' she told me, with a hint of impatience in her voice.

'What if he doesn't want to borrow any sugar?'

'That's just an example,' Hannah said with a sigh. 'The point is, someone needs to get inside his house and look around, and you're the only one who can come up with a plausible reason to go in there.'

'Plausible?' I echoed.

'Yes. Don't worry, we'll think of something.'

'I'm sorry, but I just don't follow. What is it you want me to do?'

'I'm suggesting you go inside your next-door neighbour's house and take a look around.'

'Why would I want to do that?'

An elderly couple came into the café and after that we were sporadically busy with customers and had no chance to continue our discussion. I was relieved. Hannah's odd rambling had unsettled me and I wasn't quite sure where she intended it to lead. That evening we met for a drink in the pub and she immediately returned to the proposal that I somehow inveigle my way into my neighbour's house.

'Once you get in there, you can look around and see if you can find any photos,' she explained.

I still wasn't sure what she was talking about, but when she finally explained herself, she confirmed my worst suspicions. She wanted me to look around in Richard's house and see if he had any photographs of the woman who had drowned.

'We just need to establish whether the dead woman was his wife,' she said in a low voice, when I started to protest. 'If she was, then it's obvious he killed her, thinking no one would know who she was.'

'Surely the police will find out if it was his wife?'

'They would if they had any evidence. But they'd probably need a warrant or something to search his house.'

'Could that be because he had nothing to do with the woman who drowned?' I asked drily.

Toby joined us, and quietly Hannah outlined her plan to him. She clearly thought it was an ingenious idea, but Toby looked worried.

'If you're right about Richard,' he said, 'don't you think it might be dangerous for Emily to go snooping around in his house?'

Although not worried about going to see my next-door neighbour, I thought the whole idea was creepy. Refusing to spy on my neighbour, I insisted the matter was best left to the police. Having stayed for just one drink, I made my way home, where I had left a casserole in the oven on a low heat. On my way, I passed Richard standing on his front doorstep. He called out to me and I wondered if he had been waiting for me to go past.

'I've been looking out for you,' he said, confirming my suspicion.

Suddenly I felt nervous.

'I'm on my way home for supper.'

'Please, won't you join me for a drink – or a cup of tea if you prefer – to thank you for welcoming me the other day,' he said earnestly. 'The rest of the locals haven't been quite so quick to welcome me to the village. They're a close-knit lot, aren't they?' He laughed but I could see he wasn't happy.

I nodded. 'I know what you mean,' I said.

'Was it the same when you moved in?' he asked.

I hesitated. 'A few of them were friendly from the start,' I replied, honestly. 'It only takes one to begin with.'

It was true. Maud had welcomed me to Ashton Mead from the start, and Hannah and I had hit it off straight away. I had gone into her café not long after moving into Rosecroft, for a quiet celebration at being a home owner, and she had offered me a job on the spot. Since then we had become firm friends, working together every day, and often socialising in the pub in the evening as well. Once Hannah had befriended me, the rest of the village had seemed to accept me. My relationship to my great aunt must have helped, but without Hannah's friendship I wondered how easily I would have found my place among them. Whether I would be able to help Richard settle in as easily was doubtful. Even after a year, I still felt as though I was on probation with many of the local residents. The fact that most of them seemed to regard him as a wife-killer obviously wasn't going to help his reputation with the other villagers. And I suspected he hadn't met Silas Strang yet.

Pushing his front door wide open, he beckoned to me to go in.

'I've got Poppy with me,' I murmured.

'Oh, she's welcome as well,' he replied promptly.

Cautiously I followed him. I had been inside The Laurels before, visiting the previous owner, but the place looked very different now. To begin with, Richard had installed strong central lights, making the place look bright and cheerful. He led me into his front room where the carpet and the walls were as I remembered them, but his furniture of wood and green leather looked elegant and more comfortable. I noticed a framed photograph displayed above the fireplace, but before I could walk over to look at it, he invited to me to sit down, and offered me a drink. I settled for a gin and tonic and Richard bustled off to the kitchen. As soon as he left, I leapt to my feet and hurried over to the fireplace to study the photograph. Close up I saw a woman smiling at the camera. Her hair could have been a match for the dark tendrils I had seen floating on the river, but the same could be said of any dark-haired woman. Between her and a younger-looking Richard two teenage boys were standing, one laughing, the other looking at the camera with a sulky expression typical of a boy his age. Hearing my host return, I flung myself back in my chair just as he reappeared with a tray of drinks and a few snacks.

'I haven't forgotten you,' he added, turning to Poppy with a smile. 'Here you are.'

He put a few treats down on the floor. Ignoring them, Poppy rolled over, wagging her tail which thumped softly on the carpet.

'She prefers attention to treats,' I laughed as he petted her.

'At least she seems to accept me,' he said quietly.

Perhaps holding my drink gave me courage. 'Is that your family?' I asked, pointing to the photograph above the fireplace.

He nodded. 'That's me with my wife and our two boys, in happier times.'

'Will your family be joining you here?'

He smiled wistfully. 'My boys are grown up now, and they've got lives of their own. Oh, I'm sure they'll be visiting me at some point, and I've got enough room for them to stay as long as they want, but they're both busy with their own lives.'

I took a deep breath before asking about his wife. 'Will she be joining you?'

'I'm afraid not,' he replied, his voice taut with concealed emotion that could have been grief or anger.

He looked so wretched that I hesitated to continue, but I seemed to hear Hannah's voice urging me to find out as much as possible.

'Are you divorced?'

'No, not divorced.' He sighed. 'That's never going to happen.'

'So where is she?'

For an instant he looked irritated, but then his shoulders sagged and he lowered his head.

'She won't be joining me here,' he said tersely. 'That's something else that's never going to happen. Our separation couldn't be more final. She's left me and there's no going back.'

My heart skipped a beat.

'I'm sorry,' I said, not daring to ask if she was dead, although that was what he seemed to be implying.

He looked directly at me, and I quailed at the misery in his eyes. 'Wouldn't we all like to turn the clock back if we could?' he asked.

The cheerful atmosphere seemed to have turned dark, and suddenly I couldn't wait to get out of there. Gulping my gin and tonic down as quickly as possible, I gazed around the room.

'I like what you've done here,' I ventured, but our conversation had become stilted and I think we were both relieved when I stood up to leave.

6

ARRIVING AT WORK THE following morning, I confided to Hannah that I had actually visited Richard at home. Dumping a lump of pastry on the worktop, she wiped her floury hands on her apron, and popped tea bags into a two-person pot. A moment later she ushered me into the café and set two mugs of tea on a table between us. Leaning forward, she listened, agog, as I told her how Richard had invited me into his house and offered me a drink.

'I hope you didn't accept it,' she said, her voice sharp with alarm.

'Please don't act like you're my mother. In any case, you were the one who insisted I go and see him.'

'To talk to him, yes. Not to go inside his house. What if he attacked you there, where no one could see what was happening?'

'And you call me melodramatic,' I replied, trying not to laugh. 'It was absolutely fine. He was very nice. I keep telling you, there's nothing dodgy about him.'

Hannah frowned. 'That remains to be seen. Did you notice any pictures of his wife in the house?'

'Yes, I did. And he told me –' I hesitated. 'He told me she'd gone and she wasn't coming back.'

Hannah's eyes grew wide and she pressed one hand to her mouth. She couldn't have looked more shocked if I'd told her Richard had assaulted me. 'So he could have done it,' she whispered. 'We were right all along. She's dead, isn't she?'

'He didn't say that, exactly.'

'He said she's gone and she's never coming back. What else could it mean? You have to tell the police.'

'And say what? That my next-door neighbour could be separated from his wife, or he might be a widower? Hannah, we don't know anything about his marriage. His wife could have been dead for years. And I don't know what you mean by "we were right". I've never suspected him of any wrongdoing.'

'Did you see a photo of his wife?'

I confirmed that I had.

'How did she look?'

'Like a woman looks, when she's posing for a photo with her family. She was smiling and she looked happy.'

'Did you get the impression she was frightened of him?'

'Don't be silly. It was a nice family photo. But it didn't look that recent,' I added, thinking about what I had seen. 'He looked younger in it. He had more hair. And I think he might have had a moustache. I'm not sure. And his children were young, about ten or twelve, and now they're grown up.'

'Never mind what they looked like, did she look like the woman who drowned?'

'Possibly, but I only saw the body for an instant, and the reconstruction is just that, a reconstruction. I mean, it could have been the same woman, but I can't be sure. She had dark hair and a similar sort of face, but lots of women have dark hair, and everyone has a face. Between the distorted face of the drowned woman, the reconstruction of her appearance, and the photo I barely glimpsed next door, it's impossible to reach any conclusion about whether they were the same person or not.'

'Did he say anything about what happened to her?'

'Yes, he told me he pushed her in the river as soon as they arrived, because he was confident he could get away with it in a village like Ashton Mead where everyone knows everyone else's business.'

'Emily, be serious.'

'I am being serious. You're the one who's being ridiculous with your wild suspicions.'

A small group of customers came in, and for a while I was occupied serving them while Hannah was busy in the kitchen. After that, there was a little flurry of activity, with several tables of customers coming in for breakfast, and that was followed by a lunch rush. By the time we were clearing away before tea, we were both tired and neither of us brought up the topic of the recent drowning. But that evening, in the pub, when we sat down with Toby, Hannah told him in an excited whisper how I had been inside Richard's house.

Toby looked annoyed. 'What on earth made you go there alone?' he asked me in a fierce undertone. 'Are you mad?'

'Actually, he invited me in for a drink. He wanted to thank me for welcoming him to Ashton Mead. He said no one else has been exactly hospitable. And I wasn't alone. Poppy was with me.'

Lying by my feet, Poppy opened her eyes. Her ears twitched and then she closed her eyes again.

Toby subsided, muttering under his breath.

'Tell us everything that happened,' Hannah said. 'And I mean everything.'

I sighed and took a sip of my lager. 'I've already told you.'

'Yes, but Toby hasn't heard about it yet and he wants to know what happened, don't you, Toby?'

I wasn't sure if she actually kicked him under the table, but Toby jolted slightly and nodded his head, frowning.

'There's really nothing much to tell,' I insisted when Hannah urged me again to share what I had discovered.

'He said his wife's dead,' Hannah proclaimed with an air of triumph. She glanced around and lowered her voice. 'That means he could be as guilty as sin.'

'He never said she was dead, not in so many words.'

'Well, he wouldn't, would he? Not if he'd killed her.'

'Saying she's gone doesn't really mean anything,' I protested feebly. 'It just means they're separated, or he's a widower.'

I hesitated to tell my friends the real reason I had for trusting Richard, which was that Poppy liked him. Her instincts about people had so far proved infallible, and she wasn't distracted by the prospect of a dramatic scandal. Hannah offered to buy the next round and I was about to say that I wouldn't stay, when a sudden hush fell. We looked up to see that Richard had entered the bar. I hoped he hadn't overheard what we'd been saying but, seeing me, he smiled and came over. He didn't appear in the least bit awkward so I guessed he had come in too late to hear us talking about him. Every eye in the place was watching him as he crossed the room, and I squirmed uneasily in my seat. Poppy had no such reservations. With a gentle growl of welcome, she darted out from under the table and greeted Richard like an old friend, jumping up at him for attention. Hannah and Toby stared in surprise, and I thought I detected a hint of suspicion in their expressions.

'Poppy seems very familiar with him,' Hannah muttered.

'Richard, come and join us,' I called out, in an unnecessarily loud voice, with a defiant glance at Hannah.

'Are you sure?' Richard replied. 'I don't want to intrude on your gathering.'

'Don't be daft,' I said. 'Draw up a chair. What are you drinking?'

With a smile Richard joined us, oblivious of the fact that almost everyone in the room was convinced he had murdered his wife. Pulling myself together with an effort, I introduced my new neighbour to my friends. Having invited him to join us at our table it was the least I could do. At the back of my mind was the notion that if I could persuade my friends to accept Richard, perhaps others would follow suit. When I had arrived in Ashton Mead, Hannah's friendship had persuaded the local residents to accept me. They had seen me working in the café, and socialising with Hannah and everyone she knew. But I had probably been readily accepted since I had inherited my great aunt's cottage. As far as I knew, Richard had no connection with the village, but was a complete stranger to the community.

Gazing at the hostile faces gathered around the bar, watching us, I had a horrible impression that if this scene had taken place a couple of hundred of years earlier, by now the villagers might have been chasing Richard with pitchforks, with a view to lynching him or burning him at the stake. He might not be at immediate risk of physical attack, but it seemed one had only to scratch the surface to discover the cruelty that still lurked behind the mask of human civilisation. Poppy had no such reservations but lay down at his feet, her tail thumping gently on the wooden floor. Richard insisted on buying a round, and regaled us with anecdotes about his move. While he talked, he continued to pet Poppy who had settled comfortably at his feet and was now dozing peacefully. I struggled to believe an evil man could win her trust so completely. Hannah and

Toby didn't share my confidence. When I stood up to leave, and Richard said he would walk back to the lane with me, Toby leapt to his feet and insisted on accompanying me right to my door.

Richard attempted to start a conversation with Toby, enquiring how long he had lived in Ashton Mead, but he could only elicit monosyllabic replies and soon gave up. After that, the three of us walked in silence back through the village.

'I know what you're doing,' I told Toby crossly, when we reached Rosecroft. 'And it's ridiculous. I'm going to be bumping into Richard all the time. He lives next door to me, for goodness' sake. This charade of trying to protect me is not only unnecessary, it's plain stupid. Are you proposing to camp in my front garden and chaperone me to work every day, in case Richard sees me and calls out good morning?'

'I just wanted to see you home safely,' he replied, looking sheepish.

Poppy loved Toby, but this evening she turned her back on him as if insulted by the implication that she couldn't take care of me.

'Well, goodnight,' I said, deliberately not inviting him in.

Miserably, Toby said goodbye and left. Poppy and I stood for a moment watching him stride quickly down the lane and away into the village. I almost called him back, but I resisted the temptation, and he was soon out of sight, leaving me alone with my little dog. In The Laurels, I saw a light go out downstairs, and wondered what my next-door neighbour was doing, sitting alone in the dark. With his tubby figure and friendly grin, of everyone I had ever met he looked the least likely to be hiding an evil secret. But it was possible that my impressions were misguided, and I had no reason to trust Poppy's instincts over the suspicions of everyone in the village. Despite my protestations to the contrary, that night I took Poppy out in my back garden rather than onto the grassy slopes beyond the border of my property, and I checked that my doors were securely locked and all my windows were shut, before I went to bed. Poppy watched me with a baffled expression on her face, as though she knew my disquiet was misplaced.

'Oh, what do you know?' I asked her crossly. 'You're only a dog.'

She barked once and then turned and stalked out of the room.

7

NOT LONG AGO A villager had lost her mind and locked her daughter in an underground cellar, but other than that nothing dramatic or even out of the ordinary had ever happened in Ashton Mead, at least while I had been living there. I was content with my uneventful life, but Hannah seemed determined to believe that Richard had killed his wife. She was either bored, or else genuinely scared that my new next-door neighbour was a crazy killer. Although outwardly I scoffed at my friend's suspicion, her fears had unnerved me, so I resolved to do some private investigating of my own. At the very least, I was curious to find out what had happened to Richard's wife. Whether he had committed a heinous crime or was completely innocent, quizzing him directly seemed like a bad idea. If he was guilty of murder it could be dangerous to go snooping into his private affairs. On the other hand, if he was innocent, to make him aware of any such suspicion would be cruel. I would have to proceed subtly.

Richard had told me that his wife had left, and her departure had been 'final'. Adamant that his wife was 'never' going to return, he had said, 'She's gone and there's no going back.' He had followed that claim with a heartfelt expression of regret that he couldn't turn the clock back.

In retrospect, I couldn't be sure whether he had expressed sorrow or remorse. The latter would suggest at least some element of guilt about something he had done, or perhaps had failed to do. I wondered if the police knew anything about his missing wife. Hopefully they would solve the mystery that was bothering me.

For a few days I deliberated about how to discover what, if anything, the police knew about Richard's wife. One afternoon, on my way back from work, I noticed a policeman coming out of Maud's grocery store. He had attended a Christmas gathering in the pub, and I recognised him at once. Combining an athletic gait with the slightly hunched posture common to tall men, he was approaching rapidly. In a moment we would draw level with one another. I was trying to think of a way of engaging him in conversation before he walked by, when Poppy stepped in. As though she knew exactly what I wanted, she darted forward to confront Barry, pawing at his large black shoes and wagging her tail. He immediately squatted down to pet her and she rolled over onto her back. I seized the opportunity to make friends with the local policeman.

'I'm sorry about my dog,' I lied.

Poppy opened one eye and seemed to wink knowingly at me, as though she knew I wasn't sorry at all.

'She just wants to make friends with you. She won't hurt you,' I added almost automatically.

The policeman was crouching down, rubbing Poppy's chest, while she growled ecstatically. Through the stretched fabric of his trousers his knees looked bony yet strong. The prospect of my little dog intimidating him was laughable, and I couldn't help smiling. Barry straightened up and introduced himself with a toothy grin that made him look dopey. He had sandy coloured hair that flopped forward over his eyes, and a large broad face.

'I know who you are,' I said. 'We met at Christmas, in the pub. That is,' I added, 'your aunt pointed you out to me but I don't believe we actually spoke.'

He gave another grunt. 'There were a lot of people there,' he muttered.

'I'm Emily Wilson,' I went on, extending a hand. My fingers disappeared in the warm grip of his enormous hand.

'It's very nice to meet you, Emily,' he replied, rather formally. 'Aunt Maud told me you moved into the village. I was sorry to hear about the trouble you had with your neighbour in the lane.'

For a second, my heart seemed to jump into my throat, but then I realised he was referring to the previous owner of The Laurels, the woman who had gone mad and imprisoned me, along with her daughter, in a subterranean cell. Everyone in the village had known about it, and no doubt the whole Swindon police force had been apprised of the situation at the time.

I shook my head with a smile, dismissing the incident. 'That's history,' I said, wondering how I could move the discussion on to the present resident of The Laurels.

'Of course, she moved out and someone else is living there now,' I said and waited to see if he would respond with any information.

'Well, you look after yourself,' he said with an air of finality, but he didn't walk on.

On a sudden impulse, I told him that I was meeting a couple of friends in The Plough that evening. 'You're welcome to come along, if you're free.'

Barry grunted, which seemed to be his response whenever an answer was expected.

That evening Poppy and I took our usual walk down to the pub. Hannah was already there. Not long after I sat down and settled Poppy under the table with one of her favourite dog chews, Toby joined us. When he had bought a round, I told them about my encounter with the policeman, explaining that if anyone could help us discover what had happened to Richard's wife, he might.

'This could be serious,' I said. 'Barry might be able to tell us something and if he doesn't know, he might be able to find out. He's a policeman so he must have access to all sorts of sources of information.

'Well?' Hannah prompted me. 'What did he say?'

'I tried to broach the subject but all he did was grunt.'

'Is that because he's a pig?' Toby asked and burst out laughing at his joke.

I joined in, but Hannah scolded us for being disrespectful.

'It doesn't matter. He's not here,' Toby said.

'No, but he might turn up,' I said. 'I invited him to join us here this evening for a drink.'

'You did what?'

'Oh God, is this going to become a regular thing?' Toby wanted to know.

I was dismayed that my friends weren't more impressed by my investigative skills, but before we had time to continue our discussion, Barry walked into the bar. Seeing me, he grinned and waved wildly. A woman was walking past him at that moment carrying a couple of pint glasses, and he accidentally knocked one of them, spilling beer on the floor, and on the woman's trousers.

'You clumsy oaf,' she squawked.

We couldn't hear what Barry said, but it was clear that he managed to appease the woman before accompanying her to the bar together where he appeared to pay for four pints which he helped her carry to her table. Toby, Hannah and I watched with varying degrees of amusement.

'He seems nice,' Hannah murmured.

'It's hard to believe he's a policeman,' I replied, 'I mean, considering how clumsy and gormless he is.'

'You don't know he's gormless,' Hannah hissed.

I was surprised by her ferocity, but a moment later Barry joined us and we left off glaring at one another to smile at him.

'Hello, Emily,' he said shyly.

Toby eyed him with suspicion, while Hannah smiled and fluttered her eyelashes.

'Have you got something in your eye?' Toby asked her, leaning forward solicitously.

'No, no, I'm fine,' she answered, slightly disconcerted. 'I see you've met Emily. Please, join us,' she added, looking up at Barry.

He drew up a chair.

'That's better,' Hannah said. 'You're so tall, I was getting a neck ache looking up at you.' She giggled.

But Barry was looking at me and all at once I felt awkward. He seemed perfectly at ease and offered to buy a round, which went some way towards mollifying Toby. Still unsure why Toby was so vexed about Barry joining us, I resolved to challenge him about it later. But for now, we had Barry with us, and I was determined to find out as much as I could.

'As you know, I'm quite new to the village,' I said to steer the conversation.

He grunted politely.

'But my next-door neighbour is even newer to the village than I am,' I offered disingenuously. 'He's called Richard and he seems to have moved in alone, although he has a wife. We were wondering,' I glanced at my two friends who were both staring at the table, 'we were wondering what happened to his wife.'

Barry grunted and took a swig of his beer.

'You know the village well, don't you?' I enquired, smiling at Barry.

'I've lived in the area all my life,' he replied sidestepping the question. He sighed. 'My parents died in a car crash when I was a very young lad, and my Aunt Maud took me in and raised me. I owe her a lot.' He took another gulp of beer. 'If it wasn't for her, I'd probably have gone into care and I doubt I'd be the man I am today. Yes, I have a lot to be thankful for. So,' he went on in a brighter tone, 'how do you like living in Ashton Mead? It must seem very quiet after London.'

I was surprised that he knew where I had lived before moving to the village, and said so.

'Ah,' Barry replied, tapping the side of his nose knowingly with one finger, 'you'd be surprised what we know.'

Presumably he was referring to information held by the police force.

'So what can you tell us about the newcomer to the lane?' Hannah asked directly, losing patience with the exchange of pleasantries.

'We want to be sure Emily hasn't got another lunatic living next door to her,' Toby explained. 'She's our friend and we try to look out for her.'

Barry grunted.

'So, what can you tell us about him?' Hannah prompted him.

Barry shook his head and explained that he couldn't share any information of a private or personal nature with members of the public. He was still looking at me and I saw that Hannah was fidgeting restlessly.

'It's more than my job's worth,' he added apologetically. 'And it wouldn't be right. How would you like it if I went around sharing information about you with anyone who asked?'

This wasn't going well. When Barry stood up to leave, I realised that he had only accepted my invitation to join us out of a spirit of community solidarity. As the local policeman he clearly felt it was incumbent on him to forge good relations with residents in the area. It was probably one of his official duties and he would be able to report back to his senior officers that he had spent time in The Plough talking to people and listening to their concerns.

'I'll see you again soon, I hope,' he said, looking directly at me. And then he left.

'Well, that was a big waste of time,' Toby said, leaning back in his chair with an air of complacency.

'We need to see more of him, win his trust,' Hannah told me. 'Why don't I have a go?'

'He's not a roulette wheel,' Toby said.

I heard myself grunt.

8

As Lorna's great niece, somehow I had been accepted quite readily in Ashton Mead. Lorna had lived there longer than many of the present residents had been alive, and I was viewed as a kind of extension of my great aunt. By leaving me her house, it was as if she had tacitly vouched for me. In the absence of any such credentials, Richard seemed to awaken quite unjustifiable misgivings among the established villagers. But it was the meeting with Barry that appeared to rekindle Hannah's interest in my new neighbour.

'I haven't seen much of him since we were at school,' she murmured. 'He always was tall but he used to be spotty too. Who would have thought he would have turned out like that?'

'Like what?' Toby enquired, clearly amused by her preoccupation with Barry now that he had left the pub.

'Like that,' she replied. 'So tall and –'

'You just said he was always tall,' I laughed surprised by her interest in Barry, who had struck me as nice enough, but gauche.

'Yes, but he's so confident now. He used to be such a wimp.'

'Put a man in a uniform,' Toby said, shaking his head. 'Watch yourself, Hannah.'

She sighed and I had a feeling his warning was wasted on her.

Hannah was curious, but Toby was adamant that I should have nothing to do with Richard.

'We don't know the first thing about him,' he insisted.

'You didn't know anything about me when I moved in,' I pointed out.

But we all knew that was different. We spent the rest of the evening arguing about Richard, while Poppy slept peacefully under the table. We reached an impasse, and parted without reaching any resolution about how to proceed.

The following evening I noticed a car on Richard's drive next to his red Citroën. Wondering if he and his wife had reconciled after all, I hesitated to call, but my curiosity was irresistible and I rang the bell. Poppy sat down patiently on the doorstep, waiting. After a few moments, Richard opened the door.

'I saw the car on your drive,' I began and faltered.

It was difficult to explain why I had decided to call on him just when he had a visitor. Once again, Poppy came to my rescue, barking and jumping up at Richard.

'I'm sorry,' I said. 'She can't bear to be ignored. She just wants you to say hello to her and then she'll be quiet.'

Richard laughed. 'You'd better come in then,' he said, looking down at Poppy.

She leapt forward and I followed, overcome with embarrassment, and wondering what Richard would think of me. It must have been obvious I was only calling out of curiosity. The man who rose to greet me was about my age. He could almost have been a model of Richard when he was thirty years younger. He had the same round face and penetrating dark eyes, but there the resemblance ended because he had a full head of light brown hair, and he was slim and a little taller than Richard.

'This is my son, Ralph,' Richard said, with a proprietorial beam.

Poppy trotted over to Ralph and sniffed inquisitively at his legs. To my surprise, instead of pestering him for attention, she let out a low whimper and turned her back on him. Returning to Richard, she rolled over onto her back exposing her soft underbelly, inviting him to scratch it.

'She's usually very friendly with strangers,' I told Ralph apologetically.

He scowled. 'I can see that,' he said, resuming his seat.

Meanwhile, Poppy was enjoying Richard's attentiveness. After a few minutes, he bustled off to the kitchen to open a bottle of wine, with Poppy trotting eagerly at his heels.

'And I haven't forgotten about you,' Richard added as he left the room.

'It's nice to meet one of my dad's new neighbours,' Ralph said stiffly, when we were alone together.

I explained that I had been living in Mill Lane for about a year. Ralph had heard that the previous owner was insane, and asked me whether I had met her. Reluctant to rake up unpleasant memories of the past, I gave a vague answer to the effect that I had seen her coming and going but we hadn't been friends.

Ralph nodded. 'It seems to be quite a closed community from what dad's told me. Did it take you very long to settle in and feel accepted?'

While I was explaining how my situation had differed from Richard's, he returned and poured us each a glass of white wine.

'If you prefer red, that's not a problem, of course,' he said with a smile, 'but this one is nicely chilled so I thought you might like to try it. I've only given you a taster. If you like it, we can fill our glasses.'

'I really wasn't expecting to stay long,' I remonstrated.

'Yet you called,' Ralph pointed out. There was a slight edge to his voice and Richard frowned at him, insisting that he was always pleased to see me.

'And Poppy, of course,' he added.

She was dozing by his feet, but lifted her floppy ears when he mentioned her name and he laughed. We chatted for a while about my dog, and the conversation moved on to dogs in general.

'You mentioned you were thinking of getting a dog,' I said. 'It's a lovely area for them, with so much green space just across the lane.'

Ralph wanted to know why it was called Mill Lane, and whether there had ever been a mill there. The close proximity to the river meant that was highly likely, but I hadn't researched the history of the village and wasn't sure. Richard was interested in the question, and said he would look it up and let us both know. History was a particular interest of his. We chatted inconsequentially for some time, voicing our appreciation of the chilled wine, and discussing the locality, and I lingered, hoping to spot an opportunity to enquire about Richard's wife.

'So what brought you to Ashton Mead?' I asked him at last, thinking a direct approach might, after all, be best. 'I mean, until I was left a house here, I knew nothing about the village except that I'd seen its name when I wrote to my great aunt when I was a child. So how did you hear about it?'

Richard launched into an account of how he had wanted to relocate to the country, and had been eyeing properties in the area for some time. He explained that he hadn't wanted to move too far from London.

'I suppose you wanted to be near your wife,' I blurted out and immediately regretted having mentioned her.

Richard looked pained, and his son glared at me, making no attempt to conceal his anger. Responding to the change in atmosphere, Poppy sat up and barked, and for a moment I was preoccupied with telling her to be quiet.

'I'm sorry, she doesn't bark much. It must have been a fox outside. They're everywhere. Apparently it's increasingly a problem for the local farmers.'

'I hardly ever hear her bark,' Richard conceded.

Responding to his father's composure, Ralph sat back in his chair, watching us both cautiously.

'She's a very well-behaved dog,' Richard went on amiably. 'She must be very happy living with you.'

'Let's hope she isn't the victim of an attack,' Ralph added almost under his breath.

It sounded like a threat and I turned to him in surprise. 'An attack? What do you mean? What sort of attack?'

'Didn't you just say there are a lot of foxes around here?' he replied. 'I would have thought they might attack a small dog like Poppy, if she behaves aggressively towards them, barking and that. For such a small dog, she does have a very loud bark.' He laughed, as though his comment was intended to be light-hearted.

Richard, meanwhile, was sitting quietly as though his son had said nothing untoward. Feeling uncomfortable, I assured Ralph that Poppy would be more than a match for any stray fox. She was stronger and more agile than he might think. I was tempted to add that I had a gun at home, just in case he had any nefarious ideas, but decided against it. Not only would it be an outright lie, but knowing how fast word travelled in the village, I was afraid I might receive a visit from the police enquiring about illegal ownership of a firearm. It didn't seem sensible to raise the subject of Richard's wife again, and I left soon after that. Ralph watched me go with a louring expression that left no doubt in my mind that he was hostile, and possibly even violent. Poppy's antagonism towards him only served to confirm my unease. It crossed my mind that if Richard had killed his wife, as several people suspected, then Ralph would probably know all about it and might want to protect his father. Ralph might even have had a hand in pushing his mother in the river. I would have to be careful.

9

IN A QUIET PERIOD at work the next day, I asked Hannah if I might take Poppy for a walk and was surprised when she told me she had been thinking the same. The café was so quiet, she suggested we close up for an hour and do just that. She needed to pick up some supplies from the shop which she could do on the way back. We automatically walked down to the river. It was a bright cold day in late March, and the last of the daffodils were still out, making a bright splash of colour against the grass dotted with crocuses and buttercups.

'I love daffodils,' Hannah said. 'They really signal the beginning of spring. There's no going back to winter once the daffodils come out.'

Her enthusiasm was evident in the small pots of daffodils she kept on the tables in the café, and its bright yellow paintwork and awning. I had resolved to say nothing more about my neighbour and our suspicions concerning his wife, but this time it was Hannah who raised the subject again. It seemed that whenever she lost interest in the drowned woman, I couldn't stop speculating about what had happened, and every time I decided to walk away from the subject, my friend's interest revived. The discussion started innocuously enough.

'What do you think of Barry?' she asked me.

'He seems very nice,' I hedged. 'He's not exactly my cup of tea, but he's nice.'

'Nice how?' she pressed me.

'I think he's kind, and civil, you know, and considerate, and Poppy likes him.'

She laughed. 'That's no surprise. Poppy likes everyone.'

It crossed my mind that my dog didn't like Richard's son.

'Why are you asking about Barry, anyway?' I asked her. 'Do you like him?'

She launched into a rambling account of her impression of him when they had been at school. 'I was just so surprised to see him again, close up like that, in the pub the other night. I mean, I've seen him driving around in his police car, and even walking around the village from time to time, but he looks so different in his uniform. I hardly recognised him in the pub.'

'Do you fancy him?' I asked.

She turned to look at me almost accusingly. 'Why not? What's wrong with him?'

'Nothing, there's nothing wrong with him, he's just –' I struggled to find the right words. 'He doesn't strike me as the sharpest tool in the tool box, that's all.'

'You don't know him.'

'And you do?'

'Admittedly he wasn't exactly top of the class at school, but that doesn't mean he's stupid or anything.'

This risked becoming awkward. Diplomacy would be my best course. After all, I didn't want Hannah to hold a grudge against me if she ever did end up in a relationship with Barry. At the same time, I was reluctant to encourage her to rush into a romance with someone I thought couldn't possibly turn out to be a good match for her. I decided to approach the issue from the opposite end.

'Hannah,' I ventured, 'you are one of the cleverest people I've ever met.'

'What are you talking about? I'm not clever.'

'You run your own business.'

'With money my ex gave me.'

'Yes, but you manage the place on your own. That takes brains.'

'Yet you think I'm too stupid to work out what you're getting at? If you think Barry's not intelligent enough for me, why not just come out and say it? But I hardly think you're in a position to judge. You've met him, what? Once?'

All I could do was apologise if she felt offended, and reassure her that I had no doubt she knew what she was doing.

'Thank you, but I don't need your permission to go out with someone,' she answered frostily.

'You are pissed off with me. I knew it!' I cried out, and for some reason my exclamation made her laugh.

'Now,' she went on, 'never mind my love life, or lack of it. What about your next-door neighbour?'

So I told her about my visit the previous day. She listened, her eyes wide with interest.

'Why didn't you tell me?' she asked, when I had finished relating what had taken place.

'It didn't seem that important,' I replied a little sheepishly. 'I mean, we just talked about dogs, and about Poppy, and about how it takes time to settle in somewhere new. It was all very harmless. I don't think his son liked me,' I added.

Hesitantly I told her about my enquiry concerning Richard's wife. Hannah's eyes widened even further and we stood perfectly still, staring at one another until Poppy tugged on her lead and whimpered.

'You actually asked him where she was?' Hannah whispered.

I shook my head. 'Not in so many words, no. I wasn't that blatant about it. It was more like –' I paused, trying to recall exactly what I had said to Richard in front of his son. 'Richard said he wanted to live near London and I said I thought he must have wanted to be near his wife, something like that, as if I thought she had stayed behind in London when he moved away.'

Hannah nodded. 'And? Tell me exactly, word for word what he said.'

Again I shook my head because I couldn't really recall him saying anything.

'He must have said something,' she protested.

'Then Poppy started barking and that defused the situation and we talked about dogs and Ashton Mead and stuff like that and then I left. '

Hannah looked cross but there was nothing more to say. Watching my little dog scurrying busily around, I tried to forget about Richard and Ralph and the body in the river. Poppy sniffed eagerly at a small clump of primroses growing wild on the grassy slope before lifting one leg and peeing on the little flowers. Her action seemed like a metaphor for my life in Ashton Mead, a picturesque village that threatened to be overwhelmed by a dark cloud that hung over it. But the primroses would continue to flourish, undisturbed by my dog watering them. The problems threatening to disrupt my life would not be so easily solved.

On our way back to the tea shop, Hannah stopped off at the grocery store and sent me on ahead to open up. As luck would have it, a minibus load of holidaymakers arrived as soon as I turned the sign around. We were almost out of milk, and had run out of cream completely, so my heart sank when all nine of the customers ordered cream teas. I hesitated to take the order, wondering whether to come clean or hang on and hope Hannah would be back in time with the supplies. I decided to try and spin it out and repeated the order, speaking as slowly as I could.

'So that's eight full cream teas?'

'Nine,' a strident woman who appeared to be in charge corrected me.

I made a show of counting the members of the group, who were spread out around three tables. The woman tutted, muttering crossly, that she knew how many people were in her party.

'Right you are, that's nine of you,' I agreed. 'And is it cream teas all round?'

The order was confirmed. I glanced through the window but there was no sign of Hannah. If she had stopped to chat to Maud, she might be a while yet. By now I was bitterly regretting having kept quiet about the situation. Reluctant to turn customers away, I had landed myself in an impossible position, and was going to have to tell nine women that I had taken their order knowing it couldn't be fulfilled. Somehow I had to delay serving the tea. Forcing a smile, I asked each of the women in turn whether she wanted cream or butter with her scones, and then I moved on to the jam, offering a choice of strawberry or raspberry, although I knew we only ever served strawberry jam.

At last I could drag the process out no longer, and retired to the kitchen in a state of near panic. If Hannah wasn't back soon, I would have to return to the café and admit to the waiting customers that we couldn't even provide them with enough milk for all their tea, let alone cream for their scones. I could hardly tell them I had spilt the cream and the milk. Desperately I laid out the scones with butter and jam – all strawberry – and filled the teapots. There was nothing more to do but wait and hope that Hannah would come bursting into the kitchen to rescue me. I opened the back door and looked outside in the vain hope that we might have left a carton of milk in the yard. As I glanced around, Poppy dodged past me and darted across the kitchen into the café. I raced after her but was too slow to catch her. This was a complete disaster.

I ran into the café, apologising to everyone, and assuring them that the dog was gentle and would never harm anyone. No one took any notice of me. All nine women were too busy making a fuss over Poppy who was gazing round at them, wagging her tail and growling with pleasure as they jostled each other in their eagerness to pet her.

'Isn't she adorable?' one of them cried out.

'Look at her little ears.'

'Such beautiful eyes.'

'She's so soft.'

Eventually I dragged Poppy back out to the yard where she stared quizzically at me, as if to say, 'Well, you needed someone to distract the customers from their long wait, didn't you?'

The teapots were no longer hot by the time Hannah walked in, laden with shopping bags, and I was on the verge of despair. Hurriedly I explained the situation and Hannah set about making fresh tea while I filled the milk jugs and pots of cream. We succeeded in averting a crisis, although I had to apologise for having no raspberry jam.

'What made you offer a choice of jams?' Hannah asked me when the customers had gone.

I explained that I had tried to stall by offering alternatives, and Hannah laughed.

'Next time I'll just tell the truth,' I vowed.

'Oh no, you won't,' she replied. 'That was an order for nine cream teas this afternoon, and it's not even teatime yet. If this carries on, we'll be running short of cream again. I knew I could rely on you to hold the fort.' She beamed at me.

'Well, next time, I'll go to the shop and leave you here to cope,' I told her.

'No way,' she replied. 'I might need you here if we have to keep customers waiting again. You're a natural.'

I wondered if she would be quite so pleased with me if she knew that it was Poppy, and not me, who had kept our customers entertained while they were waiting for their tea.

10

We left the café in heavy rain which showed no sign of letting up. Poppy and I hurried back to Rosecroft, skirting the puddles, and decided not to venture out again that evening. Having rubbed Poppy with an old towel and had a bite to eat, I changed into pyjamas and dressing gown, and settled down on the sofa. Everyone had been talking about the television detective series based on the Geraldine Steel books. Although I had read the books, I hadn't yet got round to watching it. Even my mother had seen it.

'You should watch it,' she told me. 'You'll love it.'

'Should' was one of her favourite words when she was addressing me. Usually I took scant notice of her advice, which had never yet proved particularly helpful, but on this occasion, I agreed with her. Poppy curled up at my feet with one of her favourite dog chews, as I made myself comfortable. With a large packet of crisps and a glass of white wine to hand, I prepared to immerse myself in what had been promoted as 'a gripping crime drama'. I was not disappointed, and was feeling duly gripped, when someone knocked at my door. Assuming it was Hannah or Toby come to visit me, having missed me at The Plough that evening, I paused the television and checked my phone but neither of them had called me. It was still raining as I reluctantly heaved myself off the sofa, sending my packet of crisps flying off my lap as I stood up. Poppy, who had nodded off at my feet, leapt up with alacrity, and I hurried to pick up the fallen crisps before she could guzzle them all.

'No,' I scolded her. 'You can't have them all. They're really salty and that's bad for you. Wait just a minute and I'll get you a treat. Let's see who's here first.'

The knocking continued and I hurried to open the front door, wondering if my bell wasn't working. To my surprise, it wasn't either of my friends on my doorstep, but Richard's son Ralph. There was something vaguely menacing about his stern expression that made me hesitate to invite him in, even though the shoulders of his coat looked damp and it was still raining. While I prevaricated, Poppy scurried over to stand beside me, growling softly. Her hostility decided me. Besides, I was in my dressing gown and slippers, had paused my programme, and was impatient to get back to it.

'Do you want something?' I asked, not caring if I sounded rude.

Ralph cleared his throat. 'My father is in a very vulnerable situation just now,' he began, and paused, looking awkward.

Poppy growled again, and Ralph's words made me shiver. It was something of an understatement, if the general suspicion was correct and his father was hoping to evade a murder charge.

'What do you expect me to do?' I asked, taking an involuntary step back.

'You live next door to him,' he replied fatuously. 'Look, it's all right as long as I'm here to keep an eye on him and make sure he doesn't do anything stupid, but I need to get home and I'm worried about leaving him on his own. I really have to go home tomorrow, and I'm not sure I can trust him in his present state. We both know what's being said about him, and it's not helping.'

I stared at him silently and he glared back me, his dark eyes forbidding under lowered brows.

'What do you want?' I demanded.

'Just to tell you that you and all your friends in the village need to watch what you say, or I can't guarantee what might happen.'

'Are you threatening me?' I asked, doing my best to hide my alarm.

'You can take it as a warning, if you like,' he replied. 'But if you go spreading any more stories about my father, you'll have me to answer to.'

With that, he spun on his heel and strode away leaving me shaking. I returned to the television but somehow the drama of a murder investigation seemed slightly less relaxing now that I was convinced my next-door neighbour had killed his wife and might be a threat to my life as well. And clearly his son was no less dangerous a man to cross. After taking Poppy out in the back garden, and checking that all my doors and windows were securely fastened, I went to bed and spent a restless night dreaming about a ghostly woman who crawled out of the river, festooned with water weeds. Pointing a bony finger at me, she accused me of throwing her in the river to drown.

I didn't intend to mention my uninvited caller to Hannah, but when she asked me if I was all right, my resolve crumbled.

'You look terrible,' she said, gazing at me with genuine concern. 'Is everything all right?'

Admitting that I hadn't slept well, I added that Ralph had been to see me to warn me not to say a word against his father. He seemed to be under the impression that I had started the rumour that Richard had murdered his wife.

'He as good as told me to watch out, because Richard might kill again once he was left unattended. He said it was safe while he was there to watch over his father, but he was worried what might happen once Richard was left unsupervised. He said Richard couldn't be trusted and there was no knowing what he might do, no guarantee. And Ralph threatened to deal with me himself if he found out I'd been talking about his father.'

Hannah seemed even more horrified than I was. She insisted I go straight to the police.

'And say what?' I replied. 'That my next-door neighbour's son asked me not to gossip about him? Seriously, Hannah, nothing's happened. He didn't even really threaten me, not in so many words.'

'A woman was fished out of the river,' she reminded me solemnly. 'That's hardly nothing.'

Just then a couple of women came in for breakfast, and we were kept busy for a while. By the time the rush was over, Hannah seemed to have reached a decision.

'I'm going to speak to Barry,' she said. 'I know he visits Maud for tea some Sundays. I'll check with her and find out when he's next going to be there.'

'She might not want you there as well,' I said. 'I mean, he must be like a son to her. If she only sees him every few weeks, she probably likes to have him to herself.'

'We're not going to tell her in advance. We'll just turn up. She can hardly refuse to invite us in.'

'Us?' I echoed, shaking my head. I wanted nothing to do with her scheme.

'You have to come with me or there's no point in my going. I don't know what Ralph said to you, do I?'

I could hardly recall the conversation myself, and said so.

'But you must remember how he made you feel?'

I nodded, because she was right. I could hardly forget the sinister expression in his eyes as he had warned me about his father's violence and his own threat to 'deal with me' himself if I refused to comply with his demands. I promised to think about it, but she already seemed to assume my agreement. That evening I took Poppy for a walk down to The Plough, planning to stop for a swift half before supper. Without even pausing to greet me, Hannah told me she had already spoken to Maud.

'What are you two plotting now?' Toby asked.

Speaking very quietly, Hannah outlined her plan.

Toby laughed. 'You just want to see Barry again,' he said.

'That's not what this is about,' she protested, blushing furiously. 'I'm thinking about Emily's safety, that's all.'

'If you're concerned, don't you think we ought to be reporting Ralph's threats to the police on official channels, not mentioning it to a local constable at a social gathering? I mean, either this is serious or it's not,' Toby said.

Having given his opinion on Hannah's strategy, he stood up to buy another round, but I said it was time for me to leave as I had left my dinner in the oven. I didn't add that I felt more comfortable walking home while it was still light. Musing over what Toby had said, I thought he was probably right to suspect Hannah was using my incident as an excuse to try and see Barry again. All the same, I found myself wishing that Toby had been a little more concerned about me. At one time he had intimated that he was keen to have a relationship with me, but somehow we had settled into a comfortable platonic relationship. It was tricky, because were I to say anything to Hannah about my feelings, she might let something slip to him. If he was no longer interested in me romantically, it would be embarrassing for us both. On balance, I decided to say nothing and hope that he would take the initiative. If all else failed, I might resort to buying some mistletoe for Christmas, but that was still eight months away, and a lot could happen in that time. Hannah and Barry might actually get together, unlikely as it seemed, and that might encourage Toby to approach me. In the meantime, the problem of Richard and his missing wife was more pressing.

11

HAVING FORGOTTEN ABOUT HANNAH'S proposal that we speak to Barry, I was surprised when she closed the tea shop early on Sunday afternoon, which was usually a busy time for us. Placing a freshly baked fruitcake carefully in a box, she reminded me about her plan, and we set off together for Maud's apartment above her grocery store. The shop seemed much larger than its floor space, because Maud managed to cram so many items onto her closely packed shelves. I wondered if she had spent her childhood addicted to jigsaws, because she seemed to fit everything together so skilfully, without wasting a single centimetre of display space. There was a small floor area where customers could stand in front of the till, but the rest of the shop allowed barely enough room for one person to walk along the aisles. Passing another customer involved people shuffling sideways. I couldn't see how the first floor flat would be very large, but Hannah assured me that Maud owned the whole building, as though it was an impressive property.

'That's nice for her,' I replied. 'And very convenient. She just has to go downstairs to get to work.'

'You do realise what it means?'

'It means she owns the shop and the flat above it.'

'Yes, but what I'm saying is that eventually it will all go to Barry.'

'I suppose so.'

'With my tea shop, and his salary and prospects, we could be very comfortable together,' she added, her usually cheerful expression becoming wistful.

'You might if you were a couple, but you're not,' I pointed out, hating to think of her being disappointed.

'Yes, thank you very much, Miss Negativity,' she replied, clearly peeved. 'I'm well aware of that. I'm just saying that if we were ever to become an item, we'd both have something to contribute to our future together.'

As would anyone else who had a property or prospects, I thought, but didn't say. I still sometimes daydreamed about Toby moving into Rosecroft with me, so I was hardly in a position to sneer at my friend's romantic fantasy. Such harmless delusions made it possible to get through the lonely times. We reached a little blue door tucked in beside the shop front. I had passed it many times, barely noticing it was there. Hannah rang the bell and we heard a muffled chime from inside. After a moment, we heard heavy footsteps, and Barry opened the door. If he was surprised to see us, he didn't show it. I made a mental note to point out to Hannah that perhaps she shouldn't take it too seriously if he didn't show any interest in her. His training as a police officer had no doubt taught him to hide his feelings behind a mask of equanimity.

Hannah put on a show of being taken aback to see him and said we would return another time, but he invited us in as we had expected.

'This is perfect timing,' he assured us. 'My aunt has just this minute put the kettle on.'

To my discomfiture, he appeared to direct his invitation at me, even though it was Hannah who had spoken to him.

She told him she had brought a fruitcake which she had just taken out of the oven, and he beamed at me as he replied that it smelt delicious. He led us up a steep flight of stairs to a narrow hallway, and into a cosy living room. A three piece suite was upholstered in pink and purple chintz to match drapes secured with tiebacks on either side of the window. A dark wooden coffee table stood in the centre of the room. A television was attached to the wall on one side of the chimney breast, and a row of glass ornaments sparkled on a shelf on the other side.

Maud seemed really pleased to see us, and she allowed me to let Poppy off her lead to explore the room.

'She's a nosy little dog,' I apologised, but Maud laughed.

She seemed unusually cheerful, which I put down to her pleasure at spending time with her nephew. She smiled at him and Hannah with a proprietorial air although, from what I could see, Barry barely seemed to notice my friend. Hannah handed Maud the fruitcake and our hostess went off to the kitchen to make the tea, leaving Barry to entertain us.

'I visit Maud for Sunday tea when I can. Strictly speaking she's my aunt, but she's more like a mother to me.' He looked at me. 'I hope you're planning to stay in the village? It's a pity, but a lot of people find it too quiet and can't wait to move away.'

Hannah seized on the opportunity to broach the subject of the most recent newcomer to Ashton Mead.

'He's not been here very long. Actually, Emily had an awkward encounter with his son recently. I wonder if she ought to tell you about it, officially, you know.'

Barry frowned. 'I'm not sure I understand.' He turned to me and spoke earnestly and a trifle pompously, as though reciting something he had been schooled in. 'Do you want to make a complaint? If you feel threatened by someone, don't feel embarrassed about notifying the police. It's our job to protect members of the community. Any victim of abusive or threatening behaviour or harassment should bring the situation to our attention. Often a quiet word from us is all it takes to persuade the aggressor to back off,' he concluded with a slightly smug smile.

Although I did my best to assure him that nothing had happened, Hannah was adamant that Ralph had verbally threatened me. Barry was keen to hear what Ralph had said to me, but at that point Maud returned with a tray. In silence we watched her set out a delicate china tea set, complete with matching pot and milk jug. Poppy followed the proceedings with interest, especially when Maud brought in a plate of biscuits. Finally we were all sipping our tea and Maud passed around the cake. Hannah returned to the subject of my next-door neighbour and his son, and I capitulated, realising it was pointless trying to be discreet about the incident, now that Maud knew about it.

'Richard accused me of spreading false rumours about his father, which I honestly never did,' I explained. 'Then he warned me not to provoke his father because he said he – Richard, that is – can be violent.'

Maud gasped and put her hand to her mouth, her eyes stretched wide with alarm, muttering, 'I knew that man was no good. He ought to be behind bars for what he did to his poor wife. '

'He said if I said anything against his father, he – Ralph – would deal with me himself,' I added.

'What did I tell you?' Maud burst out, frowning impatiently at Barry.

'Did he assault you?' Barry asked me, dismissing Maud's question with a shake of his head.

'Everyone knows Richard did away with his wife,' Maud said.

Barry looked at me. 'Is that the rumour he was referring to?'

'I imagine so, but I never started that rumour.'

'You didn't need to. It's common knowledge,' Maud muttered crossly.

'No, it's a rumour,' Barry corrected her.

'Even his own son says he's violent,' Maud replied.

'The point is,' Hannah interrupted their squabble, 'Richard's son threatened Emily.'

'What exactly did he say to you?' Barry asked me.

'He told me he was worried about his father being violent, and he warned me to be careful about what I said. He told me I'd have him to deal with if I said anything against Richard. He seemed to think I'd started the accusation against Richard.'

Barry shook his head. 'What accusation are we talking about here?'

'That Richard killed his wife, of course,' Maud replied. 'The woman Emily found drowned in the river. You must see that the two things can't be unrelated, Richard arriving in Ashton Mead just as a body turned up.'

'It's not just that a woman's body was discovered, but no one seems to know what happened to Richard's wife,' Hannah added. 'He told Emily she'd gone and was never coming back, didn't he?'

I nodded. 'And Ralph threatened to hurt Poppy.'

Barry asked me to repeat what Ralph had said about my dog.

'He said she might be attacked by foxes. Only he wasn't talking about foxes.'

Barry leaned back in his chair looking thoughtful and Hannah and I exchanged a hopeful glance, because it seemed we were getting through to him.

Barry's next words were a disappointment. 'A man is

worried that his father is being maligned, and insists you stop bad-mouthing him, and he expresses concern that Poppy might be attacked by foxes. It's a common misconception by city folk, but I'm sure she'd scare any fox off with that bark of hers.' He leaned down and held out his hand to Poppy who approached him and licked his fingers. Barry looked at me and smiled. 'You don't need to worry about her.' He reached for a second slice of fruitcake. 'Poppy is at far greater risk from ingesting raisins than from being attacked by foxes. You do know that raisins are poisonous for dogs. They're even more toxic than chocolate.' He took a bite of cake.

'But what about Richard? Aren't the police going to do anything about the man? He did away with his wife,' Hannah wailed. 'And now Emily's life is in danger.'

'Where's your evidence that he killed his wife? People pass through here all the time. Anyone could have been here just before the body was discovered. Why is everyone assuming Richard is responsible? And why would he commit a murder right on his own doorstep? You know, it's not unheard of for people to fall in the river, or throw themselves in. And there's no reason to suspect the woman who drowned had any connection to your new neighbour. I suggest you forget about your theories and focus on being good neighbours.'

Hannah looked vexed and Maud lowered her eyes and busied herself pouring more tea. By tacit consent, we said no more about Richard and the conversation drifted into speculation about the weather. It was a safe topic, if dull, and Hannah and I left soon after. Barry followed us downstairs to see us out. As we were saying goodbye, Barry detained me. To my dismay, he invited me to have dinner with him one evening. Stammering, I gave an evasive reply, aware that Hannah was looking crestfallen.

'Have you discovered the identity of the dead woman?' I blurted out.

'The one you found in the river?' Barry replied and I nodded. 'I'm afraid I can't share details of the police investigation,' he replied primly.

Even Poppy turned her back on him.

12

WALKING WITH POPPY THE day after our awkward meeting with Barry in Maud's flat, I noticed a woman walking along the grassy slopes that ran down to the river. Tall and willowy, and wearing a long black coat and black beret, she might have looked elegant yet was somehow gauche. Her shoulders were slightly hunched and she seemed to be constantly glancing around like a restless predator. As we drew nearer to one another I was able to observe her more clearly, but it wasn't until I was close enough to see her bright red lipstick that I remembered where I had seen her before. We kept walking until we drew level with one another and she called out in greeting, staring at me with penetrating black eyes.

'Hello there. It's Emily, isn't it?'

'You came to The Plough, didn't you?' I replied, answering her question with one of my own. 'You're from the paper?'

She inclined her head. '*My Swindon News*. You've probably seen my name in the paper: Dana Flack, senior reporter.'

It wasn't clear whether she was boasting, or merely informing me of her position when she emphasised the word 'senior'. I didn't respond. The reporter bent down to stroke Poppy who responded to the attention by wagging her tail vigorously and pulling on her lead to prevent me walking away, which was my initial inclination.

'You were the one who found the body, weren't you?' Dana asked me, straightening up and taking her phone from her pocket.

'What do you want with me?' I demanded, instantly on my guard.

Sensing my unease, Poppy bristled and let out a little bark, warning the reporter to back off. Dana smiled and reassured me that she only wanted a quiet word, off the record.

'You can put your phone away then,' I replied.

'I'd like to record whatever you say. I won't quote you, but it just helps me remember.'

I shook my head. 'No phone,' I insisted tersely.

She replaced her phone in her pocket, but I had a sneaking suspicion it was still switched on to record through the fabric. Shaking my head again, I started to walk away. Dana followed me.

'I won't talk to you until you can show me your phone isn't on,' I said quietly.

With a sigh, she took her phone out, switched it off completely and held it up to display the black screen before putting it away in her bag. By not returning it to her pocket, she seemed to confirm my earlier suspicion that she had hoped to record my words on her phone through the fabric of her coat. Some things were beyond Poppy's unquestionably impressive powers of perception.

'Well?' I asked rather ungraciously. 'Let's get this over with. What is it you want to know? I'll talk to you again, just this once, on the understanding that you then leave me alone and stop stalking me.'

Dana's eyebrows shot up and she vehemently denied stalking me. She told me she was on her way down to the river to view the site where the body had been found. She was adamant that she had no idea I would be there and it was sheer coincidence, our meeting like that. She had just come there to get some background on the case.

'We don't often see murder investigations in Ashton Mead,' she added by way of explanation. 'And this one is particularly intriguing because the police don't seem to have identified the woman who drowned here – unless they know something they're not sharing with the press. The public have a right to know these things,' she went on with a burst of energy, 'but the police can be a little backward in coming forward. It's two weeks since you – since the drowned woman was found and in all that time we've not heard a peep out of the police.' She threw me an inquisitive glance. 'I don't suppose you know who she was?'

'How should I know anything about her?'

'Well, you were the one who found the body.'

'I just saw her lying in the water, that's all. She was dead so I didn't bother to ask her for her name when I called the police.'

She nodded. 'You could tell she was dead.'

'Yes.'

'How did you know? Can you tell me how she looked?'

'She looked dead,' I replied, annoyed by her insistence. 'And she was in the river,' I added.

The body had been lying, face down, caught in the river weeds that proliferated along the bank, her hair waving on the surface of the water like delicate tendrils of weed. When I had caught a glimpse of the dead woman's face it had resembled a mask from a horror movie, the skin waxy, the eyes sightless and the mouth stretched in a scream that was forever silenced. Instead of offering a description, I shook my head. Something warned me to give away as little detail as possible. The less interesting my account was, the less chance there was that Dana Flack would quote me in her paper. To say the drowned woman looked dead would hardly make riveting copy for a reporter.

'Can you describe what you saw?' she prompted me hopefully.

I could tell she was itching to record my response, but I didn't answer.

'And presumably you were still here when the body was pulled out of the water?' She paused for a moment, waiting for me to speak. 'I'm sorry if this brings back bad memories for you. It must have been a traumatic experience.' She sighed. 'As far as I can tell, the police don't have a clue about who she was. Do you remember if she was wearing any jewellery?'

'I really couldn't say. Although presumably she wasn't wearing anything that could help the police identify her.'

'So she wasn't wearing a wedding ring, for example? If she was, that would narrow down the possibilities.'

It was a reasonable question, and it struck me that Dana and I were seeking the same information. She was eager for a story, while I felt an illogical connection with the dead woman, having been the one to discover her. Not only that, but I was keen to know whether or not my next-door neighbour was a homicidal maniac. For our own reasons, we were both desperate to discover the truth. Perhaps we stood a better chance of success if we worked together. Treating her with hostility wasn't going to help me find out what had happened to the dead woman.

'No,' I conceded, 'I could be wrong, but now you mention it, I'm pretty sure she wasn't wearing a wedding ring. That doesn't necessarily mean she wasn't married though. If she was murdered, her killer could have removed it to conceal her identity or it might have fallen off in the water.'

Dana smiled, realising that she had persuaded me to open up to her. We walked on, and to stop her asking any more questions, I began to quiz her about her own work. She confided that she had been working for the local paper for six years and was frustrated that her career had stalled.

'News print is dying on its feet,' she said miserably. 'And new reporters are coming along all the time, with their degrees in journalism, clamouring to work as unpaid interns, just to get the experience, but where does that leave the rest of us experienced reporters? The fact is, they can't do the job as well as us, but they're free and keen and then as soon as we take them on, they mostly turn out to be useless, and the ones that are any good are breathing down our necks hoping to replace us.'

'Slave labour,' I muttered.

'Exactly. Most of my colleagues have been slung out, after years on the paper, and I'm barely hanging on by the skin of my teeth. I need this story, Emily. It could be my big break. If I can make it out of this backwater I might stand a chance of building a career, doing what I love, but I'm not going anywhere if all I ever get to write about is the birth of triplets, or a garden shed blowing over in a gust of wind.'

While she was talking, we had walked down to the water's edge and I realised with a slight shudder that we were roughly at the spot where the body had been discovered. The police cordons had been removed and it was an idyllic scene, with sunlight shimmering on the river as it flowed slowly by and a few late daffodils swaying in the warm breeze. Poppy was sniffing around, scratching at the earth, looking for worms and moss. Out of the corner of my eye I caught sight of something glinting.

'No, Poppy. Poppy, drop it!'

Pulling her back, I leaned down and picked a gold chain out of the mud. A dark green stone hung from it, encased in a gold setting. The chain was made of stout gold links, and before hiding it in my fist I noticed a long scratch down the back of the pendant's casing. Dana and I stared at one another and I saw my own excitement reflected back at me from her eyes.

She held out her hand. 'What's that you just picked up? Give it to me.'

'No. We mustn't touch it any more.'

Poppy looked up at me with a puzzled expression as I pulled one of her dog waste bags out of my pocket, but this bag wasn't for her. She watched, mystified, as I swiftly slipped the chain into the bag and slid it into my pocket before the reporter could see what was hidden in my fist. It was possible Poppy had found a clue to the identity of the dead woman.

Dana stepped forward, one hand outstretched. 'I need you to give me whatever you just found,' she said. 'It doesn't belong to you, and you have no right –'

'It doesn't belong to you either,' I retorted. 'And I have as much right as you to keep it or take it to the police. What I do with it is none of your business.'

'The public have a right to know –' she began, taking another pace towards me.

We would never know whether we would have resorted to a physical scrap, because Poppy sensed the hostility that had arisen between us. Positioning herself in front of me, she barked furiously at Dana who took an involuntary step backwards.

'Watch out!' I cried out, seeing her perilously close to the water's edge.

Swearing vigorously, she moved away from the river and thankfully away from me, while Poppy followed her, still barking ferociously.

'That animal should be put down,' Dana snapped as she retreated.

I gathered Poppy up in my arms and smothered her with kisses, much to her dismay. Desperate to be released from this undignified restraint, Poppy wriggled and growled, but she must have understood that she had rescued me from the unwanted attentions of the senior reporter from *My Swindon News*.

13

IF ANYTHING, HANNAH WAS even more excited about what Poppy had found by the river than I was. She was convinced the chain had to be connected to the drowned woman, since Poppy had come across it on the river bank right where the body had been discovered. Although Hannah was eager to see the chain and pendant for herself, we agreed it was best not to handle it again. If the woman *had* been murdered, which we agreed was at least possible, then there might be some residual fingerprints left on the chain or the stone by her killer. So we decided to leave it where it was, safely hidden away in a small plastic bag in a pocket of my jeans. Hannah had to be satisfied with my description of it. The likelihood was that the damage to the pendant had been sustained when its wearer drowned, or possibly even when she had been pulled out of the water, but it could turn out to be an identifying feature if the pendant had already been scratched before the woman fell in the river. It was a thrilling possibility.

Hannah made a huge fuss of Poppy, which was nothing unusual.

'What a clever little dog you are,' she said, squatting down to pet Poppy who was very happy to respond by rolling over onto her back to have her tummy stroked. 'Do you know you might have discovered a vital clue that will help the police identify that poor woman who drowned?' Poppy growled softly and Hannah laughed. 'It's almost as though she understands what I'm saying. I wish my mother's dog had half Poppy's brains.'

'Jack Tzus are an intelligent breed,' I replied modestly, although secretly I was ready to burst with pride.

'That explains it,' Hannah replied.

'Yes, but I think she's exceptional, even for a Jack Tzu,' I added.

Our immediate concern was what to do with the piece of jewellery hidden in my pocket. We considered the various options, whenever the café was empty, taking care to abandon our discussion the instant a customer came in. Dana had already seen the chain. We didn't want anyone else to hear about it, although it would probably be impossible to keep it to ourselves now that a reporter knew about it.

'I can't believe we have something that could be a vital clue in a murder case.' My friend's eyes shone as she spoke.

We chatted about the situation on and off all day, and the upshot of all our feverish discussions was that we had only one real choice, and that was to hand the item over to the police. As long as we kept it, we were potentially withholding evidence from the police in a murder investigation. That was a serious matter, and I had no wish to end up with a criminal conviction for obstructing the police. I might even face a custodial sentence. Alluring though it was to speculate about how we might use the pendant to track down a killer, we had to accept that it wasn't feasible for us to do that.

'They can't send us to prison for finding a pendant,' Hannah laughed, but I could tell she was worried.

'I could be prosecuted for withholding evidence,' I pointed out, 'and you would be involved as an accessory.'

'Only if the police knew that I knew,' she said. 'I'd deny all knowledge of it once you accused me and leave you to face the music alone.' She laughed to indicate that she was joking.

'Of course, I wouldn't drop you in it,' I hastened to reassure her. 'There's no point in both of us risking getting into trouble. But even if there's no chance of you being implicated in any way, *I* don't want to go to prison.'

We agreed that I should take the jewellery to the police station in Swindon.

'If you give me the morning off, I'll go first thing tomorrow,' I said. 'That's reasonable, isn't it? No one could accuse us of holding onto evidence if I take it in then. It's the first reasonable opportunity and, after all, it's probably got nothing to do with the drowned woman anyway.'

We agreed that was the sensible course to take.

'So that gives us time to do a little ferreting around, and see what we can find out,' I added.

Hannah had been thinking the same. We needed to come up with an excuse for me to visit Richard again, so that I could try to take a closer look at the photograph of his wife and see if she was wearing a gold chain with an emerald pendant. Even if the pendant wasn't visible, a chain around her neck would provide a strong indication that the woman in the river could be Richard's absent wife. The chain might have been dropped, and have no connection to the body at all, but that seemed unlikely. And if we were able to find anything to indicate that the chain might have belonged to Richard's missing wife, I could pass that information on to the police when I handed in the chain.

'We might even call the police tonight,' I added, 'if I can get a look at Richard's photos and see a pendant matching this one visible round his wife's neck.'

'Whatever happens, once this is done you need to promise me you'll keep well away from your new neighbour.'

In the meantime, I had to make one more visit to Richard's house. Hannah suggested I smuggle a magnifying glass in with me, so that I could study his wife in the family photograph when he was out of the room.

'Do you think you'll be able to manage it without him seeing you?' she asked, suddenly getting cold feet now that we had come up with a plan.

I shrugged. 'There's only one way to find out. Don't look so worried. What can go wrong? The worst he can think is that I'm being nosy, wanting to look at his photos.'

'Through a magnifying glass?' Hannah asked. She nodded uncertainly. 'You can say photography is a hobby of yours.'

Thinking that it was probably safer to lie as little as possible, I dismissed that idea. We agreed not to tell Toby abut our plan until after I had visited Richard. Toby would want me to hand the chain to the police straight away, and he would make a terrible fuss about letting me go and see Richard on my own. Of course, taking Toby with me to Richard's house would be sensible but, as I said to Hannah, my neighbour would have no idea about my real motive for visiting him so there was actually no danger to me in going there. And as far as the police were concerned, one day's delay wasn't going to make much difference. I intended to take the chain to the police station in Swindon the next day, whatever happened at Richard's house in the meantime.

'It's not as if there's a police station in Ashton Mead I can take it to,' I said. 'It's perfectly reasonable to wait and go tomorrow.'

'They won't know that Poppy found it today,' Hannah pointed out. 'She could have come across it tomorrow.'

'Except that the reporter from *My Swindon News* was there today.'

Remembering that Dana Flack had been snooping down by the river, where she had seen me pick something up, we agreed it was important that I take the chain to the police first thing the next morning. That meant I needed to look at Richard's photograph that very evening. As a reporter, Dana was almost bound to succumb to the temptation to create a story around Poppy's latest discovery. We had to act fast so that I could hand the chain to the police before Dana had time to write her report. Hannah nipped home before tea time to fetch a magnifying glass. I left the café early, with Poppy in tow, and set off for Mill Lane. The sun was out and it was one of those lovely spring days when the weather is warm and there are birds trilling and bees buzzing, sharing the joy of being alive. I even saw a butterfly; Poppy pulled on her lead, desperate to chase it. Not until I had rung Richard's bell did I experience a flicker of fear.

Until that moment, I had been caught up in the urgency of my mission and hadn't stopped to consider the plan. Now I regretted having brought the chain with me. If Richard were somehow to catch sight of it, the situation would be awkward, to say the least. Telling myself that he could have no idea his dead wife's jewellery was stashed in the pocket of my jeans, I forced myself to remain outwardly calm and waited. Sensing my disquiet, Poppy whimpered softly and pressed herself against my leg as though to reassure me that she was there.

'That's all well and good, but it's your fault I'm here at all,' I whispered crossly to her, and she whimpered.

Richard looked surprised to see me, and he admitted as much. I smiled foolishly, and muttered inanely that we were next-door neighbours, so how could we not see each other. Instead of inviting me in, as I had expected, he just stood there, smiling warily at me, waiting for me to speak. I could hardly invite myself into his house, yet somehow I had to get inside to look at his photos.

'It's just a neighbourly visit,' I said.

Once again, Poppy came to my rescue, straining on her leash, and making it clear that she wanted to go indoors.

Richard laughed. 'Oh well, now you're here, I suppose you'd better come in.'

Under normal circumstances I would have felt awkward, inveigling my way into Richard's house for a third visit when I hadn't asked him round even once, but I was too focused on my mission to worry about social niceties. Feeling like an undercover agent, I entered his house with the pendant and the magnifying glass concealed in my jeans. He led us into the living room where we sat down. I unclipped Poppy's lead and she set off at once on a voyage of discovery around the room, sniffing in corners and under furniture. Finally she settled down beside Richard so that he could lean down and tickle her. She closed her eyes and growled very softly.

Richard laughed. 'Your dog thinks she's a cat.'

Despite my tension, I found his laughter infectious. 'Dogs make that low rumbling sound when they're happy. She's not really purring. It's more like a gentle growl.'

'Well, it certainly sounds like she's purring.'

I was wondering how to persuade Richard to leave the room when Poppy sat up, with her tongue hanging out.

'She might be thirsty,' I fibbed.

'Oh, I'm sorry, where are my manners? Let me get you both something. I'll give Poppy some water in the kitchen and can I bring you tea or coffee, or a glass of wine if you prefer?'

I felt guilty putting him to the trouble of acting as a host when I was only there to spy on him, but I accepted the offer of a cup of tea. Making tea would keep him in the kitchen for longer than pouring a glass of wine. As soon as he left the room, with Poppy trotting at his heels, I leapt to my feet and whipped the magnifying glass out of my pocket. It had a round lens attached to a long handle, like ones I'd seen in pictures of Sherlock Holmes, which seemed appropriate to my prying. Hurrying over to the fireplace, I screwed up my eyes and stared at the dark-haired woman in Richard's photograph. Both of her hands were resting on her sons' shoulders, and she was wearing what appeared to be a dark dress. Raising the magnifying glass, I leaned forward to scrutinise her throat. My heart seemed to pound when I saw she was wearing a chain round her neck, but it was impossible to be sure that it matched the one hidden in a waste bag in my pocket. As I was trying to hold the lens in the best position, Richard spoke. He must have entered the room without making a sound, before I had a chance to conceal the magnifying glass. Hearing his voice, I froze in silent terror.

'You're admiring my photo,' he said. 'Those were good times. I'm afraid they won't return.' He heaved a loud sigh. 'Yes, those were happy times.'

As long as my back was turned towards him, he couldn't see the magnifying glass clutched in my hand, but when I turned round he was bound to see it. As though she could sense my panic, Poppy ran over to me and rose up on her hind legs, scrabbling at my jeans with her front paws. Quickly I reached down and slipped the magnifying glass between her jaws. She ran off with it, and crouched down, her tail wagging, expecting me to give chase. Seizing one of my belongings so that I had to run after her was one of her favourite games.

'What has she got there?' Richard asked.

'I didn't see. She must have picked something up from the floor.'

Richard put down his tray, took the magnifying glass from her and frowned, turning it over in his hand. 'This isn't mine.'

Poppy barked. She turned to look at me accusingly, as though asking me why I had allowed Richard to step in and spoil our game.

'Perhaps Ralph left it here?' I suggested, taking my tea from the tray and sitting down.

'Yes, that must be it. Oh well, I'll put it by and try to remember to return it to him when I next see him,' he said. 'I don't suppose he's missed it because he hasn't asked about it.'

Sipping my tea, I felt increasingly nervous in case Ralph phoned and Richard learned that the magnifying glass didn't belong to his son at all. If that happened, I would just have to deny having brought it into the house myself and suggest Poppy that must have found it in a corner somewhere, left behind by the previous home owner. I would have to replace Hannah's magnifying glass, but that problem faded into insignificance beside the need to extricate myself from Richard's house before my lie could be exposed.

14

AT AROUND TEN O'CLOCK that evening, my phone rang. Seeing that it was Hannah calling, I answered at once. It was obvious why she wanted to speak to me, because I had agreed to call her with any news after visiting my next-door neighbour. Sure enough, she asked me what had happened with Richard. I hated to disappoint her, but had to admit that my visit had been a complete failure. Not only that, but I had unfortunately had to leave her magnifying glass behind. Miserably, I explained how that had happened, and promised to buy her another one. She assured me she didn't care about her magnifying glass; she was just pleased I had escaped with my secret intact. On reflection, she said, she should never have encouraged me to go there alone. If Richard really was a killer, and realised I was spying on him, the situation could have been extremely dangerous for me.

'You could still be at risk,' she added earnestly. 'He lives right next door to you. Are you quite sure he didn't suspect what you were up to?'

'He couldn't have. All we did was sit and drink a cup of tea and talk about Poppy.'

Reassured that there was no way Richard could have realised my motive for going to his house, Hannah asked me about the photograph that was the whole point of my visit. I had already intimated to her that I hadn't discovered anything, and now had to explain how Richard had returned before I had a chance to study the photograph closely. All I had been able to ascertain was that his wife had been wearing a chain around her neck, but that didn't really tell us anything.

'It tells us a lot,' Hannah protested. 'Don't you realise this means that the chain Poppy found could have belonged to his missing wife? And if we can prove that it did, then that means she came to Ashton Mead and we'll know the identity of the drowned woman. We still won't know exactly how she came to fall in the river, but once we've established it was her, it'll be up to the police to interrogate Richard until he confesses. The fact that she lost her chain when she fell in the river must mean she was pushed violently.'

'You've been watching too many police dramas on TV,' I told her.

That night I didn't sleep well, fretting about having concealed potentially important evidence from the police. In the end I went to the kitchen and downed a glass of wine, hoping it would send me to sleep. It worked for a while, but I woke up after a few hours and immediately felt compelled to check that the chain was still safely stowed in the pocket of my jeans. Seeing me up and about, Poppy decided it must be time to go outside for a nose around the garden. Although she didn't normally go out during the night, it seemed not only churlish but also slightly risky to refuse her entreaties. Hoping this wasn't setting a precedent, I took her into the garden where she promptly watered the grass.

'This is just a one-off,' I told her. 'We're not doing this every night.'

By the time we went back indoors I was feeling really tired and finally went back to sleep, only to wake up feeling groggy when my alarm went off. Grumbling to Poppy that I might as well not have gone to bed at all that night, for all the good it did me, I had breakfast and dropped Poppy off at Jane's house. There must have been a downpour during the night, while I was asleep, because the ground was damp and dotted with puddles, but the rain had given over by the time we went out. Poppy was excited to see Jane's elderly dog, Holly, who greeted her with a yawn of resignation. Poppy scampered around, darting backwards and forwards, doing her best to persuade the sleepy old dog to jump up and play. Holly never stirred in response, but Poppy was relentlessly optimistic.

Before long I was on the bus, staring at the world speeding by the window. As country lanes gave way to built-up streets, I was thankful to be living in a village, where life was very different to my former existence in London. Poppy would have hated it there. Alighting at the bus stop in the town centre, I set off to find the police station which was situated near a busy main road. The noise reminded me of my former home, and I was impatient to return to the relative peace of Ashton Mead. But I had come to the town for a purpose and was determined to complete my mission before leaving. Approaching a huge white and red brick building, I saw a police sign displayed on the wall. An attempt had been made to make the exterior space attractive, with ground cover cultivated in flower beds. There was even a small pond behind low metal railings, where red and white carp were swimming around. Every few seconds, one would change direction with an insouciant flick of a tail. I stood watching them, procrastinating, afraid the police would rebuke me for the delay in bringing the ring to their attention instead of contacting them as soon as Poppy found it.

Summoning my courage, I crossed the road and entered the police station. High automatic glass doors opened onto a spacious reception area where a uniformed policewoman greeted me from behind a long polished wooden counter. I explained the reason for my visit and she invited me to take a seat, assuring me that someone would come and speak to me shortly. The row of blue chairs were surprisingly comfortable, and I did my best to distract myself by studying boards of notices and signs about domestic abuse and burglary and other crimes. An array of leaflets seemed to cover similar issues. Absorbed in studying the display, I didn't notice the detective approach and was startled when she called my name.

'Emily Wilson?'

I looked up, brushing my hair out of my eyes, and nodded, immediately recognising the tall female detective who had spoken to me when I had reported the body. She stared levelly at me, with a hint of recognition in her sharp eyes.

'We've met before,' I muttered.

There was no point in trying to deny that I had found the body and was now returning with a chain that might be important evidence. I could only hope that the detective wouldn't consider my find a bit of a coincidence, and suspect I knew more about the drowned woman than I was sharing with her. That said, I did live very close to the site where the body had been dragged from the river, so my discoveries were both quite plausible. All this ran through my mind as the detective invited me to follow her. There was something about her voice that reminded me of my head teacher at school, who had expected instant obedience. I resolved to try and imitate their tone when attempting to train Poppy to do tricks. Without a word I rose to my feet and followed the detective through a swing door into a corridor and through another door into a room furnished with a small table and two chairs. We sat down facing one another and she stared intently at me for a moment, while I tried to breathe deeply and convince myself there was no reason for me to feel nervous.

'Emily Wilson,' she said, with a frosty smile, before introducing herself as a detective inspector. 'Fifteen days ago you reported a drowning in Ashton Mead.' It sounded like an accusation.

'That's right,' I replied, doing my best to keep my voice steady. 'It was actually my dog, Poppy, who found the body. I would have walked straight past it. In fact I would never have gone so close to the water's edge. My dog can dash about a bit – she's really fast – and she loves to chase birds. There are sometimes ducks or even swans in the river so...' I broke off, aware that I was gabbling nervously.

'So it was your dog that found the body?' the detective repeated, careful to add nothing to what I had told her.

'Yes, that's right. And I called 999. Like I said, it was my dog who found the body.'

The detective thanked me formally for calling the police to report the discovery. 'I understand you must be feeling curious, but I'm afraid I can't tell you anything about the progress we're making,' she said. There was an air of finality to her words, as though she was preparing to end our meeting.

'Actually,' I said, clearing my throat nervously, 'that's not why I'm here. You see, the body isn't the only thing my dog found.'

Without moving a muscle the detective somehow managed to look faintly surprised.

'What a busy little dog you have,' she murmured. Once again, I thought her words sounded like an accusation. 'You haven't come here to report finding another body, have you?' she added. She might have been joking, but her expression remained stern.

'No, not another body,' I replied, aware that I was smiling foolishly. 'Nothing like that.'

'But your dog has found something?' Her voice sounded as even as ever, but she glanced impatiently at her phone and I had the impression she thought I was wasting her time.

My hand shook as I drew the dog waste bag from my pocket. For once, the detective failed to conceal her surprise. Her eyebrows shot up as she registered what I was holding out to her.

'What is this?' she demanded, her voice as cool as before, but her eyes alight with annoyance.

'It's not what you think,' I blurted out. 'I know it looks like a poo bag, I mean, it is a poo bag, but I just used it because it was all I had on me. It's a pendant we found – that is, my dog found it. The chain was lying in the mud by the river, near where we saw the body. I put it in this poo bag, because I didn't want to touch it any more than I already had done. It just seemed like a good idea to put it straight into a plastic bag. It may have my dog's saliva on it, because she found it. I told her to drop it and she did, otherwise it might have been a trip to the vet.' I giggled, embarrassed. 'Anyway, we discussed it – my girl friend, that is, not my dog – and we agreed the chain might have belonged to the woman who drowned.'

A faint frown crossed the detective's face and I realised how stupid the hypothesis sounded. The chain we had found could have belonged to anyone. It was hardly likely to have made its way up from the river onto the bank. But it was too late to retract my statement now. To my surprise, the detective didn't laugh at my suggestion but instead picked up the bag, and thanked me for being so careful. Instructing me to remain where I was, she left the room, with the jewellery still in its protective plastic bag. It seemed the police were taking Poppy's find seriously after all.

After a short time, the detective returned and quizzed me about finding the chain. Even though I had nothing to hide, I felt guilty. Admittedly I had attempted to investigate what had happened to Richard's wife, but I made no mention of that. All I had actually done was visit my next-door neighbour, and that was not a crime. The detective seemed sceptical, and repeated several of her questions, studying me closely as I replied. Only when I explained that a reporter from the Swindon paper had been with me when Poppy found the chain did the detective lower her gaze to note down Dana Flack's name. I realised that until that point she hadn't been sure whether to believe my story about Poppy finding the gold chain. For the first time it occurred to me that I was lucky to have had an independent witness to corroborate my statement. Having found a body, and potentially some key evidence, the police might have suspected my involvement in the case was not chance. Far from being a nuisance, as I had previously thought, the reporter had done me a huge favour.

Keen though she was to interrogate me, the detective was cagey answering my questions about what had happened.

'I'm afraid I can't discuss an ongoing investigation with you. The dead woman's face was unfortunately unrecognisable,' she added more gently, 'but we're hoping to identify her from her clothes. The pendant you have handed in may help – although I'm not sure how our crime scene investigators missed it when they searched the site,' she added, sounding slightly irritated.

15

ALTHOUGH THE DETECTIVE HAD treated me courteously, I was shaking by the time she escorted me to the exit, and hugely relieved to be back on the street. More than anything, I was thankful that she hadn't asked me why I hadn't called the police as soon as Poppy found the chain, instead of waiting until the following morning to bring it to the police station. Barely glancing at the carp swimming lazily around their pond, I hurried back to the main road and the bus that would take me home. As I walked away from the intimidating atmosphere of the police station, a few trees along the road began to sway in a light breeze, and I felt my spirits lift. Hannah was not expecting me to return to work until the following morning, and I was free to do whatever I wanted for the rest of the day. Having fulfilled my civic duty, I deserved to indulge myself, for a few hours.

Poppy would be happy enough with Jane's old dog, Holly, for company. At first the two dogs had been wary of one another, and Poppy had irritated Holly by constantly pestering her to play. Holly was too old and sedate to enjoy being chased around the grass by an energetic puppy. Despite Holly's crabby reaction, I had taken to leaving Poppy with Jane during the day when the weather was too wet or cold to leave her outside in the yard behind the tea shop. Having been forced to spend a lot of time in each other's company, the two dogs had developed a mutual tolerance, and had settled into a comfortable companionship. When she wasn't digging for worms or moss, Poppy was happy scampering after flies and squirrels and barking at birds in the garden, while Holly dozed nearby. When Poppy grew tired of her sport, she would lie down beside the old dog and they would fall asleep together. So I was happy to leave Poppy with Jane, while I enjoyed myself for an hour or so window shopping and maybe even trying on new clothes.

I hadn't mooched around the shops since leaving London a year ago. It was not yet midday, so I decided to explore the shopping centre, and possibly even treat myself to lunch before setting off home. Even though I went into the least expensive-looking shops, I was shocked to discover how significantly prices had risen since my last shopping spree. Determined to be sensible, I bought a shirt and a new pair of jeans, which I needed, after which I decided to do without lunch in order to make my final purchase, a pair of boots that cost more than my entire limited budget. The leather ankle boots not only looked cool, but they were really comfortable. I justified my extravagance by telling myself the boots would last for years. Satisfied with my outing, I made my way to the bus stop and waited for my bus, excited at the prospect of being reunited with Poppy. Feeling as though I had been away for weeks, not just a few hours, I alighted in Ashton Mead with my purchases, and took them straight home before going to Jane's house to collect Poppy.

Having tried on my new shirt and jeans once more, I put my clothes away and shut my new boots in my wardrobe, where Poppy couldn't discover them. She had a predilection for chewing my shoes. By the time I was aware of this, she had completely destroyed one of my favourite pairs. Since then, I had learned not to leave my shoes on the floor. With my boots safely stowed in the wardrobe, I went to collect Poppy, who was overjoyed to see me and jumped up at me, licking my hands furiously, and grabbing my sleeve with her teeth to prevent me leaving her again. Having assured me the two dogs had passed a congenial day in the garden, Jane invited me to stay for tea.

'I won't take no for an answer,' she went on. 'Hannah's coming by after work so you might as well wait and see her.'

Hannah had arranged to meet me in the pub that evening, so she could hear all about my visit to the police station, but the offer of tea and cake was irresistible.

'That would be lovely,' I replied. Remembering that I had missed lunch, I was suddenly ravenous.

Jane bustled off indoors to make the tea, leaving me to reflect on my good fortune at having come to live in such an idyllic place. It was a warm spring day, I was surrounded by trees in blossom and camellias displaying beautiful red and pink blooms, and Poppy was stretched out in the sun, snoozing beside me. After a few moments basking in the spring sunshine, Poppy woke up and rolled over for a tummy rub. Apart from the spectre of living next door to an affable murderer, everything about Ashton Mead was perfect. While I was chilling out waiting for Jane to return with the tea, my phone rang. Expecting to hear Hannah's voice, I answered without checking the screen.

'Hi,' I said, 'It's done. And guess what?'

I was about to tell her that I had been questioned by the detective who had been down by the river dealing with the body, when my mother's voice interrupted me.

'Seeing as I have absolutely no idea what you're talking about, it's difficult for me to guess anything.'

'Oh, hello, mum,' I said, laughing with relief at not having mentioned my trip to the police station to her.

My mother was well-meaning, and she only wanted me to be happy, but our views on life didn't generally coincide. If she heard that I had been to see the police in relation to a murder investigation, she would start fussing. The longer I could keep the truth from her, the better, as far as I was concerned. The situation was proving challenging enough without my mother nagging me and worrying unnecessarily. She was bound to pester me to return to London, where she kept my bedroom exactly as it had been when I was living with my parents, even though I had made it quite clear that I had moved out permanently. Now that I had inherited Rosecroft from my great aunt, there was no possibility of my ever returning to London, but my mother was relentless in pursuing her own agenda for me. It was all a bit of a game, really. I suspected she would find an excuse to put me off quickly enough, if she ever thought I was actually planning to move back in with her and my dad.

Still laughing, I apologised for my misunderstanding. 'Sorry, mum, I thought you were someone else.'

'Clearly,' she replied with a disapproving sniff.

'So how are you?' I went on, quickly adding that it was lovely to hear from her.

Mollified, my mother began giving me a detailed account of her various aching joints, starting with her swollen ankles. 'It always happens,' she grumbled, 'as soon as the weather turns warmer. I've been to the doctor about it, but they're useless. It's no fun getting old.'

'You're not getting old!' I protested. 'Nowhere near.'

'Well, it's sweet of you to say so, but I feel old sometimes.'

Having finished with her ankles, she was moving on to her knees, when Jane emerged from the house carrying a tray of tea things. Scenting food, Poppy leapt to her feet and trotted over to investigate.

'Listen, mum,' I butted in before my mother could carry on with her litany of minor ailments, 'I'm just about to go out, but why don't you come and visit me? It's been ages since you were last here.'

'That's not my fault. You haven't invited me since Christmas,' she responded, somewhat churlishly.

'How about this weekend?'

I didn't expect her to agree to a visit at such short notice, and was taken aback when she accepted my invitation without hesitation.

'That's settled then,' I said, doing my best to sound pleased. 'Call me when you leave Swindon and we'll meet you at the bus stop.'

'We?' she enquired sharply.

'Me and Poppy,' I replied.

'Oh yes, of course, Poppy,' she repeated, making no attempt to hide her disappointment.

Before she could launch into one of her habitual complaints about my single lifestyle, I hung up.

'That was my mother,' I told Jane. 'She's coming to stay with me this weekend.'

'That's nice,' Jane replied as she poured the tea and offered me a slice of a fruitcake she had baked that morning.

Jane's baking was, if anything, even better than Hannah's whose cakes and buns were hard to beat. When I started working at the café, Hannah had been keen for me to share the baking but despite my repeated efforts, my scones were never anything other than passable for home cooking. They certainly weren't good enough to meet Hannah's high standards.

'We want customers to come back,' she told me ungenerously. 'We don't want to send them away thinking they can do better themselves and might as well stay at home.'

Jane's round face beamed with pleasure when I told her the cake was scrumptious. We sat outside in the late afternoon sun, watching Poppy chase a stray butterfly while Holly dozed, occasionally flicking an ear as Poppy scampered past her. After the stress and excitement of my day in town, I was happy to be back in the village that had become home to me and my dog. It was hard to believe that barely a year had passed since I moved there. Had my great aunt not died and left me her house, I might never have known Ashton Mead existed. Yet even in a quiet haven like the village of Ashton Mead, dark forces were at work, and I shivered, remembering the woman Poppy had found floating in the river.

16

HANNAH ARRIVED AT JANE'S and after eating rather more cake than was good for us, washed down with several cups of tea, we took Poppy for a walk on the way back to Rosecroft. Keen to know the identity of the dead woman, Hannah was impatient with me for failing to prise any information out of the detective.

'We're not talking about an amateur sleuth,' I retorted, stung by her criticism. 'You try getting anything out of a professional detective. This woman's an inspector, trained and experienced in dealing with people like us.'

'People like you,' Hannah muttered, as though she would have succeeded in persuading the inspector to talk.

'She's never going to let anything slip,' I insisted. 'It's just not like that. I can't explain it, but it was like every word she spoke was carefully chosen.'

'Well, I suppose you did what you could,' Hannah said grudgingly. 'We'll just have to look elsewhere for our information.'

Before I could ask her what she meant, she reminded me that Barry had invited me to have dinner with him. Smiling at her persistence, I assured her that was never going to happen.

'Why not? Give me one good reason.'

'For a start, I don't fancy him, and it would be mean to lead him on by pretending I like him in that way.'

'Don't be silly,' she replied with an impatient shake of her head that made her blond curls bob up and down. 'You don't even know him. You've barely exchanged ten words with him. You might find you like him more than you think you will. Don't be swayed by first impressions. You can't have forgotten your last boyfriend. He seemed, oh so perfect, and he was certainly good-looking, but he dumped you when you lost your job and only came back when he learned you'd inherited a house.' She snorted. 'What a creep he turned out to be. Trust me, Barry's nothing like that. He's more like: what you see is what you get.'

'Yes, but where does all this leave *you*?'

'What about me?'

'Stop being disingenuous. I know you like Barry.'

'I did, it's true, but I'm over him. It was just a passing fancy. Honestly, what's the point when he's clearly not in the slightest bit interested in me? There's no point in dwelling on it. So, with me out of the picture, why shouldn't you go out with him? He's obviously got the hots for you.'

'I suppose if I agree to see him, just once, and go out of my way to put him off, he might look elsewhere,' I suggested thoughtfully.

Hannah laughed. 'The point of all this is –' she began.

'I know, I know,' I interrupted her. 'I get it. You want me to use my feminine wiles to charm him into telling me everything the police have discovered about the drowned woman.'

'Exactly.' She laughed again.

The trouble with Hannah's plan was that I had already rejected Barry's advances, so it was difficult to see how I could persuade him to invite me out again.

'Leave that to me,' Hannah grinned. 'I'll have a word with Maud in the morning.'

Worn out from my busy day, I went home and had an early night. The next morning I had almost forgotten about Hannah's machinations, but by lunchtime she had arranged everything, just as she had promised.

'Barry's going to call you,' she said, checking a message on her phone.

'What? How come?' I stammered. 'Why? What did you say to Maud? I mean, what did she say to Barry?'

'I told Maud it was a pity you had such a terrible experience with your last boyfriend – which is true – and it's sad that you've allowed that to put you off men altogether and feel you can't trust anyone. But at the same time, I told her in strict confidence that you're lonely and would love to be in a relationship with a nice, steady, reliable man. I was pretty sure she already knew that Barry likes you. Anyway, she took it all on board and I could see the cogs whirring.' She laughed. 'You know Maud. Her eyes positively light up at the first hint of any gossip, and she couldn't keep a secret to save her life. If Barry doesn't call you today I'd be surprised.'

Listening to Hannah, I frowned, reluctant to lead Barry on. I didn't have any feelings for him other than a general wish to be on good terms with him. He seemed like a decent guy, but to me, steady and reliable was synonymous with dull. He was just the kind of man my mother would like me to hook up with, but I wanted to be dazzled by someone with panache, a man who would bring fun and excitement into my life. At the same time, like Hannah, I was itching to know more about the woman who had drowned in the river. Somehow, ever since Poppy had sniffed out the body, I seemed to have been living in a permanent state of guilt, towards Richard in case he was actually innocent, towards the police for my delay in handing over potential evidence, and now towards Barry for deliberately leading him on.

'I don't know what to do,' I said, and just then my phone rang.

Placing my hand over the phone, I mouthed the caller's name to Hannah who did a little jig on the spot.

'Hello, Barry,' I said, careful to keep any enthusiasm out of my voice. 'How are you?'

In spite of my reservations, I heard myself agreeing to go out for dinner with him.

'Yes, thank you, that would be lovely,' I said and hung up, hating myself for being duplicitous.

'Well?' Hannah asked. 'What did he say?'

'He's picking me up tomorrow evening and we're going out to eat.'

Hannah clapped her hands. 'Way to go, Mata Hari,' she said.

'Mata Hari was a German spy,' I pointed out. 'Not the kind of person I really want to be compared with.'

'Oh, whatever.'

Hannah and I didn't discuss the situation any further. She spent the rest of the day grinning at me with suppressed excitement, while I scowled at her, kicking myself for having let her talk me into going on a date with Barry. At least I would have an excuse to go home early, as my mother was arriving on Saturday morning and I would have to be up in good time to tidy my house before meeting her at the bus stop. And on Friday evening Poppy might need to be fed, or taken for a walk.

'It's not really fair on Barry,' I muttered to Hannah in the kitchen, when I was laying out a plate of scones. 'And in any case, we don't even know there's anything to tell. The chances are the woman fell into the river by accident and hit her head, or couldn't swim. There's probably no mystery to it at all.'

'Well, that's what you're going to find out,' she replied promptly. 'Come on, Emily, don't make this into such a big deal. You're only going out for dinner, and who knows, you might enjoy yourself. And even if you don't find him irresistible, the point is you'll be able to find out about the police investigation. I don't think Barry's going to be as tight-lipped as that detective you saw in Swindon. Just make sure you keep filling his wine glass, and flirt for all you're worth.'

'I'm not going to try and get him drunk, and I'm not going to flirt with him,' I replied sternly.

Carrying a plate out to a group of waiting customers, I slapped it down on the table, nearly tipping half a dozen scones onto an old lady's lap. I apologised at once, pretending that I had slipped, and made an effort to appear professional for the rest of the afternoon, except when I was in the kitchen with Hannah.

'Look, Emily,' she said at last, 'if you really don't want to go out with Barry then you shouldn't have said yes. Don't blame me if you've got yourself in a mess.'

The fact that she was right didn't do anything to improve my temper. I had been weak, allowing Hannah to talk me into doing something that made me uncomfortable. All the same, it would have been stupid of me to fall out with my friend over an evening out, and after a while I calmed down and resolved to make peace with her.

'You're right,' I conceded. 'This isn't your fault. I shouldn't have agreed to go out with Barry, but it's too late to change that now, and there's no harm done. I'll just have to make the best of it and try to have a good time and let him down gently. It's only one evening.'

Hannah smiled. She didn't say anything, but I could tell she was pleased, and I was relieved at being reconciled with her. She had been a good friend to me since I first walked into her Sunshine Tea Shoppe in Ashton Mead and we had fallen into a conversation which had resulted in her offering me a job. We had worked together nearly every day for a year and the more time we spent together, the more I liked her. Spending an hour or two with Barry to please her wasn't such a hardship.

17

WALKING ALONG MILL LANE to Rosecroft, my route naturally took me past The Laurels where I noticed an unfamiliar car in the drive. Richard drove a red Citroën, and Ralph's car was black. This one was silver and, without knowing anything about it, I could see it was a streamlined sports car. Different models of cars had never interested me in the slightest, and I couldn't understand the point in being able to drive above the speed limit. But even I could tell that this rather flashy car was an expensive model. As I drew closer, a man rose into view from where he had been crouching behind the car. His unexpected appearance made me jump.

'Sorry,' he called out, with a concerned smile, 'I didn't mean to startle you. I was just down here checking the tyres.'

'That's okay,' I replied, returning his smile. 'I just didn't see you there.'

'Are you here on a visit too?' he asked.

'No, I'm not visiting. I live along here.' I nodded at Rosecroft the only other property in the lane.

He walked over to me, holding out his hand. 'I'm Adam, and you must be Emily. My father's spoken about you. He really appreciates how welcome you've made him feel here.'

Like Richard, Adam seemed affable, but there the resemblance ended. Similar in appearance to his brother he was dark-haired, tall and lithe but, unlike Ralph, he had an open and engaging air about him. Poppy seemed wary of him, no doubt because he reminded her of his older brother, but I liked him straight away. He told me he was staying in Ashton Mead for a few days. Silently I cursed my mother for coming for coming to stay with me that weekend, even though I had invited her. But I had made the arrangement without knowing that a good-looking guy with a sports car would be staying next door that weekend. Not only was my mother arriving on Saturday, but I had agreed to see Barry on Friday evening. There would hardly be any opportunity for me and Adam to get to know one another.

'How do you like it here?' I asked him.

Poppy began to pull on her lead. I ignored her, so she gave up and sat down at my feet, growling discontentedly.

'I've only just arrived, but I have to say I like what I've seen so far.' He gazed at me pointedly as he said that, as though he intended to direct his compliment at me. 'Perhaps you could show me around, if you've got time, that is?'

'There's not much to see,' I began, adding hurriedly, 'but I can take you down to see the bridge over the river, and show you the local High Street. I mean, it's just a few local shops, but it's a picturesque place. We get a lot of visitors passing through and stopping off, especially in the summer.'

'That sounds great,' he replied. 'If you're sure you don't mind? I don't want to take up your time if you're busy.'

I assured him I had nothing else to do, and he went indoors to tell Richard where he was going.

'Are you sure your father doesn't mind me taking you away from him like this?' I asked. 'I mean, you came here to see him.'

'Oh, he's only too happy to get rid of me,' he replied, smiling. 'He's busy preparing our evening meal, and I'd only get in the way. Has he ever invited you over for dinner?'

I shook my head.

'Lucky you,' he said and laughed.

We walked across the grassy slope down to the river. Adam admired the scene, which looked beautiful in the soft glow of a late afternoon in spring. A few ducks were scudding around on the river, and a swan sailed past, majestic in its high-necked elegance. There was no one else around at that time in the late afternoon, and the silence was disturbed only by the occasional trilling of a bird, and the faint hum of an insect buzzing past. Poppy was perfectly happy to trot along by my side, stopping every now and then to sniff the grass.

'This is where we found a body a couple of weeks ago,' I said, afraid that Adam would find Ashton Mead dreadfully dull.

I immediately regretted having shattered the peace by bringing up so depressing a subject.

Adam turned to me in astonishment. 'A body?' he repeated. 'What sort of body?'

Haltingly I recounted what had happened, explaining that it was Poppy who had discovered the woman lying face down in the water.

'That must have been a terrible shock,' he said, gazing at me sympathetically. 'Are you all right? We shouldn't have come here –'

I reassured him everything was fine. 'Of course, it was dreadful at the time, but it was nearly three weeks ago, and it's not as if it was anyone we knew.' I broke off in confusion, hoping my comment hadn't made me sound callous.

'Who was she?' he asked.

'No one seems to know. That is, the police probably know all about her by now, but they haven't told us anything. They just tell us they can't discuss an ongoing investigation.'

I considered confiding in him about my visit to the police station in Swindon, but that would have involved telling him about the chain Poppy had unearthed, and it all seemed a bit too complicated to go into just then. Adam was a stranger, and some of the villagers seemed to think his father was responsible for the tragedy. I said nothing about my duplicitous date with Barry either. It was a beautiful evening, and I regretted having mentioned the drowned woman at all. We were silent for a moment, and then Adam thanked me again for being so kind to his father.

'It's not easy moving somewhere new where you don't know anyone,' I said.

'And he's had a really rough time of it lately,' Adam added. 'I don't suppose he's spoken about it, but my mother walked out on him after thirty years of marriage.' He sighed. 'Thirty years. Can you believe it?'

'What happened?'

He shrugged. 'They seemed happy enough, and then one day she just announced she was leaving, and that was that. She packed a suitcase and went. My poor father was devastated, but he's far too nice to cause a fuss. My mother has never been – an easy person to get along with.' He hesitated, seeming to weigh his words. 'She's always had – problems, but my father always stood by her and did whatever he could to help her. Anyway, she told him she'd met someone else, so in the end they agreed to sell up and he moved here. He said he wanted a fresh start.'

'Do you know why she left him? I mean, I don't want to pry, but there must have been a reason.' I didn't like to enquire into the nature of his mother's problems.

'She just said she'd met someone else, and she was going to live with him. My father didn't deserve that. He's a good man, honest, hard-working, and kind. But there was nothing much he could do. Apparently she'd fallen for this other man. None of us even knew she was having an affair until she announced she was leaving.'

We walked on in silence for a few minutes, watching Poppy as she scampered along in front of us, or paused to sniff the air.

'It must have been hard for you and your brother when she walked out,' I remarked at last, wondering if that was why Ralph had seemed so bad-tempered, and so protective of his father.

Adam looked away across the river. 'We'd both moved out by the time she left. She told us she waited until we'd gone and were settled in our own lives before she left our father. It was that calculated. It wasn't as though her life with him was intolerable. He wasn't abusive or anything like that. He's a gentle soul. She just wanted to be with someone else. My dad thought she was having a kind of mid-life crisis –' He stopped and gave a helpless shrug. 'He tried to be understanding and forgiving, but really his whole world collapsed when she left him. He was devoted to her.'

'I'm so sorry,' I murmured.

I wasn't sure what else to say.

'Oh well, it's all water under the bridge now,' he said, appropriately enough, since we had almost reached the picturesque bridge over the river.

Moss was growing on the lower levels of the brick construction and other tiny weeds were visible, poking green shoots through the cement. A leisurely duck swam under the bridge, the sheen on its bright green feathers fading as it moved into the shadow beneath the arching masonry.

'Are you coming to the pub this evening?' I asked, gazing at the duck as I spoke, and feeling slightly awkward.

Adam thanked me for the suggestion. It wasn't exactly an invitation, although it might as well have been.

'I'll have to see what my father wants to do, but hopefully I'll see you there.'

He smiled warmly and I felt a faint glow of excitement. Despite the sombre nature of our conversation, he seemed like someone who could be fun to know.

'I'd best be getting back,' he said, glancing at his watch.

'I'm meeting some friends at The Plough later this evening,' I told him as we reached The Laurels. 'You're welcome to join us. Both of you, that is, you and Richard.'

'I'll see what my father wants to do,' he repeated. 'I know he's been busy preparing dinner. But thank you. And if not tonight, maybe tomorrow evening?'

On the point of replying that it was a date, I remembered that I actually did have a date the following evening, with Barry. Uttering a noncommittal grunt, I watched Adam walk away from me. Reaching home, I tried to look along the lane to see if he and Richard went out, but didn't spot them. They wouldn't be walking past my house which was in the other direction to The Plough.

After an early supper I went along to the pub. On my way, I paused outside The Laurels, hoping that Adam would join me in the lane. He didn't. So after a few minutes I walked on, with Poppy trotting happily beside me. Hannah wasn't there when I reached The Plough, but I spotted Toby, chatting to an elderly man, a regular at the pub. I had never seen the old man arrive or leave, but he was always in the bar, seated at the same table in the corner. Catching sight of me, Toby stood up and came over to join me. We sat down together but I was distracted, watching out for Adam, and after Toby had accused me several times of not listening to him, he downed the last of his pint and left. We waited for a while but neither Hannah nor Adam turned up, so we went home.

18

THE FOLLOWING MORNING, HANNAH stopped me in the kitchen to challenge me about my miserable expression.

'How about service with a smile?' she asked me, taking a tray of freshly baked scones out of the oven.

The smell made my mouth water and I thought regretfully of the stone I'd gained since working at the tea shop. Hannah and Jane had both independently told me they thought I looked much healthier than when I had first arrived in the village. My ex-boyfriend used to criticise me whenever I put on weight and as a result of that I used to be very careful to control my diet. Since moving to Ashton Mead, I had been eating more heartily and also walking more, thanks to Poppy. Even my sister had made a positive comment about the improvement in my appearance.

'Customers want to feel comfortable and welcome in the tea shop,' Hannah went on, putting the scones down. 'They don't want to see you glaring at them as though they're a bloody nuisance. Come on, what is it? There's obviously something on your mind. Have I upset you? I can promise you it was unintentional.'

'It's nothing you've done,' I replied, although she had been instrumental in arranging my problem. 'It's just that

I've got to go out with Barry this evening,' I said, my voice tailing off in a wail.

'Is that all?' she snapped. 'For goodness' sake. It can't be that bad, surely. He's not an ogre. He's a nice guy who wants to spend an evening with you. Seriously, what's wrong with you, Emily? You really upset Toby yesterday.'

Seeing my surprised expression, she told me she had bumped into Toby in Maud's shop before work that morning, and he had been downhearted at my dismissive attitude towards him in the pub the previous evening.

'God, this place,' I cried out, exasperated. 'Is everything that happens to me someone else's business?'

Seeing her looking put out by my outburst, I felt I owed her an explanation of sorts. I told her about meeting Adam, my next-door neighbour's younger son. 'He's gorgeous,' I concluded, 'and he's only here for the weekend. And now I'm saddled with seeing Barry this evening, and my mother's arriving tomorrow, and I've got no hope of seeing Adam on his own again.'

'Adam sounds interesting,' she said, and I grunted crossly. Before I could tell her any more about Adam, a customer came in, and the moment passed.

Hannah gave me the weekend off as my mother was arriving in Ashton Mead on Saturday morning and staying until Sunday evening. Even though it was likely to be busy, my friend insisted she could run the tea shop without me. Jane had offered to call in late morning to check that she had everything under control, and to help out if Hannah was rushed off her feet. With her mother available to help out if necessary, Hannah assured me she would be fine.

'If you're sure,' I said, reluctant to let Hannah down when she had always been so kind to me.

'Of course, I'm sure,' she replied. 'How do you think I coped before you turned up? I'm not completely helpless, you know. I ran the place with my mother coming in part-time for over a year before you turned up.'

'I don't know how you managed on your own,' I said. 'Tell you what, I'll keep my phone on, and if you're desperate, call me. I can bring my mum along and I can nip in the kitchen and give you a hand while she has a cream tea. I'm sure she'd love that. Plus she'll get to see how well we're doing.'

Hannah insisted she wouldn't think of letting me join her. Reminding me that my mother was only staying for one night, she said my mother was travelling to Ashton Mead to see me, and certainly wouldn't want me to be at work all day. So it was agreed that I would spend the weekend with my mother.

Barry arrived promptly at seven thirty to take me out. I had agonised over what to wear for the evening. I didn't want to lead him on by wearing anything that could be construed as flirty, but my vanity prevented me from choosing an unflattering outfit. In the end I settled on my jeans, which were figure hugging, and a loose long sleeved T-shirt that was casual but quite smart. It was one of my favourites and really comfortable. I hoped that Barry wouldn't be wearing a suit and tie, which would have embarrassed us both, but he turned up in what looked like a new shirt, and jeans. He grinned nervously and I breathed a silent sigh of relief. When I asked him where we were going, he surprised me by suggesting we eat at The Plough where Poppy would be welcome. I felt a rush of gratitude for his consideration. Not many men would have worried about my leaving my dog alone at home.

'That's very thoughtful of you,' I said, completely forgetting my resolution to offer him no encouragement whatsoever but to remain aloof and even slightly hostile throughout our date.

Barry smiled and we set off. Previously I had only eaten in the bar of The Plough, or out in the garden, but Barry had reserved a table in a corner of the dining area, which was on a mezzanine level from where we could look down at the drinkers in the bar. We sat down and studied the menu, even though the choice was a foregone conclusion for both of us, it being fish and chips night at The Plough. Poppy settled down under the table with a large chew toy. She was generally no trouble when I was eating, and understood that it was not a time when she could distract me. If she was well-behaved, she would inevitably receive her reward, and she was particularly partial to fish. So she sat patiently, waiting, while we ate, knowing I would leave a few choice morsels for her.

While we were sipping pints, and waiting for our food to arrive, I considered how best to broach the topic that was uppermost in my mind. Apart from my own curiosity, Hannah was expecting me to exploit this opportunity to mine Barry for information, and I didn't want my evening with Barry to be wasted. But now that the time had arrived, I was conscious only of the awkwardness of my situation. The last thing I wanted was for Barry to realise that I had only agreed to have supper with him so that I could quiz him about the murder investigation, which he quite possibly knew nothing about anyway. I decided to take a circumspect approach to the topic.

'It must be very exciting being a police officer,' I hazarded, smiling encouragement at him.

'Oh not really,' he replied, but he looked gratified by my interest. 'I guess it's like any other job, once you get used to it.'

'But it must be more varied than – well, than what I do, for example.'

'Tell me what happens in a typical day in the tea shop,' he said, deftly turning the question on me.

I smiled at his unconscious cunning. 'We take orders, tea, scones, buns, sandwiches, you know the kind of thing, and then we serve the customers. That's all there is to it. Hannah does all the baking because she's a whizz in the kitchen, I mean, really talented.' It occurred to me as I was talking that I might as well put in a good word for my friend. 'But you've probably already sampled her baking.'

'I ought to come to the tea shop more often,' Barry said, gazing intensely at me.

'Yes, I'm sure Hannah would like that,' I replied. 'Now, I've told you what happens at the tea shop. What about you? Tell me about your day.'

Barry nodded and launched into a lengthy and dull account of how he took care of his uniform, and polished his boots. I refrained from commenting that it must take a long time with feet as large as his. Other than that, he seemed to spend most of his day making sure his records were kept up to date.

'You're right, it's not as exciting as I expected,' I conceded.

He laughed. 'I'm sorry to disappoint you, but the truth is most police officers don't spend all their time involved in car chases, or kicking down doors to arrest armed drug dealers. Our work isn't generally that dramatic.'

'But there was a murder in Ashton Mead a few weeks ago,' I reminded him, lowering my eyes and taking a sip of my beer. 'That must have been dramatic.'

Barry shrugged. 'I wasn't in the response team,' he admitted. 'And once there's any suggestion of foul play, the CID take over and we don't get a look in. Not that I'd want to be dealing with something like that.'

'Like what?'

Just then our food arrived. I watched Barry squirt tomato ketchup over his chips, after which he busied himself with vinegar and salt. I had to wait while he munched his way enthusiastically through half his chips before we were able to continue our discussion.

'You were saying detectives are investigating the murder of the woman who was pulled from the river,' I prompted him, hoping he wouldn't remember that he had said nothing about the drowned woman being murdered.

If he at least confirmed that she had been murdered, that would be something for me to tell Hannah.

Barry nodded. His hair fell forward over his face and he brushed it back from his eyes with his huge hand. 'Yes, it's a job for the CID,' he agreed cheerfully.

'So she was murdered?' I asked, raising my eyebrows and doing my best to look as though this was an innocent enquiry.

Barry merely shrugged and changed the subject. 'How's your supper? If you ask me, they make the best chips in the county here. Who needs to go into Swindon?'

I took a deep breath. 'Are you hoping to be promoted to CID?' I asked.

My attempt to return to the subject in a roundabout way proved to be a mistake. Barry began to explain how transferring to CID wasn't a straightforward question of promotion. There were different branches of police work, he said, and each had its own clearly defined career structure.

'I could, if I wanted, progress to the rank of sergeant, and after that inspector, without moving across to become a detective.'

There was quite a lot more along those lines but I stopped listening after a while. If I had been interested in joining the police force I might have learned something. As it was, his detailed account of the police hierarchy didn't interest me in the slightest. I pretended to be listening, out of politeness. Out of the corner of my eye I saw Richard enter the bar below us, with Adam at his side.

'Oh, there's my new neighbour,' I blurted out.

We had finished our food so I suggested we go down and greet them, since Richard was a newcomer to the village and hardly knew anyone.

'We ought to make him feel welcome, don't you think?'

Barry grunted.

19

HAVING CAREFULLY SCRAPED ALL the crispy salty batter off my fish, I leaned down to offer Poppy a few flakes from my plate, which she bolted down so fast it was hard to believe she could even have tasted the fish, let alone enjoyed it. With supper over, our plates were whisked away by a scowling Tess who favoured me with a grimace when I thanked her. I was on the point of standing up when Barry dashed round the table to pull my chair back for me.

'Allow me,' he began politely.

Unfortunately, he was in such a rush to impress me with his good manners, that he failed to notice Tess who had just returned with a tray of food for the customers at the next table. Barry's elbow knocked into the tray which flipped up and crashed to the floor. Tess darted backwards too late to avoid a mess of fish, vinegary chips and tartar sauce landing on her. If she hadn't been wearing a long stripy apron, her clothes would have been soiled. As it was, she stood transfixed while a broken piece of fish and a handful of chips slid slowly down her apron to land on the floor with a series of soft plops. Poppy leaped forward and began devouring the fallen battered fish and chips. Quickly I grabbed her, before she could gorge herself on greasy chips smothered in salt and vinegar. Nearby, someone burst out laughing and a few other people joined in. Tess looked furious, and Barry was clearly mortified.

'I'll pay for the food, and the damage, and the cleaning,' he stuttered, glancing at me in consternation.

In that moment, he seemed more concerned about the impression this fiasco was having on me than the mess he had caused. I bit my lip, looking down and trying not to giggle at his discomfort. The couple seated at the next table had mixed reactions. The man, who was skinny and had knobbly knuckles on his bony hands, sniggered as he peered at the mess on the floor. His companion, who was fat and middle-aged, seemed quite put out by the incident, but she recovered her good humour when Barry assured everyone that he would pay for replacement portions of fish and chips. She peered at the floor through black-rimmed glasses and announced that she was glad she didn't have to clear up the mess.

'Can't say fairer than that,' Cliff said, coming up to see what the rumpus was about and taking in the scene with a quick glance around.

Only Tess continued to glower at Barry, muttering darkly under her breath that he was a 'clumsy oaf'.

'These things happen,' I said, holding Poppy tightly as she wriggled in my arms, eager to jump down and scavenge further. 'No, Poppy,' I told her as she tried to get down, 'you've had enough. The chips are covered in salt which is very bad for you. If you eat any more you'll throw up.'

'That's all I need,' Tess snapped, swearing at me, at Barry, and at the world in general.

Cliff gave a broad grin and sent Tess off to clean herself up, while he and Barry scraped up the remnants of the ruined meal and dumped them on the tray.

'I'll pay for another dinner,' Barry said, apologising to Cliff and to the customers whose fish and chips had landed on the floor. 'I'll pay. This was entirely my fault. I'm so sorry.'

'You can't be expected to have eyes in the back of your head,' I pointed out. 'It was Tess's fault for not letting you know she was there.'

'Best not repeat that when Tess comes back,' Cliff warned me, his customary smile slipping a little at the prospect. 'Now, how's about another drink while you're waiting for your fish and chips?' he asked the customers whose food had been ruined. 'Barry here's paying.' He grinned and jerked his head at Barry who nodded.

'Yes, yes, let me get you a drink,' Barry echoed. 'It's the least I can do.'

When order had been restored to the dining area, Barry and I went downstairs and found Richard and Adam sitting at a table near the bar. They both looked up and smiled at me as we approached. Richard leaned down to pet Poppy, who jumped up at him in excitement.

'She's a bit hyper,' I apologised. 'She's just been eating fish and chips.'

Richard looked surprised. 'Are fish and chips good for her?'

'It wasn't exactly what I'd planned for her,' I admitted. 'Too much salt isn't good for her. But she finds scraps on the floor.'

While we were chatting, Adam stood up and I introduced him to Barry who offered to buy a round. What with one thing and another, it was turning out to be an expensive evening for him.

'He seems friendly,' Richard said as we sat down and watched Barry make his way to the bar.

'He's the local policeman,' I explained. 'That is, he's a policeman who grew up in the village. He lives near Swindon now, I'm not sure exactly where.'

As we were talking, Hannah and Toby came over to say hello. When the introductions were completed, Toby pulled another table over so we could all sit together.

Hannah nudged me. 'I see what you mean about Adam,' she whispered, giggling. 'He's gorgeous. So, what's happened with Barry? I thought he was taking you out this evening?'

I shook my head. 'I'll tell you all about it tomorrow,' I replied.

Barry returned with more drinks and we all sat down. Hannah had contrived to place herself next to Adam and I could see her chatting and flirting with him, while I was stuck between Barry and Toby, who was watching Adam curiously.

'So,' Barry said, addressing Richard, 'how are you settling in?'

Perhaps that was how a policeman might speak to a suspect in a murder investigation, but it was equally possible that the police weren't interested in Richard at all or, if they were, that Barry knew nothing about it. On the other hand, the fact that Barry seemed to want to question Richard might be significant, so I listened to their conversation as closely as I could. Toby meanwhile began talking to me. As quietly as I could, I muttered to him to keep quiet. Without understanding my reason for not wanting to engage in conversation with him, Toby fell silent and sat quietly, looking downcast, but I was too interested in what Richard and Barry were saying to take much notice of Toby. He would have to wait for my explanation.

'So you moved here from London?' Barry was saying.

Richard nodded. 'That's right. It's very different here in Ashton Mead, but I have to say I love it. I'm guessing it's going to take a while to feel at home in the village, but I can't imagine ever wanting to leave now I'm here.'

'Emily moved here from London a year ago,' Barry said. 'You should ask her about village life.'

'I will. She lives right next door to me,' Richard said, smiling complacently at me. 'Emily and Poppy,' he added.

Hearing her name, Poppy abandoned Toby, who had been disconsolately tickling her under her chin, and trotted over to Richard. Since Barry and Richard didn't seem to be saying anything interesting, I turned my attention to Adam and Hannah who by now seemed to be deep in conversation. Adam glanced over at me and caught me watching him.

'Hannah was just telling me that you work in her tea shop,' Adam said.

'Hannah saved my life when I arrived here,' I replied.

'Saved your life?' Adam echoed.

'Not literally,' I replied. 'What I meant was that she befriended me when I didn't know anyone, and gave me a job when I was totally broke.'

I smiled at Hannah who smiled back guiltily. I guessed she had been chatting Adam up. Still, there was no reason why she shouldn't pursue him just because I had mentioned that I liked him. Apart from anything else, I was still supposed to be on a date with Barry, although even he seemed to have forgotten about that. The conversation moved on to the village, and how picturesque it was. No one mentioned the body that had recently been fished out of the river. Tess came over to collect some empty glasses and hovered for a moment, listening to what was being said about the village.

'The bridge needs renovating,' Barry said. 'That is, it's perfectly safe, but it's beginning to look rather the worse for wear.'

'That's part of its charm,' Hannah protested. 'It looks authentic.'

'How old is it?' Adam wanted to know.

'According to my Aunt Maud, it dates back to the Romans,' Barry replied. 'My aunt knows everything there is to know about the village. She's lived here all her life.'

Richard frowned. 'No, it's not a Roman bridge,' he said. 'It's far more recent than that. That's not to say there wasn't an earlier bridge across the river there, of course. But I'd say the existing bridge is no older than a hundred years, probably less. I'd guess it was built for farmers to reach the water mill.'

'He's not been in the village five minutes and already he's telling us about it,' Tess commented, overhearing what Richard was saying.

'My dad's a historian,' Adam explained. 'He was a professor of history at the University of Westminster,' he added with a touch of filial pride. 'He's something of an expert on Roman architecture. He's written books about it.'

'Oh, that was then,' Richard said dismissively. 'Now I'm just a villager living in Ashton Mead.'

'Just a villager,' Tess sniffed as she walked away with a tray of glasses.

'Don't take any notice of the barmaid,' I muttered to Richard. 'I've been living here for a year, drinking in The Plough nearly every night, and she still regards me as a stranger.'

As though he appreciated my kindness towards his father, Adam smiled at me and I looked away, feeling slightly flustered. Beside me, I heard Barry grunt.

20

On Saturday, I was up early, preparing the spare bedroom for my mother's overnight visit. Poppy jumped around, sensing that something unusual was about to happen. In the end, I put her out in the garden while I aired the spare bed and put fresh flowers on the table in the kitchen. At last everything was ready, and only just in time, because my mother's bus was due soon. We had agreed that she would call me if she was delayed. If I didn't hear from her, I would be at the bus stop in time to meet her as she arrived. Poppy darted around my feet, happy to be going for a walk into the village, and stopping every few feet to sniff the ground or water it.

One consequence of my day off work was that I would have no chance to tell Hannah about my rather prosaic date with Barry, or to discuss Richard's interesting son or his wife's affair, until after the weekend. Poppy and I had just reached the end of Mill Lane and were turning onto the road that ran parallel with the river and would lead us round the corner to the High Street when someone called my name. Turning, I saw Adam walking down the lane towards us and stopped to wait for him. Poppy strained at her lead and did her best to pull me on towards the bus stop, but she had to wait with me. Adam caught up with us and stopped to chat. He told me Richard had sent him out to the local shop because they had run out of milk.

'Where are you off to?' he asked.

I explained that my mother would be arriving on the bus from Swindon, and we walked on together, with Poppy sulking at my heels. We chatted inconsequentially for a few moments about his father and the village. He accompanied me to the bus stop and waited with me. My mother's bus was due in a few minutes and we stood waiting in silence. All at once, Poppy growled and looking round I saw Silas Strang striding purposefully towards us. Immediately I began talking to Adam, to show Silas I was not alone. Even so I was relieved when Silas walked straight past, glowering. Before long we spotted the bus coming along the road. I was surprised by how excited I was at the prospect of seeing my mother again. She stepped down from the bus, and beamed at me. She was neatly turned out, as always. Her naturally mousy hair had been skilfully dyed blond, her make-up was flawless, if a trifle heavy for my taste, and she looked vibrant, as though she had just been on a long holiday. She put her bags down and flung her arms around me, while Poppy jumped up at her, clamouring to greet her. We hugged and when we drew apart I was touched to see tears in her eyes. Catching sight of Adam at my side, her expression immediately changed and she turned to me, her eyes now bright with curiosity.

'This is Adam,' I said. 'He's here visiting his father. Adam, this is my mother.'

'It's a pleasure to meet you, Mrs Wilson.'

'Call me Linda, please,' my mother replied, smiling.

It was evident she approved of Adam even before he insisted on wheeling her case along the lane to Rosecroft.

'What about your milk?' I asked him.

'I can come back for that.'

'Absolutely not,' I said. 'We can't take you out of your way like this.'

'I insist,' he replied, seizing the handle of my mother's case. 'It will do me good to stretch my legs.'

It came as no surprise to me that my mother thought Adam was wonderful.

'You know he's single,' she told me, with a smug grin, as though that meant he must be looking for a girlfriend or, if my mother had her way, a wife.

It hadn't occurred to me to enquire about Adam's marital status. It was typical of my mother to have established that at their first meeting, while he was taking her case to Rosecroft. I could only hope that she hadn't been indiscreet. It would be typical of her to try and pitch me to a stranger as what she would call 'a good catch'. Shrugging off that humiliating notion, I determined to enjoy her visit. The weather was fine and we took Poppy for a long walk before ending up at Hannah's tea shop for afternoon tea and cakes. My mother merely sniffed when she learned that I was still working there, but at least she was tactful enough to refrain from nagging me to find a better job while we were there. I had a sneaking feeling that would come later.

'You can do so much better for yourself than waiting at tables,' she had insisted on her last visit.

Despite my protestations that working for Hannah suited me perfectly, and Poppy was welcome to stay out in the yard if Jane wasn't at home to look after her, my mother had remained adamant that the job was beneath me.

'You can't organise your working life around a dog,' she had told me.

As luck would have it, Barry followed us into the tea shop. I wondered if he had done so deliberately. In any case, I invited him to join us. He was in uniform so explained that he couldn't stay long, but he sat with us for a few minutes. My mother was pleased by this unexpected development and immediately set about telling him how skilful a cook I was – which was a downright lie – and praising my kind and generous character. She meant well, but if everything she said about me was true, I would have been insufferably perfect.

'Of course, working here is just a stopgap,' she added, smiling at me. 'Emily used to run a corporation in London.'

This was so absurd, I burst out laughing. 'I worked for a small company,' I corrected her, 'and I was a receptionist and general dogsbody. There was no way I ran the company, and it wasn't a corporation.'

My mother smiled, momentarily sold on her own fantasy. 'She's very modest,' she murmured to Barry.

'Really, mother, you are incorrigible,' I scolded her when he had gone. 'Everyone sees through your delusions about me.'

'One day, someone will see you through my eyes, and you'll know he's the one,' she replied with conviction.

'Well, it won't be Barry. He knows I've been working here for a year and I have no intention of leaving.'

'He seems very nice,' she whispered to me, ignoring my complaints.

'Yes, mother, he's nice.'

'Well, I must say, Emily, this place isn't as dull as I thought,' my mother said as we were walking home. 'That's three eligible young men you've met here in the space of a year. Surely you must like at least one of them? You can't carry on pretending you want to live by yourself, like my poor Aunt Lorna.'

'Great Aunt Lorna was hardly poor,' I pointed out, vexed by my mother's harping on about my being single.

'You seem to have forgotten she left me Rosecroft. And she wasn't alone,' I added, watching Poppy as she sniffed the grass.

My mother sniffed, which was her way of signalling her disapproval.

'You might not want to believe it, but I like living here. And I've got Poppy.'

My mother had the sense to offer a placatory smile. 'Yes,' she agreed. 'You've got Poppy, and thank goodness for that. Who knows what might happen to a woman living alone in a remote place like this if you didn't at least have a dog to protect you. So,' she went on, turning to scrutinise at me, 'are you seriously telling me you don't like any one of the three men, because they are all clearly besotted with you?'

I told her that I didn't even know which three men she was talking about, which was true.

'Barry, Adam and Toby,' she replied promptly.

I laughed. 'Barry's a dope,' I said.

'That's not possible. He's a policeman. That's a responsible and steady job.'

'Adam is only here this weekend visiting his father and I hardly know him. We've only really met once, so how you can possibly think he likes me is beyond me.'

'Well, what about Toby?' My mother sighed. 'I had high hopes for you and Toby when you first moved here. Remember how he looked after you last Christmas, when you had that accident?'

'Toby's a friend,' I replied. 'There was never anything more than that between us.'

I felt slightly uncomfortable saying that, because I really liked Toby and at one time had hoped we might become more than friends. But somehow it had never happened.

That evening we ate at home. I cooked. Contrary to my mother's claim, my culinary skills were limited, but she seemed happy enough with homemade macaroni cheese and salad, followed by one of Hannah's apple pies with lashings of cream. Sitting at home, half-listening to my mother's gossip about my sister and her family, with Poppy curled up on the sofa beside me, it was hard to believe that a woman had drowned only a few hundred yards away from my front door. And we still didn't know if she had been murdered.

21

MY MOTHER CAUGHT A bus after tea on Sunday afternoon, so she could be home in time for dinner. I had a feeling we were both looking around for Adam as we walked along Mill Lane, but there was no sign of him. Watching my mother wave energetically at me through the bus window, I felt unexpectedly bereft. As the bus began to move, she turned away, probably to tell the woman seated beside her that she had been visiting her daughter. I smiled, wondering what silly boasts she would be making about me as the bus accelerated away down the road, leaving me alone with my dog. Seeming to understand how I was feeling, Poppy pressed her warm little body against my leg and nuzzled my ankle.

'I know,' I told her, leaning down to scratch her neck, 'I've got you. What would I do without you? I'd be all alone in the world.' An image of the drowned woman flashed across my mind and I shivered. 'No one would even notice if I didn't come home at night if you weren't there.'

As though she had heard enough, Poppy turned her back on me and began to dig frantically in the grass verge. Even worms were more interesting than my maudlin ramblings. I laughed and she raised her head and looked round at me, her bright eyes quizzical above her muddy nose.

'Yes, I'm over my fit of self-pity,' I assured her. 'And your nose is dirty.' She let out a bark and brushed her nose with her paw. 'I swear you understand everything I say,' I told her, surprised by her reaction. 'Come on, then, let's go home.'

We walked slowly along the street to Mill Lane. As we approached The Laurels, I saw Adam putting a bag in the boot of his car. Poppy growled and crouched down, refusing to walk any further. Vexed by her refusal to be friendly with my new acquaintance, I picked her up, muttering crossly that Adam wasn't Ralph. I could understand her aversion to Richard's elder son, but she couldn't hold that against Adam.

'Are you leaving as well?' I asked as we drew level with The Laurels.

'As well?' he queried, looking up.

'I've just seen my mother off at the bus stop.'

Adam slammed the boot of his car and turned to give me his full attention, his dark eyes soft with sympathy. 'You'll miss her?'

'Well, yes, I suppose I will, although I've been here for a year and I haven't lived with my parents for years.'

There was no point in going into details of how I had dropped out of university to live with my ex. He was history now.

Adam laughed. 'It can't be all that long ago.'

'Well, maybe not, but it feels like a lifetime.'

We both laughed.

'Where do you live?' I asked him.

'In London,' he replied vaguely.

My mother had informed me he wasn't married, but that didn't really mean anything. Eager to know if he lived alone, and whether he had a girlfriend, I held back, not wanting to sound intrusive. Instead, I asked him when he was leaving Ashton Mead. He told me he was staying for the evening and would set off later. I was about to invite him to my house but just then Richard emerged from The Laurels. He smiled when he saw me and Poppy, who ran over to say hello, her tail wagging with glee.

'I wondered where you had got to,' he said to Adam. 'Are you coming in?' he added addressing me.

'I think it's my turn to invite you over,' I replied, slightly embarrassed that he kept asking me in and I hadn't reciprocated.

'I've just made a pot of tea,' Richard replied. 'Is your mother with you?'

'She's just left.'

'Come on in,' Adam said. 'We're going to have tea in the garden.'

And that seemed to settle the matter.

Poppy was unusually quiet as we sat down on Richard's garden chairs. She lay down by my feet, as if guarding me and growled when Adam approached me with a plate of scones.

'My father baked these himself,' he announced, with a smile.

'It hardly seems worth the effort, when Hannah's cakes and scones are so much better than anything I can produce,' Richard said.

'Don't be so modest,' Adam chided him. 'We'll let Emily be the judge, shall we?'

He winked at me as he said that, and Poppy growled quietly at my feet. 'She really doesn't like me, does she?' He laughed uneasily.

'She's just not used to you,' I replied, helping myself to a scone.

The scone was perfect, light and with just the right amount of sweetness without being cloying. Realising she wasn't going to be given any as a treat, Poppy lost interest and fell asleep. Her nose twitched as a bee buzzed lazily past her head, but she didn't even open her eyes. Nearby a blue tit was trilling its tiny siren call and somewhere we could hear the pigeons cooing and further off the faint tapping of a woodpecker.

'Did you really make the scones?' I asked Richard when I had finished my mine.

He nodded.

'They're fantastic. You ought to be helping Hannah in the tea shop. She's constantly baking. I'm sure she could do with an extra pair of hands. She wanted me to help out in the kitchen but I'm afraid my scones are nowhere near good enough to serve to customers and I practised making them for months. How do you do it? You've obviously got the knack.'

'It's all in the consistency,' Richard replied and he started giving me detailed instructions.

'I do all that, but they never turn out anywhere near as good as these,' I told him. 'Nowhere close.'

We finished our tea and Richard took the tray inside. If Adam was going to express any interest in me, this was his opportunity. He leaned towards me, his dark eyes alight with curiosity.

'Tell me,' he said, and I nodded hopefully. 'Emily,' he added, and I held my breath. 'Do you like living here in Ashton Mead?'

I considered my answer. He was probably making small talk, but it was just possible he wanted to know whether I would ever consider moving back to London, where he lived.

'It's a lovely village,' I replied at last, before the silence could become awkward. 'And I have my own house here. My great aunt left it to me. You should come and see it.'

I broke off, afraid of sounding as though I was trying to reel him in. My mother would have approved.

Adam nodded. 'It looks pretty from the outside.'

That must mean he had walked past to have a look at Rosecroft. Once again, I held my breath, waiting to hear what he would say next. But he remained silent. Annoyingly enough, I was reminded of my friend Toby, who had often appeared to be on the point of asking me out, but never did. Perhaps it was my fault for setting my expectations too high.

'Is it me?' I asked Poppy, when we were home with the front door closed behind us and no one else could hear us. 'I mean, am I deluded in thinking all these men fancy me? First there was Toby, then Barry, and now Adam. They all seem to find me attractive but none of them ever do anything about it. Well, that's not strictly true because Barry did ask me out but he took me to The Plough, for goodness' sake.'

Poppy whimpered.

'Yes, I suppose that was nice of him to think of you, but nothing happened, did it? Not that I wanted anything to come of it. He's hardly my dream date.' I giggled, remembering how he had tipped a tray of fish and chips over Tess. 'But I want a real relationship with a boyfriend who puts me first. Is that too much to ask? Right now you're the only creature on this earth that I can have a serious honest conversation with, and all you can do is whimper and bark. At least Ben made his feelings for me clear.' Not that my relationship with my ex had been a success. Quite the opposite. I looked at Poppy and sighed. 'What do you think I should do? Adam will be gone soon and who knows when he'll be back? And I really like him.'

Poppy growled.

'You're no better than Barry, with his grunting,' I told her crossly. 'I don't know what you've got against Adam. I keep telling you, he's nothing like his brother. As if you can understand anything I say anyway.'

Poppy turned away and trotted out of the room. 'Now even you've abandoned me,' I complained. She didn't come back so I followed her to the kitchen and made our supper.

22

As it turned out, I did see Adam again before he left Ashton Mead. It was a mild evening, and dry, so I walked to the pub after supper, hoping to see my friends. Adam's car was still parked outside The Laurels. I rang the bell, wanting to say goodbye to him, but no one answered. I was pleasantly surprised to see him seated in the bar of The Plough with his father. Hannah was sitting with them and they were all laughing. Seeing Hannah with Adam, I felt a stab of jealousy which I stifled at once. Hannah was free to be friendly with anyone she liked, and I was a mere casual acquaintance to Adam, a neighbour who had been kind to his father when most of the villagers treated him with suspicion. I had no more claim on his time than she did.

Catching sight of me, Richard stood up and pulled another chair over to their table. I did my best to hide my pleasure at finding myself sitting next to Adam.

'Hannah was just telling us about her plans to expand the tea shop,' Richard told me.

Suspecting Hannah was making a play for Adam, I decided to be generous. She was my friend, and she had been very kind to me. 'The tea shop's great,' I said. 'Hannah's a shrewd businesswoman, but the key to her success has got to be her scrummy pastries and scones. Like I told you before, she's a wizard in the kitchen. But Hannah,' I added, turning to her, 'I'm afraid you've got a rival.'

Hannah's eyebrows shot up. 'What are you talking about?' She glared uneasily at me and for an instant I suspected she was thinking about Adam.

'Have you tasted Richard's scones? I mean, they really are almost as good as yours. I'm not sure I could even tell them apart. Seriously, Hannah, he's a natural. You have to recruit him to help in the kitchen.'

Richard threw his head back and guffawed, his fluffy white hair quivering as his shoulders shook. 'I don't think so,' he spluttered. 'Apart from anything else, I intend to enjoy my retirement. I'm not looking for a job, and certainly not as a pastry chef.'

I chuckled. 'I wasn't looking for a job as a waitress, but look at me now, working in Hannah's tea shop. It's been a year and I'm still at it. You wait,' I told Richard. 'Once she's tasted your baking, she'll have you working there whether you like it or not. Before you know it, you'll be running a second tea shop for her.'

'I'm perfectly happy with the tea shop I've got, thank you,' Hannah said, but it was obvious she was pleased with the way the conversation was going.

'She doesn't like to admit it,' I said, 'but she's ambitious. The Sunshine Tea Shoppe is going to be a national chain one day.'

'Today Ashton Mead, tomorrow the world,' a familiar voice chimed in.

Looking up, I saw Toby standing behind me. He dragged a chair over to sit between me and Adam, and nodded at everyone in turn, before turning his attention to Poppy who had scurried to greet him. Adam watched, looking faintly puzzled.

'My round, I think,' Richard said, clambering to his feet.

He smiled warmly at me, and I had the impression he wanted to thank me for introducing him to some of the people who lived in the village.

'Poppy's an affectionate little dog,' Toby hazarded, glancing at Adam who looked down. 'She seems to like all of Emily's friends.'

Toby was generally kind to everyone, but it sounded as though he had placed extra emphasis on the word 'friends' and it struck me that he could be making a dig at Adam. Everyone must have noticed how Poppy shunned Adam. What Toby didn't know was that it was Adam's brother whom both Poppy and I disliked. It was impossible to explain the situation then and there, in front of everyone else, but I determined to put Toby straight about Adam at the first possible opportunity. If there would ever be a chance that Adam and I might become romantically attached, it would help if my friends didn't take against him. I didn't want to lose Toby's goodwill but I was annoyed with him. Richard had gone to the bar to order drinks for everyone, and Adam was sitting on the other side of Toby, talking to Hannah.

'How was your mother?' Toby asked, still stroking Poppy who had settled comfortably at his feet.

'Fine,' I replied tersely.

'That's good. You must have been pleased to see her.'

I didn't answer. He nodded, but before he could continue our stilted conversation, I stood up abruptly and made my way to the bar to help Richard carry the drinks over. It was generous of him to buy a round when there were so many of us gathered together, but he was clearly keen to make a good impression on my friends. I understood his motivation. Buying a round at The Plough was a good idea for someone hoping to be accepted by the locals. As I returned with three pint glasses carefully balanced in my hands, Adam leapt to his feet and offered to help me. Seeing Toby glare at him confirmed my suspicion that there was some personal animosity between them. Remembering what my mother had said about Toby, I wondered if she had been right in thinking he liked me more than I realised, but I dismissed the idea. Coming from my mother, it deserved little credence. She was convinced that every eligible man I met was eager to propose to me when, in fact, she was the only person who wanted to see me married.

Anyway, if Toby *was* interested in me in that way, he was certainly very slow in coming forward. Even Barry had asked me out, admittedly only to The Plough, but he had made his intentions clear. Toby was either not at all interested in me romantically, or else he was a bit feeble-minded. He had told me once that he had never had much luck with women. It seemed to me that it was a miracle that he had ever been in a relationship at all. Although he was by no means unattractive, he seemed to have no interest in forming a relationship but was devoted to his career as a science teacher, and to his mother who was in a wheelchair.

The evening passed slowly after that, and I waited for Adam to leave. At last, Toby put the question that was on my mind.

'So when are you setting off back to London?' he asked.

'Oh, I thought I'd stick around for the rest of the week,' Adam replied airily.

I couldn't help smiling, Richard nodded cheerfully, and Hannah looked smug, but Toby was barely able to suppress a scowl.

'Don't you have to get back to work?' he asked.

Adam shook his head. 'It's not like that when you work freelance,' he replied. 'I've not had a break for a while, and I've decided to take a week off. I'm enjoying myself far too much here to want to rush home.' His smile seemed to encompass Hannah and me as he turned to Richard. 'It's nice to be able to spend some time with my dad for a change.'

'What do you do?' Toby asked. 'When you are working?'

'I'm freelance,' Adam replied, without offering any more details.

'Well, you're obviously doing all right,' Hannah interjected. 'Have you seen his car, Toby? He drives a Ferrari.'

Toby muttered inaudibly as he leaned down to scratch Poppy under her chin.

'So,' Richard said brightly. 'What are the sights we should visit in the area, while Adam's here?'

'Oh, let's not rush about like excited tourists,' Adam said before anyone had a chance to respond. 'You're *living* here now. There's plenty of time to see the sights. I'm happy to just chill out and sample village life, go for walks, have tea at Hannah's tea shop, and come to the pub in the evening.'

Richard smiled. 'Sounds good to me,' he said. 'Perhaps Emily and Poppy can come for a walk with us one day? I'd like to take you out for lunch. It's the least I can do when you've been so kind. How about tomorrow?'

'I'm really sorry to rain on your parade, but she does have a job,' Hannah said. She turned to me apologetically. 'You've already taken time off for your mother's visit. If you could agree to take a day off later in the week, it will give us a chance to catch up from the weekend.'

I nodded, thinking about the ovens that probably hadn't been cleaned while Hannah had been on her own in the tea shop.

'Later in the week it is then,' Richard agreed amiably, without specifying a day, and I had to be satisfied with that.

23

On Monday Hannah kept me hard at work all day. I couldn't complain, because she always put in at least as much effort as me. Admittedly it was her café, and she stood to benefit from any profit we made, whereas for me it was only a job, and not a particularly desirable one at that, as my mother liked to remind me. But Hannah had been a good friend to me, and the position suited me perfectly. At least for the time being, I had no incentive to look elsewhere. Monday was generally a fairly quiet day, and between customers we scraped and polished the oven and hob and scrubbed every surface in the kitchen, from top to bottom, until every worktop, cupboard and hob was gleaming and the floor tiles shone. I was pleased we were too busy to sit and chat, because I wasn't sure whether to tell Hannah what Adam had told me about his mother's affair. The longer I kept quiet, the more awkward I felt. Hannah was my best friend, but it wasn't my place to share something Adam had told me in confidence. Finally, Hannah was satisfied, and we put away the mop and cleaning materials and sat down to share a well earned pot of tea with a couple of slices of chocolate cake that wouldn't be fresh enough to serve the next day. I put my feet up with a sigh of exhaustion, and for once Hannah was too tired to scold me for putting my feet on a chair. We drank our tea in silence for a few moments, both of us too shattered even to gossip. When we were drinking our third cup of tea, Hannah asked me about Adam.

'I don't really know anything about him,' I admitted.

'You must have found out something.'

'Only that he's Richard's younger son, and he works for himself, but he didn't say exactly what he does. He lives in London and he drives an expensive car, so I suppose he must be doing all right.'

Hannah nodded thoughtfully. 'Anyone can spend on borrowed money.'

That was certainly true, as I knew to my cost, my ex-boyfriend having run into debts he had been unable to repay. His profligacy had cost me a lot of money. Only in retrospect did I realise how stubbornly naïve I had been to keep on trusting him every time he had promised to pay me back.

'So we don't know much about him at all,' Hannah sighed. 'It's difficult to know what to believe, isn't it?'

'I don't think Richard's son can be all that bad,' I began and hesitated, remembering Ralph. 'But you're right. Who knows what he's really like?'

'You like him, don't you?' Hannah asked, watching me closely as she put her question.

'He seems nice enough,' I replied. 'But I don't exactly have much of a track record when it comes to knowing who can be trusted, at least when it comes to men.'

'You're being evasive,' she said with a smile. 'But I know you like him, and I don't blame you. He's fit, isn't he?'

'Are we going to fight over him?' I laughed.

Hannah shook her head. 'I think we both know which of us he fancies. He can't take his eyes off you.'

'He's just grateful to me for helping his father find his feet in the village.'

'I don't know whether it's false modesty with you, or if you really are that dense, but you never seem to notice when men are obviously interested in you.'

'Now you sound like my mother.'

But I was secretly pleased that Hannah thought Adam liked me, and I hoped she was right.

Poppy had spent most of the day in the yard behind the tea shop, because Jane hadn't been around to keep an eye on her. So on our way home, I took a detour across the grass by the river, to give her a chance to stretch her legs. Poppy loved snuffling around on the open ground, snapping her jaws at gnats and the occasional butterfly or bee that flew past her. She sometimes stopped to dig for worms and I would have to drag her on to prevent her from making muddy holes in the grass, which she knew she was only allowed to do at home in our back garden. As we walked parallel with the river, taking care not to go too close to the water's edge, I recognised Adam. He had his back to us and was scuffing at the earth with his toes, as if looking for something along the river bank. He straightened up when he noticed us, and glanced around as though checking that no one else had seen him.

'What are you looking for?' I asked him, as we drew close enough for him to hear me.

'Nothing,' he replied, sounding tetchy, and frowning uneasily.

His reaction startled me and seemed odd, because he had definitely appeared to be searching for something.

'I was just examining the weeds along here,' he went on, with a return to his customary easy manner. 'It's quite extraordinary how many different varieties there are.'

'I guess so,' I stammered, distracted by his eyes that were gazing at me, dark and mysterious. 'I didn't know you were interested in plants.'

'It's more my father's thing. Since he moved here he's really been getting into domestic life, cooking and gardening and all that. He never showed any interest in anything like that before he moved here. He was happy to leave all that to –' He broke off with a pained expression.

'To your mother?' I enquired gently, my sympathy engaged.

He nodded. Almost without noticing, I followed him a few steps away from the river.

'What happened?' I asked. 'I mean, he seems so kind and – well, he's so nice.'

'My mother left him for someone else, as I said before.' Adam said dully. 'When Dad found out she'd been having an affair, he said she had to choose between them. He said if she went home, it would all be forgotten. He was prepared to forgive her, unconditionally.' He paused. 'She chose the other man.' His voice was flat, but an expression of suppressed fury flickered across his face.

'I'm so sorry,' I said. 'That really sucks.'

He didn't say anything else, and for a moment neither of us spoke. If he had given me the slightest encouragement I would have reached out and hugged him. As it was, he looked away, and I suppressed the urge to comfort him, uncertain how he might react to my flinging my arms around him.

'You and Barry,' he began, and hesitated.

I could hardly breathe, wondering what he was going to say. It sounded as though he wanted to know whether I was in a relationship with someone else.

'Me and Barry?' I echoed at last. 'What about me and Barry?'

'I just wondered how close you are. How well you know him.'

'We're not an item, if that's what you mean. He's not my boyfriend. I don't have a boyfriend at the moment.' I spoke firmly, keen to make my single status clear.

Adam looked at me, nonplussed. 'I just wondered how well you knew Barry, that's all. He seems like a nice guy,' he added lamely.

A depressing thought struck me: Adam didn't seem to be enquiring about my status at all. He sounded interested in Barry. Not knowing how to reply, I just nodded. I hardly knew Barry, really. Hannah had told me he fancied me, so it didn't seem likely he was gay, but it wasn't my place to draw conclusions about someone else's sexual orientation, especially someone I had only met a few times.

'You know Barry's a policeman,' I said brightly. 'He sometimes wears a uniform.' I stopped, conscious that my words sounded childish. At the same time, I couldn't resist watching Adam carefully to see how he reacted.

'I wonder how much he knows about the crime rate in Ashton Mead.' Adam grinned suddenly, and I had the impression he was deliberately changing the subject. 'I'm guessing there isn't actually much crime in this sleepy little village. Still, it might be interesting to have a chat with our local bobby, see what he can tell us, from the inside. I wouldn't want to think my father was living in the crime capital of Wiltshire. Although compared to London, I dare say it's going to seem pretty tame.' He laughed. 'Of course, there was the woman who drowned here not long ago, the woman you found. Has Barry been able to shed any light on that? Surely the police must be all over it if they think she was murdered.'

'You'd think so,' I agreed. 'But I'm not sure Barry has much to do with the investigation into the drowning.'

'More of a traffic cop, is he?'

'Something like that, I think. I don't really know him that well. You need to ask Hannah. They're old friends. She was at school with him.'

Adam looked surprised, and I wondered what Hannah had told him about me and Barry, as we walked slowly back to the lane. Its proper name was Mill Lane, but everyone in the village referred to it as 'the lane' and I had fallen into the habit of calling it by its generic local name. As we drew closer, we saw Richard out in his front garden, seemingly studying the façade of his house. He turned round on hearing Poppy bark at him, and smiled at us. As soon as we drew close, he invited me in, as he habitually did. As usual, I tried to refuse, embarrassed by always accepting his hospitality and never inviting him back. The truth was, I wasn't sufficiently efficient with my domestic arrangements to receive guests without any notice. If I offered Richard tea, the chances were I would have run out of milk, or biscuits. When I started working at the tea shop, Hannah used to insist on loading me up with cakes, scones, pastries and buns, and whatever goodies she had left over at the end of the day. They were difficult to resist, but after a couple of months I began to refuse her offerings, afraid that none of my clothes would fit me if I kept stuffing myself with leftovers from the tea shop.

Richard insisted, telling us he was planning to make a jug of Pimms. It would be his first attempt, and he was excited for us to try it.

Adam grinned affectionately at his father. 'You're not exactly selling it to us by asking us to be your guinea pigs.'

But when Adam added his exhortation, I agreed to join them for one drink before going home. I liked Richard, but Adam was the one who drew me. Every time he smiled at me, I felt my stomach flip. As for Poppy, she continued to treat Adam with caution, because he reminded her of his brother. She would get over it. If I had my way, Adam and I would be spending a lot more time together, and Poppy would just have to get used to him. Adam led me into the back garden and we sat on Richard's patio waiting for him to emerge with his Pimms.

'Your dad seems very happy here,' I said.

Adam nodded. 'He puts a brave face on it, but he was heartbroken when my mother left. He's a broken man.'

'Do you think she'll come back?'

He shook his head. 'She won't come back.'

'You can't know that.'

With a sigh, Adam replied that she was never going back to Richard. With misty eyes, he described how he had tracked down his mother, who was living with her boyfriend in London. He had gone to see her the day before he had come to Ashton Mead, intending to plead with her to think better of her move and return to the family.

'What happened?'

He shook his head. 'I know she was there because I saw her going into the house with him. She was clinging onto his arm as though she was afraid he would run away. But when I rang the bell and asked to speak to her – my own mother – the man she was living with told me she didn't want to see me. He threatened to call the police if I didn't leave her alone. My own mother!'

'How terrible.'

Just then Richard appeared holding a large jug of Pimms packed with different fresh fruits, slices of apples and early strawberries, and garnished with mint. It looked more like a fruit salad than a drink, but we all agreed it tasted gorgeous. A robin came and perched on the fence and began trilling; for such a tiny bird, it had an amazingly loud and penetrating chirp. As the alcohol went to my head, I understood that it wasn't just the drink, but life itself that was glorious.

24

'IT'S SUCH A SHAME about Adam's mother,' I said quietly to Hannah at work the next day.

In common with most weekday mornings, we had been fairly quiet once the early breakfast rush was over. Having finished cleaning up, we were sitting down to enjoy a pot of tea for two, and were ready for a natter.

'What about her?' Hannah asked.

I repeated what Adam had told me the previous evening, and Hannah stared at me in amazement.

'You do realise what this means?' she asked.

'That Richard's wife isn't going to go back to him, ever. Unless she changes her mind again.'

'It means that it can't have been her body you found in the river, not if Adam saw her and she's alive. It means Richard didn't kill his wife. We misjudged him all along.'

I had never actually believed that Richard was a murderer, so I wasn't as excited as Hannah by the news that his wife was alive and well and living in London. Far from being relieved that I wasn't living next door to a psychopath, I just felt sorry for my next-door neighbour, as well as for Adam who was clearly very upset about his mother's decision to choose her lover over her husband.

'It must be hard for Adam,' Hannah said. 'Knowing his mother walked out on his father like that. I mean, he walked out on Adam as well, and his brother.'

In a way that was an emotive interpretation of what had happened. Neither Adam nor Ralph had been living at home for some years, and their mother's departure couldn't really have made any difference to their daily lives. But I didn't comment on what Hannah had just said. A couple of elderly women came in just then and after that, although we weren't busy, we had a steady stream of customers throughout the day. What with serving at tables and checking on Poppy and taking her for regular walks to prevent her becoming restless, there was no chance to chat with Hannah again until the teatime customers left.

'So what's going on between you and Adam?' Hannah asked me, looking up from a pot she was scouring.

'Nothing.' That was true, although I didn't add that it wasn't for lack of trying on my part. 'Actually he's made it pretty clear he's more interested in someone else. In fact he indicated that's the reason he's staying here for the week.'

Before I had a chance to mention my suspicion that Adam was interested in Barry, Hannah reached out and grabbed my arm.

'Do you really think he fancies me?' she blurted out breathlessly. 'I can't believe it. I've waited so long for someone like Adam to come along, but I never thought it would actually happen. I can't believe Adam would be interested in me, with you around.'

'What do you mean, with me around?'

'Oh, come on. Look at me and then go and stand in front of a mirror. Since my disastrous marriage I've really let myself go, and men don't even notice me any more, not in that way. You don't know what it's like to be fat and frumpy. I might as well be invisible.'

'What are you talking about? You're stunning.'

Hannah laughed. 'You must be the only person who thinks so. You and my mother.'

Although it was true she wasn't exactly beautiful in a traditional way, she was undeniably attractive with her soft blond curls and blue eyes, but more appealing than her physical looks, was the warmth and kindness she exuded. And in addition to that, she baked the best cakes I had ever eaten. I couldn't imagine any man preferring me to her. Admittedly Barry had chosen to invite me out, when he could have asked Hannah who really liked him. I hoped his choice hadn't dented her confidence. But Barry and Hannah had known each other since they were children, which could explain why he didn't regard her in a romantic light. There was no reason why someone like Adam, who didn't know either of us, should prefer me to Hannah. It was true I found Adam attractive, but Hannah was my friend. Besides, Adam had made it clear he wasn't interested in me, so I decided to see whether I could pull off a little matchmaking. Of course, if my suspicion was correct, and Adam was gay, then there was no hope of persuading him to ask Hannah out. But I was going to give it my best shot. No one need ever know, especially not Hannah.

I was on my way home, still wondering how to try and bring Adam and Hannah together, when I spotted him outside The Laurels. He was fetching something from his car. Of course, I stopped to chat, although Poppy did her best to drag me away and turned her back on me in disgust when I refused to budge. Adam asked me whether I'd be going to the pub that evening.

'Probably,' I replied, still thinking about Hannah.

I did my best to hide my surprise when Adam enquired how well Hannah and I knew each other, just as I was thinking about her. I told him how kind Hannah had been to me when I first arrived in Ashton Mead, offering me not only a job when I needed one but also her friendship.

'She's the kindest person I know, and you really should try her cooking. She's amazing. Like I said, she'll probably be at the pub this evening, so why don't you come along and I'll introduce you properly. I think you'll find you have a lot in common.'

With that, I turned and walked quickly away before he could ask me to be more specific about what he and Hannah might have in common. Poppy trotted happily beside me as we walked home. As soon as we were back at Rosecroft, I phoned Hannah to tell her that Adam was going to be at the pub that evening.

'Did he want to know if I would be there?' she asked eagerly.

'Not exactly,' I equivocated, 'but he asked about you.'

'What did he want to know?'

'He asked me how long we've known each other and I told him you're going to be at The Plough this evening so he can speak to you himself if he wants to get to know you better. He's definitely interested in you. If he turns up it'll give you a chance to get to know him. I thought you'd want me to let you know.'

That evening, Hannah and Adam were already at the pub by the time Poppy and I arrived. Having greeted Hannah enthusiastically, Poppy allowed Adam to stroke her before she lay down at Hannah's feet, growling softly. Hannah and Adam seemed to be getting on well, and I needed an excuse to leave them alone together. As I was saying that Poppy wanted to go outside, Toby arrived with Barry.

'You've just been for a walk,' Barry protested, hearing my fib.

Strictly speaking, it wasn't a lie, because Poppy always wanted to go outside, but I could hardly insist, since Poppy was so obviously content to doze at Hannah's feet. Toby suggested I could go to the bar if I fancied a walk, but Adam insisted on buying a round.

'You've all been so kind to my father,' he said. 'It's the least I can do.' He smiled at Hannah as he was speaking and she looked down to hide her broad grin.

'He's so generous,' she murmured, watching him go up to the bar.

'Someone's smitten,' Toby muttered as he bent down to pet Poppy.

Barry sat down and looked generally bemused, which seemed to be his habitual expression. Meanwhile, Hannah went over to Adam to help him carry the drinks back to our table and we spent a convivial evening, swapping stories about our recent near disasters. Hannah described an incident in the café, where a doddery old man had missed his cup and poured almost an entire jug of milk over the table, completely oblivious to his mistake. Fortunately it hadn't been boiling hot tea. Toby had a few stories to tell from his week at school where some eleven-year-olds had discovered how to make stink bombs, much to the disgust and amusement of the staff and other pupils. Adam just smiled and listened, while Barry seemed lost in his own thoughts and barely joined in the conversation.

'How about you, Barry?' Adam enquired, kindly trying to draw him into the conversation.

Barry shrugged. 'I had a good week,' he replied.

'You must have a store of entertaining anecdotes,' Adam pressed him.

Barry shook his head. 'Nothing I'm at liberty to discuss.'

'Come on,' Adam urged him. 'You're among friends here.'

Sensing Barry's discomfort at being pressed, Poppy barked, and Adam let it go. But I noticed he looked slightly disgruntled, and made a mental note to watch him and Barry closely in future, in case there was anything between them that Hannah ought to know about. Soon after that, Richard joined us. He too offered to buy us all a drink, but Toby and Barry insisted on sharing the next round.

'Makes no odds to me,' Tess interrupted the discussion as she collected our empty glasses. 'As long as you keep drinking and someone pays.' She twisted her face in an unappealing kind of smile before stalking off with the empty glasses. As Toby and Barry went to the bar, I spotted Adam's hand brush Hannah's, and she smiled. For no reason, I felt a spasm of unease. I had as good as engineered their meeting, and I really knew very little about Adam. I hoped my friend wasn't going to end up getting hurt.

25

THE NEXT DAY I woke early with the sun streaming through a gap in my curtains and Poppy snuffling at the back of my neck. Laughing, I pushed her away and she jumped off the bed and bounded to the door, whimpering at me to hurry up. There was a day outside waiting to be explored. Opening the curtains, I gazed down at my back garden. What I could see over the fence in Richard's garden looked neat and well-cultivated, compared to the overgrown tangle on my own property where, despite all my efforts, weeds flourished in the borders and the grass was riddled with moss and clover and pitted with holes where Poppy had dug for insects or buried chew toys. She enjoyed sniffing around the daisies and bright buttercups, and I quite liked them, and I didn't object to her occasionally digging up the turf, even though she knew she wasn't supposed to. If it was in her nature to dig, it was better for her to do so in my back garden than under Cliff's begonias and geraniums at The Plough, or in other people's flower beds.

It was a lovely day, and on our way through the village Poppy insisted on stopping every few paces to sniff the ground and sometimes water it. We made very slow progress, and after dropping her off at Jane's house for the day I barely made it to the tea shop before Hannah turned the sign round.

'Sorry I'm late,' I puffed, hurrying to fetch my apron and notepad.

Not a moment too soon, because a young couple entered and sat down almost immediately. They told me they were going to Wales for a holiday, and passing through Ashton Mead on their way. The village had been recommended to them as a picturesque place to stop. Having left home very early that morning, they were ready for breakfast. A quick glance at the menu was all they needed, and before long I returned with two plates laden with full English breakfasts. While I was serving them, a tall dark-haired woman entered the café and sat down near the door. I didn't immediately recognise her, and went over to take her order.

'I'd like another word with you,' she said in a low voice. 'Please, sit down.'

Recognising the detective inspector, I nodded. We had met by the river when I reported the body, and again at the police station when I had handed in the chain Poppy found.

'I'll just tell my boss that you're here or I'll be in trouble for skiving,' I replied and scurried to the kitchen.

'What does she want?' Hannah asked, her eyes wide with curiosity, when I told her who had come in.

'I'll let you know when I've spoken to her.'

There was no reason for me to feel uneasy. All I had done was accidentally stumble on a dead body, after which my dog had found a pendant on a chain hidden nearby. None of my actions could be construed as criminal in any way. On the contrary, the fact that I had reported both discoveries to the police more or less straight away meant I couldn't be suspected of being implicated in any foul play. I lived very close to the spot along the river where the drowned woman had been discovered, so it was hardly surprising my dog had found both the body and the chain. But learning that the police were snooping around again, wanting to question me, made me nervous. For a start, it suggested that a crime had been committed, and the woman had not drowned by accident.

'Can you tell me why you're here?' I asked quietly as I sat down.

I tried to keep my voice level, but my consternation would have been obvious to anyone, and I had the impression the detective's shrewd gaze missed nothing. Without answering, she pulled a grainy printed image from her pocket and placed it on the table in front of me. Barely able to hide my growing alarm, I stared at a picture of Adam. As if in a dream, I heard the detective ask me if I recognised the man in the picture.

'Have you seen him before?' she asked, with a hint of urgency in her voice.

I hesitated only briefly. There was no point in equivocating. Half the residents of the village would be able to identify him.

'That's Adam Jones,' I whispered. 'Richard's son.'

The detective nodded briskly and put the picture away.

'But why do you want to know? What are you doing with a picture of him? Has he done something wrong?' My voice rose and the other customers looked up from their breakfast.

The detective's severe features softened slightly. 'There's no need to worry. This is a routine enquiry. Now, tell me what you know about Adam.'

For the second time, I was being quizzed about Adam Jones.

'Not a lot,' I replied honestly. 'That is, I can't say I really know him. His father moved into the village recently, and

Adam's come here for a few days to visit him. He arrived on Thursday and was originally planning to leave after the weekend, but he decided to stay on with his father for a few more days.'

'For someone who doesn't really know him, you seem to know a lot about his movements,' she remarked drily.

I explained that Adam's father lived at The Laurels, next door to my house, Rosecroft. She nodded and I had the feeling she wasn't hearing anything she didn't already know. Just then, Hannah came over and offered the detective tea, which was refused.

'Is everything all right?' Hannah asked, leaning over the table and lowering her voice so the young couple who had come in for breakfast wouldn't hear her. 'Only what with the body being found in the river the other week, everyone's a bit jumpy at the moment, as you can imagine, and you turning up in the village isn't going to help,' she added.

It was obvious that Hannah would be more comfortable if the inspector were to accept a pot of tea. That way, she would look like just another customer. I watched the detective closely, but she showed no sign of dismay or irritation at Hannah's words.

'How long are you staying in the village?' Hannah asked.

'Until I find out everything I need to know,' the detective replied calmly.

She pulled out the picture of Adam again and looked quizzically at Hannah. There was no need for her to ask whether Hannah knew Adam. Her face indicated her instant recognition, even before she stammered Adam's name.

'How well do you know him?' The detective asked, and I discerned a gentleness in her voice that had not been there when she had posed the same question to me.

But Hannah was not so easily drawn. 'He's staying with his father in the village,' she replied. 'Everyone here knows Richard. We're a close-knit community. So we've all met his son, Adam. But I've only met him a couple of times at the pub, and I can't really tell you anything about him. Why do you want to know?'

The detective paused. 'We think something may have happened to his mother,' she said at last.

'Oh no,' I blurted out, thinking I could see where this was heading. 'Adam's mother's fine. That is, I happen to know that she's living with her boyfriend in London. She left her husband, Richard, the one we were telling you about. That's why Adam's here. He wanted to see that his father's all right,' I added, seeing the detective looking slightly perplexed.

'Adam's like that, thoughtful,' Hannah added.

The detective's frown deepened. 'You both said you hardly know him, yet you seem to know him very well.'

'People chat at the pub,' Hannah replied breezily. 'Like I said, we're a very close community here.'

There was a faint commotion behind us. The couple had finished their breakfast and were ready to pay. Thanking us for our time, the detective rose to her feet and left.

'What the hell was that all about?' Hannah asked once everyone had gone. 'And why was she so interested in Adam?'

'You heard what she said,' I replied. 'It's nothing. The police thought something had happened to Adam's mother, but it turns out that was a misunderstanding. She's living somewhere in London, that's all. My guess is that tongues were wagging in the village and the police got wind of the fact that people were saying Richard killed his wife. It was probably Maud,' I added thoughtfully.

Hannah nodded and her worried frown cleared. 'Yes, you're right. That must be it,' she said.

Privately I wondered whether the police knew something about Adam that they weren't sharing with us. If Adam had been telling me the truth, he had seen his mother in London only a week earlier, but we only had his word for it that he had seen her there at all. It was looking increasingly likely that he had lied to me. Remembering how I had encouraged Hannah to see Adam, I felt a frisson of unease.

26

WORN OUT BY MY recent anxieties, I stayed at home that evening and didn't learn about Hannah's disappointment until the following day when I arrived at work to find her looking dreadful. She refused to look at me with her bloodshot eyes, and was uncharacteristically silent as she stood with her back to me, busying herself at the oven. We had always shared our problems, but she dismissed my questions with a wave of her hand, insisting that she was fine. Obviously something was amiss, and I urged her to confide in me, but she shook her head.

'I told you, there's nothing wrong,' she said, stubbornly facing the oven.

'And I told you, I don't believe you.' I hesitated. 'This hasn't got anything to do with Adam, has it?'

Hannah drew in a breath sharply and didn't answer.

'Come on, Hannah, tell me what's happened. Whatever it is, you can't keep it to yourself forever.'

During a quiet spell we sat down with mugs of hot chocolate and slices of banoffee pie, which was a particular favourite of hers. She tucked in without speaking while I waited patiently for her to open up. At least her misery didn't seem to have affected her appetite.

'Come on, Hannah,' I cajoled her when she seemed

determined to maintain an obdurate silence. 'What happened with Adam? I thought the two of you were getting on so well.'

She gazed down at her plate and tears gathered in her eyes. 'I thought so too,' she murmured.

'So what went wrong?'

'He's gone,' she whispered. A solitary tear trickled down the rounded contours of her cheek.

'Oh for goodness' sake,' I burst out, exasperated. 'Is that what all this is about? That's no reason to be down. You knew he'd be going home soon, and he'll be back before you know it.'

For the first time, it crossed my mind that Hannah might end up joining Adam in London. If the Sunshine Tea Shoppe in Ashton Mead were to close, I would lose my job. But I was more worried about Hannah's state of mind than my income.

'No, no, he won't, he won't be back,' she said. 'He's gone for good.'

A cold feeling seemed to slice through me like a knife. 'You mean he's – dead?' I stammered, shocked. 'What happened?'

'No, no,' she replied. 'It's nothing like that. God, do you have to be so stupidly melodramatic about everything?'

I knew she was upset, so I let that go.

'He's not dead,' she went on, sniffling. 'He's gone away and he said he's never coming back. He told me he had a terrible row with his father and now they're not speaking to each other. He left the village. He's gone and I don't know where he is. I asked him where he was going so we could keep in touch, but he just said there's nothing to keep him here.' More tears slid down her plump cheeks as she spoke. 'He said he had no reason to return here, ever. He's never coming back.' She let out a sob. 'I'll never see him again.'

I resisted an impulse to fling my arms round her and comfort her. If we had been standing up, facing one another, I would have hugged her. But mine weren't the arms she wanted to feel around her and, besides, we were sitting down with a table between us making physical contact difficulty.

'He'll be back,' I said lamely. 'Don't worry. I'm sure he'll be back.'

'He wouldn't even tell me where he lives. He said he didn't know where he would be.'

Hannah was in no state to see customers so we agreed she would spend the day in the kitchen while I served the tables. That was the way we normally split the running of the café anyway, so it made no difference to me. Hannah usually liked to pop into the café every once in a while, to chat to customers and check that everyone was happy, but today she kept out of sight. Very few people seemed to miss her.

'No Hannah today?' one regular customer asked.

'She's busy baking.'

'That's good to hear.'

Hannah had not recovered her usual good humour by the time we closed the café for the day. When I tried to cheer her up, she grew angry with me.

'You were jealous of me right from the start,' she snapped.

'Jealous of you? I don't understand. What do you mean? You're my best friend. How was I ever jealous of you?'

'You wanted Adam and you couldn't bear it that he chose me –' She broke down in sobs.

'No, no, that's not true. Hannah, you have to believe me. I did fancy Adam, it's true. Can you blame me? But as soon as I realised how you felt about him, I did everything possible to convince him how wonderful you are.'

'So you're saying he only spent the night with me because

you persuaded him to? Did you tell him how desperate I was? Was that how you sold me to him, as an easy shag?'

I hadn't been aware that Hannah had grown so close to Adam so quickly, but I understood she was feeling distraught and probably not thinking clearly.

'What? No,' I replied. 'It wasn't like that. I had no idea he spent the night with you. Why would he do that if he didn't really like you?'

'Then why has he gone off without even telling me where he went? Where is he?'

'I'm guessing he's feeling confused. His mother walked out on them and his father's in a state because of it.' I paused. Richard hadn't seemed particularly upset to me, but people can hide their emotions, especially from strangers. 'Perhaps he started to have feelings for you and just couldn't cope with it right now. He might be finding it difficult to trust women after what his mother did to his father. You need to talk to him, Hannah. I'm sure he can explain.'

'How can I talk to him, when he's disappeared?' she snapped before breaking down in tears again. 'He told me – he told me he thought he was really falling for me. And I – I told him I loved him. Oh, how could I be so stupid?' she cried out. 'He spent the night with me in the room above the shop and then he just announced that he was leaving and buggered off. How could he do that? What's going on, Emily? It might sound daft to you. I never believed in people having soulmates and all that kind of thing, but somehow everything seemed different when Adam came along. I really thought he was, you know, 'the one'. It just felt so right.'

I resolved to speak to Richard myself and find out where Adam was living. If necessary, I would confront him and find out why he had treated my friend so callously, and whether there was any chance he might be reunited with her. If not, at least I would have the satisfaction of telling him exactly what I thought of the shabby way he had behaved. And so it was that, on our way home, Poppy and I stopped outside The Laurels once again. While I was dithering, working out what to say to Richard, his front door swung open slowly and he emerged. Assuming he had spotted me and come out to say hello, I wasn't entirely convinced by his expression of surprise on seeing me standing there. I wanted to speak to him, yet now the opportunity had presented itself, I dithered.

'I was just going out for a walk,' he said.

Summoning all my courage, I broached the subject that was bothering me. 'I hear that Adam has left the village.'

Richard nodded. 'Yes, he had to get back to London. It's a pity. I was hoping he'd be able to stay a few more days, but a job came up and he's not in a position to turn work down.'

While he was speaking, I had moved closer so that he could hear me talking quietly. Somehow it seemed more appropriate, given that I wanted to raise a delicate matter.

'I hope you didn't part on bad terms,' I said.

Richard's eyebrows shot up comically and then lowered in a bemused frown.

'Bad terms? Why on earth would we be on bad terms?'

'I just thought – I mean, he left so suddenly – it seemed –'

'Really,' he interrupted me, grinning, 'where do you get your fanciful notions from? There was no dramatic falling out. I'm afraid the truth is far more pedestrian. He had to work.'

Mumbling an awkward apology for my mistake, I was about to turn away and head home, when a flash of indignation shook me. Adam had invented a pathetic excuse for walking out on Hannah like that. He was a liar and a coward, and he shouldn't be allowed to get away with his atrocious behaviour. Before I had time to think about what I was saying, I heard myself asking for Adam's phone number.

'We were going to exchange numbers, but we forgot,' I added.

I was shocked to discover how easily lies rolled off my tongue, but I was doing this for my friend, and remained firm. One way or another, I was determined to confront the rat who had seduced my friend and let her believe he loved her, when it now appeared she had been no more than a casual fling to him. Richard happily passed me Adam's phone number, after warning me that Adam might not answer but would almost certainly call me back if I left a message.

'I was hoping he'd stay here for his birthday, but he couldn't,' he said, with a sad shrug.

'When is his birthday?'

'Saturday.'

That was three days away. With a flash of inspiration, I asked Richard for Adam's address, explaining that if I sent a card the next morning, first class, it might arrive in time for his birthday. Richard happily obliged. After two little lies, I now knew Adam's phone number and where he lived. One way or another I was going to persuade him to face Hannah and apologise for the despicable way he had treated her, and possibly even get them back together again. I considered giving the number to Hannah, but decided it might be better to speak to Adam myself first, and find out what was going on. At the very least he ought to know how serious Hannah was about him. This was becoming complicated, but I had engineered the date between Hannah and Adam and I owed it to my friend to put matters right between them, if that was possible.

27

THAT EVENING I PHONED Adam. Either Richard hadn't given me the correct number, or there was a problem with the line. Whatever the reason, the number turned out to be unobtainable. After trying to call him on and off all evening, I gave up. I still had Adam's address and on looking it up discovered it was close to a tube station. The following day was Thursday, which wasn't usually very busy at the tea shop, and that gave me an idea. Inventing an excuse about my mother being sick, I asked Hannah for the day off work. I had decided to speak to Adam in person. So, on a drizzly day, Poppy and I set off on a secret mission to reunite Hannah with the man she had fallen for. Poppy trotted along in front of me, stopping to sniff and leave her little messages on the way to the bus stop. She hadn't travelled on the bus very often, and had never been on a train, and I could only hope that she would behave herself. She sat quietly on my lap on the bus journey into Swindon, watching the countryside trundle past and whimpering only occasionally. She didn't bark once and the other passengers could hardly have been aware of her presence. I hoped she would be as docile on the train.

I had forgotten how much a train ticket to London cost, and was taken aback at the price, but I owed it to my friend to discover Adam's true intentions. So far he appeared to have behaved very badly, sleeping with her and telling her he cared for her, only to scarper the next day without even saying goodbye properly. The more I thought about what he had done, the angrier I felt, and the more determined to tell him what I thought of him. At the very least, I hoped to make him feel ashamed of his callous treatment of my friend. She was the kindest of people, and had done nothing to be treated that way. But there was a possibility that he had a credible excuse for his conduct, and was genuinely fond of Hannah and meant to return to Ashton Mead to see her as soon as he could. Perhaps his departure had led to a cruel misunderstanding on her part.

While I was plotting what to say to Adam to make him appreciate the consequences of his conduct, Poppy behaved beautifully on the train, dozing quietly on my lap the whole way. The journey took us almost an hour, but once we arrived at Paddington, we still had a half-hour journey to get to Archway on the tube. If I hadn't lived in London and known my way around the underground system, it might have taken even longer as we had to change trains at King's Cross. I carried Poppy all the way around the large station, concerned that she would be frightened by the hordes of people hurrying by. Snug in my arms, she seemed quite happy and watched everything around us with intense curiosity.

The address Richard had given me was less than a mile from Archway station and although it took us a while to get there, it wasn't difficult to find. We walked along Dartmouth Park Hill, past a park which Poppy was desperate to explore. Having just spent so long on public transport, she was due a frolic on the grass. The rain clouds had vanished and the sun was out. We spent twenty minutes stretching our legs while Poppy sniffed her way across the grass. With difficulty I yanked her away from the park and we found Dartmouth Park Avenue where we turned right into Bramshill Gardens. Adam's address was on the ground floor of a three-storey Victorian terraced property. I surmised from Adam's address, and a series of bells beside the front door, that the building was divided into flats which were rented out. The building was poorly maintained, with chipped paintwork on the crumbling wooden window frames and brick walls in need of repointing. Since becoming a home owner myself, I had become attuned to maintenance issues with property, and this building was clearly in urgent need of repair. I studied the names beside the series of bells, but Adam Jones wasn't there. Richard had told me he lived on the ground floor; I rang that bell.

A blonde girl opened the door. I caught a whiff of strong perfume as she turned her head and her shoulder-length blonde hair flicked past my face.

'Is Adam in?'

'Who do you want?'

She was very pretty, with a neat turned-up nose, blue eyes and a slender figure.

'Adam,' I repeated. 'Adam Jones. I'd like to speak to him. Please. It's important.'

'Oh, Adam,' she replied, her puzzled expression clearing. 'He's not here.'

She was already closing the door so I spoke quickly. 'When are you expecting him back?'

'Roy!' she turned and called out. 'There's someone here asking for Adam.'

'Who?'

A tall, gangly, ginger-haired man came into view and his freckled face peered at me over her shoulder.

'You're asking about Adam?' he repeated.

'Yes, Adam Jones,' I said, trying to hide my impatience. 'When will he be back, only I haven't got all day?'

Roy looked faintly bemused. 'I don't know. Whenever. I haven't asked him over. Are you expecting him?' he asked the blonde girl.

'Why would I ask him here?' she replied defensively, making me wonder what had happened between her and Adam that she was keen to hide from Roy.

'I don't understand,' I blurted out. 'He lives here, doesn't he?'

'Not when I last looked,' Roy replied with a sharp glance at his companion.

The blonde girl shook her head, scowling, and disappeared into the flat.

'Has he moved out?' I asked.

Roy gazed at me warily and heaved a sigh. 'All right, are you the police?'

'The police? No. Whatever gave you that idea?'

'Oh, nothing.'

At my feet, Poppy let out an indignant yelp, as if to ask whether Roy thought she looked anything like a police dog. It seemed the police had been there before me, asking for Adam.

'Listen,' I said, 'I'm not a police officer, I'm just a friend of Adam's and I've come a long way to speak to him. Can you tell me where I can find him? I mean, if he's not living here, he must be living somewhere. Do you know where he is?'

I must have sounded quite aggressive, but I was irritated by what appeared to have been a wasted journey. Sensing my frustration, Poppy whimpered. As far as she was concerned, we had just travelled for two hours to walk in a London park when we had fields and farm land on our doorstep.

'My ticket was expensive,' I added crossly.

Poppy whimpered again, reminding me that she had suffered too, spending a long time cooped up on a bus and two trains for this.

'Look, lady, I'm sorry if you've come a long way to see Adam, but I don't see what you expect me to do about it. He's not here, and I've no idea where he is. And if I never see him again, that's fine with me. But I dare say he'll pop up again one day, knowing Adam,' he added with a good-natured grin. 'He likes to move around. I swear he's got gipsy blood in him.' He laughed as though that was a long-standing joke between him and Adam.

'But he must have moved out quite recently?' I asked, hoping to draw him out, but Roy had lost interest, or patience.

'Adam doesn't live here and he never has done, at least not in the three years I've been here. If he's a friend of yours, as you claim, then why don't you ask him? Now, if you don't mind, I've got my own shit to deal with. I hope you find him and when you do, you can tell him from me that he owes me a beer and a curry.' With that, he shut the door.

'Thanks, Roy,' I muttered. 'You've been a great help.'

All I had succeeded in discovering was that Richard had given me an out-of-date address for Adam, and a phone number that was incorrect. My journey had been a complete waste of time.

'Come on, then, Poppy,' I said. 'Time to go home.'

She looked up when she heard her name and wagged her tail.

'You never let me down, do you?' I murmured, stooping down to pet her.

28

Poppy seemed as pleased as I was to return to the relative peace and rural beauty of Ashton Mead. As the train carried us closer to home, she grew excited and I was afraid she would urinate on the train. In a way, that might be even worse than if she defecated, because the pocket of my jeans was stuffed with dog poo bags. Thankfully there was no one sitting beside me to witness her leaving a deposit on my lap. It wouldn't be pleasant, but it could be dealt with discreetly. If she urinated on me, that would be more difficult to conceal. I had brought a small towel with me in case of such an emergency and could only hope it would suffice if it were needed. Nothing happened to disturb our journey, but I was relieved when we arrived at the station and could take a walk outside as far as the bus stop.

We left Swindon behind us and travelled along country lanes, stopping in small villages and hamlets along the way, through open fields and gently rolling grassy slopes, and I felt a wonderful sense of release. My home was no longer in London, but in Ashton Mead. Poppy had never lived in the big city, but I could tell she was becoming increasingly relaxed as we moved closer to familiar territory. No one knew anything about my pointless trip to London, so there was no one to whinge to about my exasperating experience, and no one with whom I could discuss the mystery of Adam's address. Either Richard had no idea that Adam had given him a false address, or he had deliberately prevented me from speaking to his son, perhaps at Adam's request. Either way, it would be embarrassing for us both if I were to confront my neighbour with the truth.

The following day, I was almost thrown when Hannah enquired about my mother.

'My mother?' I repeated stupidly, remembering just in time that she was supposed to be sick. 'Oh, she's all right. She just panics. I think she wanted to see me,' I added, frowning. 'Don't worry, it won't happen again. I told her in no uncertain terms that she wasn't to summon me like that again without good reason. And I warned her she might end up like the boy who cried wolf, you know. One day she really might be ill, and I'll ignore her,' I added darkly. 'So, I hope you weren't too busy yesterday, and you're not too exhausted?'

Hannah reassured me she was fine and had coped on her own without any trouble. If anything, she said it had done her good to be busy. Work had taken her mind off her broken heart. So that was one positive outcome from my trip to London, at least. We slipped back into our comfortable routine, but I couldn't help noticing that Hannah had lost her usual buoyancy and was unusually quiet when we had no customers. She also stopped coming to the pub in the evenings, insisting she had a lot to do at home. She had recently renovated the small flat above the café and moved in there. I didn't believe her and was sure she was moping. Toby agreed and he did his best to cheer her up. But there was no doubt she was feeling low and I pondered how I might contact Adam to find out what he was playing at. But as the days passed, and he failed to return or even contact Hannah, it grew increasingly clear that he had dumped her without telling her.

When Dana Flack came to the cafe for afternoon tea, I thought little of it. As far as I was concerned, she was just another customer. But once the other tables had cleared, she wiggled her finger, beckoning me to her table.

'Would you like anything else?' I asked automatically. 'Some more hot water?'

'Sit down,' she hissed, gazing around as though we were spies, surrounded by enemy agents.

'I'm sorry, I can't join you. I'm working.'

'What time do you finish?'

'At six, after we close and clear up for the day.'

She glanced at her watch and grunted. 'Very well,' she said. 'I'll wait.'

With that, she took out her phone and began studying a document on her screen. Reluctant to fend off any more of Dana's intrusive questions, I resolved to slip away unseen through the back exit. But when she heard about my conversation with Dana, Hannah insisted I hear what the reporter had to say. Hannah had a point, since Dana was unlikely to give up, and I didn't relish the prospect of her pestering me at home. Somehow, I had the distinct impression that Dana was not one to withdraw without getting what she wanted. So at six o'clock I collected Poppy from the back yard, and we walked round to meet Dana on the pavement at the front of the café. From there we made our way towards the grassy slope near the river. Dana was tall and she strode swiftly, with an air of purpose, as though impatient to get somewhere. By contrast, Poppy kept stopping to sniff around. I made no attempt to keep up with Dana, nor did I apologise when she had to keep stopping to wait for us. As far as I was concerned, Dana could walk away and never come back.

She waited until we left the High Street before addressing me.

'Thank you for agreeing to talk to me,' she began.

'I agreed to listen, not to talk,' I pointed out, 'and it'll just be for a few minutes while we take Poppy for a walk.'

Poppy's ears pricked up at the mention of her name.

'She's adorable,' Dana said. 'And so well-behaved. She's clearly a very contented little dog.'

Refusing to unbend in the face of her blatant flattery of Poppy, I remained aloof, waiting in silence to hear what she had to say.

'I just wanted to hear your views on the news that is about to hit the headlines,' Dana said. 'I'm sure the public would be interested in your response. And if there's any information you can add to this startling development, it would be better if you told me first so I can make sure the facts are accurately reported. There is always so much gossip and misinformation attached to news of this kind.'

'What news?' I asked, intrigued despite my determination to say nothing to her. 'I'm afraid I don't read your paper, so I have no idea what you're talking about.'

'I thought Barry might have been as indiscreet with you as he was with me,' she said with a sly grin.

Her insinuation infuriated me, but I said nothing, instead turning my head away from her.

'I know he has a soft spot for you,' she went on.

'I still have no idea what you're talking about.'

'Barry met me for a drink last night.' She shook her head and smacked her lips with a disapproving frown. 'He really ought to learn to hold his tongue.'

'You mean you got him drunk?' I countered with poorly controlled irritation. 'Really, is there no depth to which you won't sink?'

Dana chuckled. 'I've been called scheming and unscrupulous, and worse, far worse, more than once in my career.'

'Hardly a career,' I muttered crossly. 'Reporting for a scrappy local paper. It's barely even a job.'

My words clearly stung, because she winced, but she dismissed the insult with a grim smile. 'I can see you're desperate to hear what your friend Barry told me.' She hesitated, suddenly serious. 'This is off the record, Emily. I can't reveal my source or he might lose his job.'

I scowled at her. 'So you got him drunk, wheedled some information out of him, and then blackmailed him into telling you more by threatening to ruin his career? Is that how you work?'

She shook her head. 'It wasn't like that. You can't blame me if your friend has a loose tongue. But he realised straight away he'd been indiscreet, and he begged me to keep his name out of my report. I gave him my word his name wouldn't be mentioned. So if you repeat a word of what I'm about to tell you, it will be on your conscience, not mine.'

'I didn't think you had a conscience.'

'You must keep Barry's name out of it – unless you want to deliberately undermine his prospects and probably ruin his life.'

'It would be your fault if that happened.'

'No, he has only himself to blame. He spoke out of turn. I think he wanted to impress me. But I'm a journalist, not a gossip.'

'And the difference is what, exactly?' I scoffed.

Dana shook her head. 'You can't seriously expect me to suppress this information. Of course, I don't have to tell you anything, but I would like to know what you can add to what Barry told me, and to quote your reaction to it.'

'What do you mean?' I asked.

'May I quote your response to what he told me?'

I nodded, privately determined to say nothing in exchange for learning what she had discovered. But I knew I would only be able to hear the information from her. Having blabbed once, from now on Barry was going to be very careful about what he said.

'It concerns the woman who was pulled from the river,' Dana said solemnly. 'She didn't drown.'

'What do you mean? I saw the body.'

'Yes, I know. But the truth is she was murdered. Her body was dropped in the river after she died, in an attempt to make her death look like an accidental drowning.'

I didn't say anything, although there were questions I was desperate to ask.

'The police know,' Dana went on, answering my first unspoken query. 'It was the post-mortem that proved she hadn't drowned. After Barry told me the woman had been murdered, I managed to speak to the pathologist.'

'I'm sure you did,' I murmured under my breath, wondering how she had wormed her way into the pathologist's presence.

'There was no water in the dead woman's lungs, no froth in her airways, none of the usual signs of drowning,' she went on with sudden animation, like a bloodhound baying at a scent. 'The woman you thought had drowned had stopped breathing before she entered the water. Someone dropped her in the river, because she sure as hell didn't fall in by herself after she was dead.'

'How *did* she die?' I asked, shocked into speech in spite of my earlier resolve to remain silent.

Dana shook her head. 'I'm afraid I couldn't access that information,' she replied, unexpectedly formal, as though she regretted her surge of enthusiasm. 'So,' she went on, smiling encouragement, 'my readers would like to know what you think, now you know the dead woman was the victim of a murder committed right here in Ashton Mead.'

Even if what Dana had just told me was true, there was nothing to suggest where the murder had taken place. Refusing to be drawn by her provocative question, I turned without a word and hurried away, dragging Poppy behind me. She barked in protest at being forced to trot across the grass, when she wanted to take her time, sniffing as she walked, but I was keen to get away from Dana as quickly as possible. Our interview was over.

29

THAT EVENING, TO MY surprise, there was nothing about the alleged murder on thc local news. With a mixture of relief and disappointment, I started to wonder whether Dana had fabricated the murder story, hoping to rile me into revealing a snippet of information previously hidden from her. She knew my dog had discovered the body of the drowned woman, and she had been eager to prise details of the scene out of me. She had obviously been frustrated by her failure to wheedle from me a gruesome description of a dripping corpse, but I remained firmly convinced of my good sense in sharing as little as possible with her. It was not hard to imagine how she might have exaggerated anything I told her, twisting it into a scene far more ghoulish than the reality, horrible though that had been.

The following morning, as I walked past the village store on my way to work, Maud summoned me through the open door. Even from a distance, I could see she was flapping her hand vigorously as she called my name. Catching her elation, Poppy bounded towards her, barking happily.

'Have you seen the paper?' Maud asked me, as soon as I set foot in the shop. 'Have you seen the news? Well? Have you seen it?'

Her beady eyes glowed and her nose seemed to twitch with excitement, while her mop of grey hair quivered as she nodded her head at me. Vaguely apprehensive, I asked her what she was talking about. For answer, she brandished a copy of the local paper at me. A cold sensation crept down my spine as my attention was arrested by a headline emblazoned boldly across the front page. 'Murder in Ashton Mead' I read, while the paper trembled in my grasp. There followed a report which stated that the dead woman pulled from the river had not drowned, as had first been assumed, but had been, as the paper put it, 'bashed on the back of the head'. After the victim had received a fatal blow to the head, her body had been deposited in the river to make the murder appear to be an accidental drowning.

'Yes,' Maud crowed, her face alight with glee, 'there's been a murder, right here in the village. An actual murder!' She lowered her voice conspiratorially, although we were alone in the shop with only Poppy to hear us. 'I knew there was something not right about that poor woman's death. Isn't that what I've been saying all along? Didn't I say it was no accident, her falling in and drowning just when that man moved into the lane? The police ought to have done something about it straight away, not left single women unprotected, with a murderer living in the village.' She rolled her eyes dramatically and shuddered.

I had no recollection of hearing Maud say she thought the woman had been murdered, but several people in the village had suspected Richard of murdering his wife, including me. On reflection, it made perfect sense for the rumour to have begun with Maud. She spoke to most of the local residents regularly, and was always spreading gossip. But it turned out we had been wrong to suspect Richard, because Adam had assured me his mother was alive and living in London with her lover. The only mystery now was the identity of the dead woman. According to Dana Flack, Senior Features Editor of *My Swindon News*, her death had not been accidental. Whoever the woman was, there no longer seemed to be any doubt that she had been murdered before her body ended up in the river. No one seemed to know anything about her, so I decided to arrange a meeting with Barry, to find out whether he had heard anything.

'It's important to keep an open mind and not jump to conclusions,' I told Maud. 'We only have the word of a journalist that the woman was murdered. The police haven't said anything about it.'

I might as well have saved my breath, because Maud assured me that Dana Flack wouldn't have written such a report without evidence to back it up.

'She's a journalist,' I replied. 'They're all desperate to find something sensational to write about, and Dana Flack would sell her soul for a scoop. Everyone knows you can't believe everything you read in the paper. They've got my name and my age wrong, for a start.'

Maud insisted that Dana's editor wouldn't have printed an unverified story. She was convinced the police would issue a statement soon. Feeling uneasy, I turned to leave.

'Are you going to pay for that paper?' Maud asked. 'Only I can't sell it now you've crumpled it.'

With a sigh, I paid for the paper and went to work where, busy attending to the demands of the day, I had little time to dwell on the murder story. Not knowing who the victim was, nor anything about her other than that she had been killed, made my discovery of her body seem somehow distant and unreal, and even unimportant. When I mentioned the matter to Hannah, she dismissed my interest in the murdered woman with a shrug. Hannah was right. The dead woman was nothing to do with me.

In fact, had Poppy not been the one to discover the body, reading Dana's report in the paper wouldn't have interested me personally. As it was, I reread every word carefully.

MURDER IN ASHTON MEAD

> Residents of Ashton Mead have been shocked to learn of a murder committed in their tranquil village. The body of a young woman was dragged from the river three weeks ago. At first believed to be an accidental drowning, the death is now being investigated as a suspected homicide. The victim is believed to have been brutally battered to death before her body was thrown in the river upstream of Mill Bridge, where it was discovered by 22-year-old resident Emily Wilton. Police are urging anyone who may know the identity of the victim to come forward.

The report was accompanied by a contact number for the police, and an e-fit sketch of the dead woman's face, reconstructed from her remains. I was one of the few people who knew what she had really looked like when she was pulled from the river with glassy eyes and barely any lips. The memory of it still made me feel queasy.

No one was happy with the confirmation that someone had been murdered in the village, and there was a sense of unease in the pub where people seemed to be muttering darkly in secretive cabals. It might have been groundless paranoia on my part but, as a relative newcomer to Ashton Mead, I seemed to be the target of several hostile glances. With the publication of one article in the local paper, the atmosphere in the village had changed. Hannah was guardedly pleased, as the news resulted in an influx of people from the surrounding area coming to gaze at the spot where the body had been found. Many of them stopped at the tea shop where we were busier than at the height of summer, although it was still only the end of May.

'It's an ill wind that blows no one any good,' she told me cheerily.

I resisted the impulse to reproach her for gloating over some poor woman's death, but she must have read my disapproval in my face, because she hurried to defend herself.

'It's not as if we killed her,' she protested. 'And if we can benefit from the situation, why shouldn't we? It doesn't do her any harm, does it? We can't help it if people are interested in seeing where the body was found. Go and preach to the ghouls who've come here to gawp at the river, and don't come virtue signalling to me. You were the one who found the body in the first place. If you'd left it where it was, it might have floated on down river and been picked up miles from here. So if anyone's to blame for this, it's you.'

Her reasoning was flawed, and I told her so. Before we could continue with our disagreement, a group of customers came in, and we were kept busy for the rest of the day. By the time we closed up, if our argument wasn't completely forgotten, at least we had both resolved not to fall out over it.

30

A WEEK OR SO passed, and the murder remained a topic of conversation in the village where most people seemed to consider Richard the obvious suspect, despite my assurances that Adam had seen his mother alive and well and living in London.

'Of course, he's going to say that, isn't he?' Maud retorted when I repeated what Adam had told me. 'He's covering up for his father.'

'Surely he wouldn't lie about his own mother's death,' I replied.

'Think about it,' Maud said. 'When Richard's wife left him, she abandoned her children too. Naturally they're going to stick up for their father, especially if it means lying to cover up such a vicious crime. Adam and his brother have already lost their mother. They don't want to lose their father too. It doesn't take a genius to work out that man's going to be locked up for a very long time once the truth comes out.'

'You can't go around making wild accusations like that without any evidence,' I protested, laughing at her outrageous claim, in spite of my indignation. 'You don't know that Richard had anything to do with it. You don't know anything about him.'

'It seems pretty obvious to me,' she replied with quiet conviction. 'Richard's wife left him for another man and a few weeks later her dead body washes up outside his house. I can draw my own conclusions about what happened to her.' She nodded grimly and refused to budge from her position.

On our way home one day, Poppy and I saw a stranger standing in Mill Lane, looking around. His hair was white and his hunched posture made him appear elderly, when seen from a distance. Drawing closer I saw that his face was unlined, and he looked as though he was in his late fifties or sixties. He seemed unaccountably nervous as we approached, but he smiled at Poppy who treated him with caution, quite unlike her usual boisterous behaviour with strangers. Since there were only two cottages in the lane, it seemed likely that he was lost. My impression was confirmed when he asked me the name of the road we were on. In return I enquired where he wanted to go and he told me he was looking for Richard Jones's house.

I pointed out The Laurels to him. 'It's right here. Are you a friend of his?'

'Not exactly.' He gave a wry half-smile. 'No, I wouldn't say we were friends. Actually, Richard's not really the person I want to see. I've come here to speak to Isobel.'

'Isobel?' I repeated, puzzled. 'I don't know anyone in the village called Isobel.'

'Isobel Jones, Richard's wife.'

'Oh, yes, of course.' I had forgotten the name of Richard's wife, if I had ever known it. 'Well, I'm afraid she's not here,' I went on. 'She left Richard before he moved here.'

'Did someone tell you to say that?' he asked.

It was a strange question and my surprise must have shown on my face, because he continued. 'Yes, she left him,' he agreed, 'but she went back to him.' He sighed.

'I've come here to find out if there's a chance she'll change her mind again. She was never happy in her marriage. But you don't want to stand here listening to me talking about such personal matters. I'll go and speak to her myself.'

'Wait. Who are you?' I asked.

'My name's Steve Collins.'

'What's your relationship with Isobel?'

It was his turn to look surprised, but he answered me readily enough, telling me that he was a friend of Isobel's. He just wanted to see she was all right. A horrible suspicion gripped me, making me reluctant to proceed, but I had to know the truth.

'Did she leave Richard for you? I mean, were you having an affair with her?' I asked.

Steve looked puzzled. 'Well, yes, as it happens I was. Why? Has Isobel talked about me? What did she say?' There was a note of urgency in his voice as he fired questions at me.

'One of her sons told me that Isobel's been living with you, in London.'

He sighed again. 'She was, but she left me nearly six weeks ago when she decided to return to her husband. I've come here to make one last appeal to her to change her mind and come back to me.'

I shook my head in confusion. Steve was telling me that Isobel had returned to Richard just after he moved to Ashton Mead but, as far as I knew, she had never arrived. If Isobel had drowned – whether accidentally or otherwise – that would explain her disappearance, but not why Adam had told me she was still living in London. If Isobel hadn't decided to run away altogether from her difficult situation, caught between two men, then either Steve was lying, or Adam had been covering up for his father. If that was the case, then presumably he had discovered that Richard had killed Isobel in a fight. And there was another possibility: Adam himself might have killed his mother. Whatever the truth of Isobel's alleged disappearance, I felt desperately sorry for Hannah. It was looking as though either the man she had fallen for might be a killer, or his father was. It was hard to take this in and I must have looked shocked, because Steve frowned. Quickly I assured him that his supposition was wrong; Isobel hadn't returned to her husband.

'What do you mean, she's not with Richard? Listen here, who are you?' he demanded, suddenly hostile.

In a shaky voice, I assured him I was a friend of the family. 'Can you just tell me one thing,' I added. 'Did Isobel wear a pendant?'

He scowled angrily. 'What business is that of yours? I thought you said you were her friend. Why don't you ask her?'

'Was it a green stone on a gold chain? Please, I need to know. This is important.'

'Very well then, yes. She did have a green pendant. Her father gave it to her before he died, which is why she always wore it. And now, I have to speak to her, to be sure. I have to hear it from her own lips that she has abandoned me after all we went through together.' His voice shook as he continued. 'I left my wife for her and now my children won't speak to me. I don't blame them. But it can't all have been for nothing. I turned my back on my family to be with her. I can't have done so for – this. For nothing.' He paused and inhaled deeply, before continuing in a calmer tone of voice. 'But how do you know about the pendant? What do you know about Isobel? Tell me where she is.'

'I think it's time you spoke to Richard,' I replied, suddenly nervous of this agitated stranger. 'This really has nothing to do with me.'

Without another word, I turned and hurried towards The Laurels. As we reached the gate, Richard opened his front door.

'I thought it was you,' he said, staring at Steve. 'What do you want? I have nothing to say to you.' He broke off, as though unable to continue. 'How – how is she?' he asked at last.

Steve shrugged. 'That's what I want to know. I need to know what she intends to do.'

Richard looked baffled.

'Where *is* Isobel?' I blurted out.

My question was greeted with silence.

'There was a woman –' I began and broke off. The two men turned to stare at me, as though remembering my presence for the first time. 'The woman who drowned in the river was wearing a green pendant.'

No one spoke for a moment and then Richard shook his head, murmuring that Isobel was a strong swimmer. He turned on Steve suddenly, his jovial features twisted in savage fury.

'This is your fault,' he hissed. 'Why couldn't you leave her alone?'

'I never laid a finger against her in anger, not like you,' Steve retorted, his expression grim.

'What the hell is this?' Richard asked. 'More lies, more lies.'

'I would never hurt her. I love her.'

'This is all your fault,' Richard repeated. 'If you hadn't enticed her away from me, none of this would have happened. We had a happy marriage, for years.'

'She was never happy with you,' Steve snarled.

Poppy had been whimpering and now she began to bark. I took the opportunity to leave the two men to their anger and grief, hoping that there wouldn't be a second murder in Mill Lane. I considered summoning the police, but all I could report was that two men were having an argument over a woman. Feeling thoroughly wretched, I went home, where even Poppy was unable to distract me from my dark thoughts.

That evening Richard came to find me in the pub. He seemed set on speaking to me and shoved a chair into the space beside me.

'It wasn't Isobel,' he said urgently. 'It can't have been. She was a strong swimmer and the current is slow at this time of year. That man –' he looked sour as he referred to Steve, 'he said she was coming back to me. Did you hear that?' He looked around the table where Hannah and Toby were sitting with me. 'She was coming back to me. I knew she'd come to her senses and come back to me. I knew it!'

'So where is she?' Toby asked.

Richard shook his head and ran his fingers through his wispy hair. 'She needs time to sort herself out,' he replied at last. 'She's probably feeling ashamed of her behaviour, leaving me on some crazy impulse. I know my wife. I know she struggles to control her emotions. But the important thing is that she left him. She saw through his shallow protestations, and she's coming back to me.'

There was something pathetic in his insistence that his wife was returning to him, even though I was convinced he had killed her when she had arrived in Ashton Mead. No one had known she was there, and they must have had a violent argument. It even made sense that Adam had lied about seeing his mother in order to keep his father safe. But the truth had been bound to come out in the end.

'If the woman who drowned wasn't Isobel, then who was she?' Hannah asked. 'I mean,' she went on with an apologetic glance at Richard, 'doesn't it strike you as a coincidence, the body turning up just when your wife vanished?'

None of us mentioned the pendant Poppy had found down by the river, which seemed to prove beyond doubt that the dead woman was Isobel. Her body had been callously disposed of, or perhaps thrown in the river by a killer who had panicked.

'Richard's very keen to convince us all that his wife's still alive,' Hannah said after he had gone.

'He could be trying to convince himself,' Toby suggested, 'deluding himself that he didn't kill her.'

I kept quiet about Adam's role in seeking to hide his father's guilt. The whole situation had become weird, and I resolved to have as little as possible to do with Richard or anyone in his family. And in the meantime, I decided to return to the police station and tell the detective what had transpired. Richard and his son had been at pains to convince everyone that Isobel was living with her boyfriend, but that had now been exposed as a lie. The dead woman was clearly Isobel Jones, and Adam had lied about having seen her alive.

31

WHEN I DISCUSSED WHAT was on my mind with my friend, Hannah accused me of jumping to conclusions. At first she insisted that Adam must have been mistaken in thinking he had seen his mother. The idea that Steve had come to Ashton Mead pretending to be looking for Isobel when he knew perfectly well where she was, made no sense. Admitting that it was unlikely Adam would have mistaken another woman for his own mother, Hannah suggested he might have seen her in London before she was killed, but that didn't fit with what Adam had told me. Seeing how upset she was, I didn't press her to explain why Adam had lied to me about his mother, but it was clear that he had.

In the meantime, we were busy with other matters. It was Toby's birthday and Hannah had decided to close the tea shop early, even though it was a Saturday, so that we could throw a party for him. Toby's mother, Naomi, had wanted to pay for everything. With typical generosity, Hannah had negotiated some sort of arrangement with her, since she knew Naomi wasn't well off. As Toby's friend, I offered to contribute as well, but Hannah laughed at me and said she must be paying me too much if I could afford to give her any money. In the end, we agreed that I would pay for the birthday cake, and I was secretly relieved that

Hannah hadn't accepted my original offer, which she must have known had been more generous than I could easily afford.

Naomi insisted no one told Toby about the plan in advance. I wasn't convinced that was a good idea, having experienced several surprise parties that had not gone according to plan. At one party that my mother hosted for my father, he had gone off to play cricket with a local amateur team, oblivious to the guests who had begun to arrive to celebrate with him. Eventually my mother had succeeded in tracking him down and had sent me to fetch him. I was to bring him home immediately without giving him any reason why his presence was urgently required, and without worrying him.

'What am I supposed to say to him?' I bleated. 'He won't leave his match unless he knows why you want him to come home.'

'On no account are you to let the cat out of the bag about the party,' my mother replied firmly, patting her immaculate coiffure. 'I've spent weeks planning and preparing this, and stocking our neighbours' freezers with food so he wouldn't suspect, not to mention spending a small fortune on the catering. Now off you go and fetch him, and be quick about it.'

Eventually I had managed to persuade my father to accompany me home, cravenly pleading ignorance of my mother's motive but insisting she needed him at home for a family emergency. In a way, that was true. Dressed in his cricketing gear, hot and sweaty from the match, my father had put a brave face on the sight of his friends and family gathered to greet him, and had scurried upstairs to shower and change while my mother plied her guests with food and drink. Afterwards, my father made her promise never to throw a surprise party for him again. His mood hadn't improved when he had learned that his team had lost their cricket match.

Still, Naomi was set on throwing a surprise party for Toby, and Hannah seemed equally keen on the idea.

'He deserves a party,' Naomi told me, smiling anxiously. 'The trouble is, if I suggest anything like this to him, he'll put his foot down and say he doesn't want a fuss. So we're going to spring it on him and that way he can't refuse.' She giggled like a teenager.

It occurred to me that it was really Hannah and Naomi who were eager to have a party. If they wanted to respect Toby's wishes, they would have abandoned the idea, but the party was going ahead, and there was nothing I could do to prevent it. Sworn to secrecy, I didn't dare breathe a word of warning to Toby. Only four of us knew of the plan: Hannah, her mother, Naomi and me. If Toby were to find out, I was bound to be the chief suspect, since I was the only one who had been reluctant to join in with the preparations. Hannah complained more than once that she would have preferred to go ahead without me, calling me a 'party pooper' and a 'killjoy'. Given her distress over Adam's betrayal, I refrained from arguing with her. Clearly the party preparations were helping to distract her from her own situation, and maybe this was just the diversion she needed to lift her out of her despondency. Adam was obviously not going to contact her again, and she needed to find a way to recover her spirits. For my part, I was secretly relieved that Adam had dumped her, because I no longer trusted him. But I wished he had let her down more gently.

When the day of the party arrived, there was nothing to do but swallow my reservations and go all out to help make sure everyone had a good time, especially Hannah and Naomi. Confined to a wheelchair, Naomi didn't enjoy as many opportunities to go out and socialise as she would have liked. As for Toby, he was just going to have to make the best of it. Hannah and I spent an hour rearranging the furniture in the café, which seemed surprisingly large once the tables had been shifted to one side. We pushed them right up against the wall, before covering them with colourful disposable tablecloths and setting out the food and drinks. Hannah had gone overboard with bunting and balloons, and I had to admit the café looked sensational. Given that Toby wasn't the kind of man to choose to celebrate his birthday with bunting and balloons, at least he would appreciate that the intention behind the party was kind.

'I hope he likes it,' Hannah murmured, gazing around to admire her handiwork.

'He's going to absolutely love it,' I lied, convinced that Toby would hate all the rigmarole.

We changed out of our work clothes and were only just ready when the guests began to arrive. Hannah had clearly put Adam out of her mind, and she looked lovely in a long yellow kaftan. Maud was first through the door, flaunting the costume jewellery she had worn at Christmas. Large earrings glowed on either side of her bony face, strings of glittering beads hung down over her chest, and her fingers sparkled with bright jewels. She was accompanied by Barry, who had rearranged his work schedule so that he could join us. Other guests had entered into the party spirit, and came dressed in their finery. Even Tess had made an effort. Above her jeans, instead of a T-shirt she was wearing a shiny silver shirt that glinted when she moved in the light. Several other families piled in, along with Cliff and Tess and more friends of Toby's. It seemed as though half the village was there. Even with everyone on their feet, there was hardly enough room for the guests to move around.

Naomi had agreed to bring Toby once she received the signal from Hannah that we were ready. He was expecting a quiet afternoon tea with his mother, and I felt a tremor of sympathy for him, knowing what awaited him instead. But the atmosphere in the room was electric and the excitement was contagious. Soon, along with everyone else, I was eagerly looking forward to Toby's arrival.

'Is everyone here? I'm going to phone Naomi,' Hannah called out. 'We need to settle down. In five minutes I'll close the shutters, and that'll be the signal to be really quiet. Naomi's going to pretend to be disappointed that we're closed, but she'll ask Toby to try the door, in case it's not locked, and as soon as he opens it, we'll all shout "Happy Birthday"!'

Miraculously, the plan worked. We seemed to be waiting for a long time in semi-darkness, with the shutters closed, before the door opened. Toby stepped in, surprised to find the door unlocked, Hannah and I flung the shutters open, and as daylight streamed in everyone began shouting. Once he recovered from his astonishment, Toby took the party in good spirits.

'Hannah and my mum are enjoying themselves, anyway,' he muttered to me, as we raised a glass of punch together. 'It's great to see my mum looking so radiant. It's worth all this palaver to see her so happy.'

Although it was typical of Toby to think of others first, I was convinced he was enjoying himself far more than he admitted. The party was in full swing. Even though it was teatime, more rum punch was being drunk than tea, along with Hannah's mouth-watering pastries and cakes. The moment came for the birthday cake to be cut. Everyone stood back to allow Toby room to walk to the table where the cake had been laid out, in all its glory. Hannah had excelled herself, creating a model of the village in icing, complete with a tiny yellow Sunshine Tea Shoppe and a miniature model of The Plough. She stepped forward and lit half a dozen candles which Toby snuffed out by frantically waving his hands above them, since the old custom of blowing on the cake had fizzled out, thanks to the pandemic.

'So I'm officially six,' Toby announced, laughing. 'The number of candles on the cake doesn't lie.'

'We decided we couldn't ask you to blow out such a large number of candles just by waving your hand,' Hannah said.

'You look good for six,' someone called out.

'He's a bit immature for six,' another voice added, and everyone laughed.

In all the commotion, no one noticed the door of the café open.

'We're closed,' Hannah called out, looking round and seeing a stranger standing on the threshold. 'We're open as usual tomorrow. This is a private party,' she added, as the woman in the doorway didn't withdraw.

But I had recognised the stranger with cropped black hair and penetrating gaze. There was a shuffling of feet and a hiss of whispering voices and then silence, as the inspector held up her identity card and announced herself.

Her quiet voice carried across the room. 'I'm afraid this can't wait until tomorrow. I'm looking for Adam Jones. Do any of you know where I can find him?'

There was a faint clatter as Hannah dropped her knife. I darted forward to scoop Poppy up in my arms before she could reach the sugary blade. Other than my little dog whimpering faintly in protest, no one made a sound.

32

THE ENSUING SILENCE WAS broken by the sound of shuffling, and Richard stepped forward. Introducing himself to the inspector, he explained that he was Adam's father. The inspector thanked him and told him they needed to talk about his son, who was apparently missing.

'Perhaps you could step outside and talk to me?' she suggested. 'There seems to be a party going on here, which I'd hate to interrupt.' She glanced around, unsmiling.

No one dared point out that it was too late for her to worry about disturbing our celebrations.

'I'm sorry, I don't know where Adam's staying at the moment, if that's what you want to know,' Richard replied, making no move to leave the café. 'He tends to move around, with his work. I can give you his phone number, if that's any use. I'm sure he'll be more than happy to co-operate with you. Is there something I can help you with?'

The detective lowered her voice, but I was standing close enough to hear every word. 'Your son reported his mother missing, and we'd like to speak to him.'

Manoeuvring myself to a position behind Richard, I wondered if that was the real reason why the police were looking for Adam. I hoped I hadn't set Hannah up with a killer. Pretending to be attending to Poppy, I listened to my neighbour recite the phone number he had given me. The police were unlikely to speak to Adam on that number, but I didn't say anything. It was possible the number was correct, after all, and it had just been temporarily unavailable when I had tried to call him. With so many confusing stories, it was impossible to know who was telling the truth.

The detective left soon after she had spoken to Richard, but the festive mood had evaporated. A few small groups of people were already gathering to whisper furtively about what had just happened. Richard was red-faced and clearly feeling awkward, fidgeting with his glass and staring at the floor. He took his leave quite soon after the detective departed, as did several other people. The party was effectively over. I thought it was a pity, after all Hannah's efforts, but she seemed to think the party had been a success. She was giggling over the dregs of the rum punch she had made, and waving her nearly empty glass in the air.

'To Toby!' she called out and grinned at the answering cheer from the partygoers who had not yet left. 'Happy Birthday!'

Watching her frenetic attempt to revive the party atmosphere, I decided there and then to return to London at the first opportunity, and find out for myself where Adam had gone. There was little point in trying to discuss my idea with Hannah, who was by now very tipsy. She announced that we would leave all the clearing up until the next day, and go to The Plough where it seemed the party was going to continue. Somehow, the celebrations at the café felt tainted. Besides, as Hannah pointed out cheerfully, we had run out of punch and she, for one, needed another drink.

'You've already had too much,' I remonstrated. 'Seriously, Hannah, you're going to regret it in the morning.'

'Oh, sherious, less all be sherious,' she tittered.

'Well, don't say I didn't warn you.' I sighed. 'You're going to have the worst hangover of your life.'

Waving me away with a laugh, she shooed everyone out of the café and we all set off for the pub. I hung back from the rest of the guests; I had other plans for the evening. Before setting out, I called my mother who assured me she would be delighted to put me up for the night if I missed the last train back to Swindon. So without saying a word to anyone in Ashton Mead, I set off. Poppy trotted happily ahead of me, pulling on her lead as she always did. I had given up trying to train her to walk to heel. For all that she knew her own mind when out for a walk, she was well-behaved on the bus, and we were soon at Swindon station, buying a ticket to London. We didn't have to wait long for a train and, once again, Poppy sat quietly watching the world fly past our window without making any fuss at all. After the noise and excitement of Toby's party, I think we were both pleased to have a quiet train journey, and we were soon dozing comfortably in the warm carriage.

On our way back to the address Adam's father had given me, Poppy was eager to run into the park again, but this time I guided her firmly along the pavement. I wanted to find out where Adam was living before it grew dark. As soon as I had discovered his whereabouts, I intended to return to Ashton Mead, where I would discuss the situation with Hannah the following day, once she was sober again. Even though I probably wouldn't see Adam that evening, at least I intended to establish where he was, so I could return to the village and pass that information on to Hannah. At the very least, she deserved an explanation from him. Not only was she my best friend, but I couldn't help feeling responsible for having brought them together.

The door was opened by same blonde girl who had been at the property on my previous visit. Once again she summoned Roy, and once again he scowled on seeing me.

'Oh for Christ's sake, what now?' he demanded, his arms folded defensively across his chest. 'What is it with everyone today? I told you last time, Adam's not here. And no, I haven't seen him since the last time you came here asking for him. Now get lost and stop being a pain in the neck, will you?'

He was about to close the door, when I stopped him. 'Please,' I begged, almost in tears, 'I've come a long way to find him. It's important. It's really important. Have you got any idea where he might be?'

'You could try his mother's,' Roy said, relenting and opening the door a little wider. 'Last time we spoke, he said he was going to see her. That was a while ago, so he probably won't be there now, but maybe she can tell you where he is.'

'His mother's?' I echoed. 'In Ashton Mead?'

He looked puzzled. 'No, Chiswick Park. His mother lives in Chiswick.'

'Chiswick? I don't suppose you have his mother's address?'

It was a long shot. I didn't expect he would be able to help me but Roy turned and went back inside, calling out to his flatmate. 'Liz, where was it Adam said his mother lives?'

The reply came back, 'Chiswick Park.'

'Yes, but where in Chiswick Park?' I asked miserably.

It seemed I had reached another dead end but as I stepped back, ready to leave, the girl reappeared. This time she was clutching an envelope.

'Here you are,' she said, flapping it at me and grimacing. 'Adam was going to write to her but then he decided to go there instead, and he left this envelope behind. Why don't you go there, seeing as you're so interested in Adam and his mother? And while you're there, can you tell her to tell him –' her voice rose to a sudden screech, 'to tell the police he doesn't live here, and we don't appreciate having them round here asking for him every five minutes. We've got our own shit going on.' She shoved the letter at me and, as I took it, Roy slammed the door.

The envelope appeared to have been left in a pile of rubbish because it was damp in one corner and smelled mouldy. Having taken a photo of the address on my phone, I dropped the foul smelling envelope in a bin we passed on our way back to the station. Poppy let out a help of protest and jumped up to try and retrieve it. Clearly the stench of rotting paper had sparked her interest. According to the app on my phone, the journey from Archway to Chiswick Park would take just over an hour by tube. The reality might be closer to an hour and a half.

Since the address I'd been given was just around the corner from Chiswick Park station, I decided to go there straight away before spending the night at my mother's house as there wouldn't be time to return to Ashton Mead. Even if I made it back to Swindon, I would miss the last bus home and was reluctant to fork out for a taxi back to the village. Chiswick was close to my mother's house in Ealing, so it made sense for me to go there on the way.

Poppy had been well-behaved on the train so far, but now she grew restless and I realised she must be hungry. It was nearly her supper time and we had walked quite a long way. So I stopped off at a small convenience store and managed to find something for her and for myself because, despite having stuffed myself with cake earlier on, I was feeling peckish. Reinvigorated, we set off for Chiswick Park, and Poppy obligingly fell asleep on the tube, worn out from our day's exertions. But my adventure was not over yet. As we hurtled through tunnels, I considered exactly what I was going to say to Adam, when I finally found him.

33

IT WAS GROWING DARK by the time we arrived at the address I had copied from the stinking envelope. From the opposite side of the street I examined our destination, an elegant detached house in a pleasant suburb, where the properties had small, neat front gardens, and the pavement was interrupted at intervals by established trees. As I was studying the house, the curtains at an upstairs window were drawn. Although the figure at the window was only visible for a few seconds, I was fairly sure I saw a woman with shoulder-length hair.

One worrying explanation for Isobel's disappearance was that Richard had murdered her in a jealous rage, and Adam had agreed to protect his father by pretending his mother was still alive. The fact that the police were now looking for Adam seemed to confirm that suspicion. Still undecided what to say, and with unsettling theories floating around my mind, I hesitated before ringing the bell. Knowing I was meddling in matters that were no concern of mine, I was tempted to walk away and go to my parents' house. There was a chance that investigating Isobel's death might prove dangerous. But I owed it to my friend to find Adam, and clear up the question of his complicity in his mother's murder. The woman in the window could have been anyone. But seeing a woman who might be Richard's estranged wife gave me confidence to cross the road and approach the front door. If I could find Richard's wife alive, my fears would be allayed.

Poppy stood quietly beside me as the door opened. Somehow I wasn't surprised to see Steve, the man who had come to Ashton Mead looking for Isobel. At least I now knew I had come to the right address. Steve studied me with the kind of confused and slightly embarrassed look of someone who recognises you but can't remember who you are. When he frowned, his unlined forehead creased, and his words confirmed what his expression had already conveyed.

'I'm sorry,' he said. 'Have we met?'

'Yes, we met in Mill Lane in Ashton Mead,' I told him. 'You were looking for Richard's wife, Isobel.'

He nodded warily, which was understandable. He must have been puzzled to see me on his doorstep.

'What brings you to Chiswick Park?' he asked. I couldn't help noticing that he sounded edgy.

Poppy let out a low whimper and nuzzled my leg with her nose, as though urging me to be on my guard.

I hesitated before replying. 'I – I was passing through the area and thought – I thought I'd call on you, just on the off chance. The thing is –' Once again I hesitated, afraid of charging into a tricky situation.

'Yes?' he prompted me. 'What are you doing here?'

'My mother lives in Ealing,' I stammered by way of explanation, aware that I had no justification for turning up on his doorstep looking for Isobel, who I was fairly certain had been murdered. 'I was in the area.'

'What do you want with me?'

I took a deep breath. 'Adam wants to speak to his mother, and I thought, seeing as I'm here, I might as well call and ask if she's here, so I can tell him. I'm sure she'll change her mind about seeing him when she hears how desperate he is to talk to her. I mean, he is her son.'

Steve shook his head. 'I'm afraid she's not come back here,' he said, with a tense frown. 'I thought you knew that. The last time I saw her, she told me she was returning to her husband. There's no one here but me.'

'But –' I began and stopped, embarrassed to accuse him of lying, even though I had observed a woman at an upstairs window only a few minutes earlier.

He must have seen the doubt in my eyes because he added quickly, 'Apart from my wife, that is.'

'Your wife?' I repeated. 'Is she here as well?'

'Of course. Where else would she be? She lives here. She's my wife.'

The truth was suddenly obvious. Steve and his wife had reconciled, if they had ever really fallen out, and she was the woman Adam had spotted, going home with Steve. It was hard to believe Adam had failed to recognise his own mother, but it seemed that Isobel and Steve's wife were similar in appearance. Adam hadn't lied about seeing his mother in London, after all, even though she hadn't actually been there when he thought he had seen her. The woman he had seen wasn't his mother because, by the time he thought he saw her, Isobel had already been murdered and her body had been discovered in Ashton Mead. I could only apologise for my mistake and explain that Adam had led me to believe his mother was still living there.

'Still?' Steve repeated. 'I'm afraid you've got your wires crossed. It's only ever been me and my wife Jill living here. Isobel did – she did visit me here once or twice – but only briefly. It was just a couple of times and we both agreed it was a mistake. Isobel wanted to return to her husband straight away, and she left in a hurry before my wife came home from work. No one else knew about our brief fling, unless Isobel confessed to her husband. I did my best to dissuade her from telling him.' He shrugged. 'It could serve no purpose and would only upset him. It was over between us. There was no need to go raking it all up, hurting people. But I can't see that this is any of your business.'

'What about your wife? What did you tell her about your affair?' I asked, curious to hear how he had handled his infidelity.

'My wife knows nothing about it.'

'I don't understand. You said it was all over between you and Isobel, so why did you go to see Richard?'

Steve explained that he had wanted to speak to Isobel again, just to clear the air and apologise to her and Richard for everything that happened.

'It wasn't entirely my fault,' he added. 'That is, it takes two. But I wasn't proud of the way I'd behaved. I tried to contact her but she must have changed her phone number so I decided to visit her and Richard in Ashton Mead, where she and Richard had gone to make a fresh start. Only, as you know, she wasn't there. Richard wasn't exactly pleased to see me.' He scowled. 'But I fail to see what your interest in all this can be,' he added coldly.

It was too complicated to try and explain that I felt guilty for introducing my friend to Adam, who had broken her heart. Now I wanted to find out the truth about Adam, and discover whether he or Richard had killed Isobel, or if they were both innocent.

'Richard is my friend, and so is Adam,' I replied weakly.

It wasn't strictly true that they were my friends, but we had met, and Richard was my closest neighbour.

'Well, you can go home and tell them as far as Isobel and I are concerned, it's over. Water under the bridge.'

His mention of water reminded me that we had been travelling for hours, and Poppy had been panting on the walk from Chiswick Park station. We still had a tube journey ahead of us to my parent's house in Ealing, so I asked Steve if he would be kind enough to give my puppy some water before we set off. Seeming relieved to hear that I was leaving, he invited us in and led us to a large bright kitchen at the back of the house where he put down a bowl of water for Poppy, who lapped it eagerly. Refusing the offer of a drink myself, I made my way back to the hall, with Poppy at my heels. Steve was just reaching out to open the front door, when a figure came into view on the stairs: a slim woman in a close-fitting green dress. She looked directly at me and my breath caught in my throat. The woman was striking, with regular features and beautiful huge black eyes. Either Steve's wife looked uncannily like Isobel Jones, or I was staring at the woman in Richard's family photographs, the woman who had been dragged lifeless from the river a few weeks earlier.

34

As I stood, momentarily transfixed at the sight of the woman on the stairs, Steve stepped forward, slammed the front door and stood with his back to it, facing me. If I wanted to leave, it seemed I was going to have to barge him out of the way first. Even though he wasn't particularly tall or bulky, as a man he was bound to be stronger than me. He watched me closely, ready to react if I moved, while I struggled to conceal my shock.

'Who's she?' the woman demanded, glaring at me from her position halfway down the stairs. 'What's she doing here?'

It was a reasonable enough question, given that I was a stranger in the house, but there was something savage in the curl of her lips that made me tremble.

'My name is Emily,' I replied, forcing a smile. 'I was just leaving – my dog needed some water but now we're off –'

'I asked you a question. Who is she?' the woman hissed, without taking her eyes from me.

Steve answered. 'This is Emily. Adam sent her here. Adam Jones,' he added, emphasising the name.

'He didn't exactly send me here,' I gabbled nervously. 'I was in the area and Adam told me he wants to speak to his mother. But I see he was mistaken in thinking she lives here. I only dropped by because I was passing. My mother lives near here and I'm on my way to visit her. She lives in Ealing so this wasn't far out of my way –'

'Emily is a friend of Richard Jones,' Steve spoke over me.

'Not exactly a friend,' I said, 'I wouldn't say we were friends, exactly. And now I really need to get going or I'll be late. My mother's expecting me.'

As though agreeing with me, Poppy bounded to the front door, pulling at her lead and whimpering.

'She's a friend of Richard and of Adam,' the woman said, glaring at me. 'And now she's here.' She turned away from me and spoke furiously to Steve. 'What the hell is she doing here, snooping on us? What have you told her?'

Startled by her ferocity, I hesitated to respond. Poppy evidently shared my anxiety because she began scratching at the door, eager to be let out.

'Well, we really do need to leave now,' I called out, as breezily as I could. 'I can see I've made a silly mistake. I'm sorry to have bothered you. You've been very kind, but I really can't stay any longer. My mother will be wondering where I am. In fact, I ought to call her. If I don't turn up soon she'll be phoning the police. You know what mothers are like.' I forced a laugh.

At my mention of the police, the change in the atmosphere was almost palpable. I realised the remark had been ill-considered, but I couldn't retract my words. The woman didn't actually gasp, but her figure became rigid, and her fists clenched at her sides. Unnerved by her reaction, I pulled my mobile out of my bag intending to summon help but, before I could hit the emergency key, Steve lunged forward and slapped my arm. Startled, I dropped my phone. The woman leapt down the stairs to retrieve it. After stamping on it with her heel and smashing the screen, she snatched it up and scrabbled to remove the battery and the sim card.

Thoroughly alarmed, I made a grab at Poppy's lead which slipped through my fingers as I dashed for the front door. Just as I was pulling it open, Steve ran forward, shoved me sideways, and slammed the door shut. The back of my head hit the wall with a painful thud, and I shivered, dazed and nauseous.

'You're not going anywhere,' the woman said curtly. She turned to Steve. 'We need to keep her here while we decide what to do with her.'

'What can we do?' he asked, sounding helpless.

He didn't relax his hold on me and I was too shaken to remonstrate.

'We can't take any chances,' the woman snapped, dropping my broken phone and kicking it aside as she came over to join us. 'Not now we've come this far. We can't let this meddling bitch ruin our plans.'

Close up, she exuded a coruscating aura, and spoke with a violent intensity, even though her voice was subdued. Despite my fear, I could see there was an allure about her that was magnetic, and could imagine her being irresistibly persuasive when she set her mind to something. As she scrutinised me, a bead of sweat trickled down her forehead, although it wasn't warm in the house, and her skin had a strange tinge that looked almost grey in the dim light of the hall. She was clearly insane, but the truth that was staring me in the face was still too monstrous to believe.

'She needs to be watched,' she hissed through her teeth.

'What the hell's going on?' I squeaked. 'I haven't done anything to you. You can't keep me here. This is outrageous. You have to let me go.'

'You've brought this trouble on yourself, blundering in here like this,' the woman snapped. 'No one asked you to pry into our affairs.'

The back of my head was throbbing from where it had hit the wall. Feeling confused and utterly terrified, my only thought was that I had to get out of that house. Steve moved closer to his companion and whispered urgently to her, seeming to plead with her. While they were engrossed in their discussion, I edged towards the door but, just as I was reaching for the handle, the woman let out a warning screech. Steve spun round and caught hold of my wrist, preventing me from opening the door. I wriggled desperately, but he seized my other arm and shoved me back against the wall.

'Let me go at once!' I cried out. 'Let go of me this instant or I'll scream.'

'Don't be ridiculous,' the woman said. 'No one's going to hear you. Now just shut up, both of you, and let me think.'

Steve clung to my arms and kept me pinned against the wall, barely flinching when I kicked his shins. The woman didn't take long to make up her mind. Calmly she instructed Steve to secure my hands behind my back and carry me up to the loft. When I protested, she told him to gag me. Somehow her composure was more terrifying than her earlier hysteria. At least when she had been manic I had hoped she would be rational once she calmed down.

'I don't know why you're doing this,' I burst out. 'I don't know what's going on. I don't know anything about you, so I'm no threat to you at all. I don't even know who you are. I only came here to give Adam's mother a message, but she's obviously not here, so I'll just go away. Please,' I added, trying to sound unruffled even though my voice was quaking with fear, 'just let me go. I'll leave your house and you'll never hear from me again. You have my word on that. I won't say a word to anyone about this. It was a stupid mistake my coming here at all.'

'Yes,' the woman agreed coolly. 'It was a very stupid mistake. Who else knows about this?'

'We need to get out of here tonight,' Steve blurted out. 'It's not safe to stay any longer.'

The woman shook her head. 'Panicking won't help us. All you have to do is remain calm and stick to the plan.'

'I'm perfectly calm. You're the one who's not thinking clearly.'

'She came here alone and I don't suppose anyone else knows anything about it,' she said.

'You don't know that, Isobel. It's too much of a gamble.'

My suspicion was finally confirmed on hearing his companion was called Isobel. The woman who had taken me captive alongside Steve was Richard's wife. Isobel was alive, but the identity of the woman who had been pulled from the river remained a mystery. It was puzzling that the police had reached the wrong conclusion about her identity. With Isobel alive, I realised her pendant had been deliberately left near the river after the discovery of the body. That would explain how the police had missed it when they searched the area. Now I had worked out what must have happened, it seemed obvious, but the police didn't know they had been hoodwinked. Meanwhile, I had no way of alerting them to the identity of the real killers, who had trapped me with them in their house.

35

ISOBEL FETCHED A LONG cerise scarf which she wound round my wrists behind my back. I pleaded with Steve to let me go, but he held onto me, crushing my hands painfully against the wall while I looked around in desperation for a means of escape. Only then did I realise that Poppy had vanished; she must have slipped out through the front door before Steve had slammed it shut. I hoped she would have a better chance of survival on her own, than in the house with my captors. Poppy's absence made me more determined than ever to escape and find her before she could come to harm, but my options were now severely limited. All I could do was endeavour to control my terror, while I watched and waited for an opportunity to escape.

'So we've got her hands tied,' Steve said, watching Isobel with something approaching alarm. 'What now? What the hell are we going to do with her?'

'What's going on?' I asked. 'I don't understand.'

Steve heaved a sigh that shook his shoulders as he explained that they had encountered a little difficulty with his wife.

'What do you mean? What kind of difficulty?' I asked, my fear intensifying as I understood who had been dragged from the river.

'She attacked me,' Isobel snarled, her eyes glowing darkly. 'She screamed at me to leave him alone. As though her husband belonged to her!' she scoffed. 'She treated him like some kind of possession. What was I supposed to do when she went for me? I had to shut her up.'

'My wife hit her head in the altercation,' Steve said heavily.

I turned to Isobel, too horrified to watch my words. 'You killed her,' I whispered. 'You killed Steve's wife.'

'It was self-defence,' she retorted. 'What else was I supposed to do?'

In a flash, I understood exactly what had happened. Isobel had killed Steve's wife, perhaps in self-defence, but more likely in a fit of jealous rage. I had suspected Richard of attacking Isobel in anger, when all along it was Isobel herself who had killed her lover's wife. The two women looked similar, so they had dressed the body in Isobel's clothes to make everyone believe the dead woman was Isobel herself. They had dropped the body in the river near the bridge in Ashton Mead, not far from Richard's new home, to make it look as though he had killed her. It had probably been an afterthought to leave the pendant there, once the police had taken the body, to convince the police that the dead woman was Isobel. They planned that Richard would be blamed for killing his wife because she had left him. After that, the killers had only to pretend that Isobel was Steve's wife, and no one would ever discover the truth.

Steve looked troubled. 'I had no choice,' he said. 'I had to protect her. With the police convinced they had found Isobel's body, we knew no one would come looking for her and she would be safe. And that should have been the end of it.'

'It was, until you came along to spy on us,' Isobel added.

'Who sent you here?' Steve demanded.

'Never mind that,' Isobel said. 'By the time they come looking for her, we'll be gone.'

'But you can't just leave everyone thinking Richard killed his wife,' I cried out, struggling to believe their callous scheme. 'What has he ever done to deserve that? Isobel's still alive. It's your wife who died.'

Steve shrugged. 'What else could I do?' he asked. 'There was no other way to save her.'

Isobel laughed and the deranged look returned to her eyes. 'There's no need to fret over Richard. He wouldn't want me to go to prison,' she said. 'Maybe he didn't deserve what's happened to him, but now I've left him, he really won't care what happens to him.'

'He still has a life,' I protested.

'We had no choice,' Steve insisted.

Isobel smiled at Steve, and he gazed back at her with adoration in his face.

'You saved my life,' she said softly, reaching out to place her palm on his cheek.

'This is madness,' I cried out. 'You'll never get away with it.'

'But we have,' Isobel replied with a sly smile that made me cringe. 'We absolutely have.'

'Don't worry about Richard,' Steve reassured me. 'The police won't find any proof that he killed his wife, so no jury will be able to condemn him, even if they want to. They'll say that Isobel's death was an accident, and she hit her head when she fell in the water.'

'But the dead woman isn't Isobel, she's your wife, and *you* killed her,' I said, turning to Isobel. 'How can you let Richard be tried for killing you, when you're not even dead?'

'No one else knows that I'm still alive. They all think it was my body that was dragged from the river. Our plan worked beautifully.' She smiled. 'Anyway, Steve's told you, everyone will say it was an accident and Richard will be let off. So stop fussing, will you? We've already told you, there's no problem... apart from what to do with you.'

Something about the story didn't make sense. 'I don't understand,' I said to Steve. 'Why did you come to Ashton Mead to look for Isobel, when you knew she was here all along?'

'Do you have to be so stupid?' Isobel snapped. 'He had to behave as though I was missing.'

'I told my neighbours around here that my wife had returned to me,' Steve added. 'But I had to make it look as though I wanted to find Isobel, so no one would suspect I knew where she was. And now,' he said, turning to Isobel, 'what are we going to do with her?'

Isobel shrugged. 'Enough talking. It's making me tired.'

'But what are we going to do with her?' Steve repeated.

'Collateral damage. She knows too much. We'll have to dispose of her before we leave the country.'

'I won't tell anyone,' I lied, my curiosity giving way to terror once more.

'As soon as the new passports arrive we leave here, my love,' Isobel said as softly as if she was making normal holiday plans. 'Don't worry. We'll take her with us in the boot of the car and dispose of her at a quiet spot on the river, just like we did last time. What does she matter to us, as long as we have each other?' She turned to me and hissed ferociously. 'You brought this on yourself, you stupid fool, and now we've got another problem to clear up. You came here snooping on us, so we don't have a choice.'

'There is always a choice,' I replied sadly. 'You don't have to do this.'

Isobel returned my gaze with stony eyes. I turned to

Steve, intending to appeal to him, but Isobel had already moved to his side and was kissing him.

'Not long now, my love,' she whispered, pressing her body against his. 'Be strong for me.'

As he responded to her embrace, I wrenched myself free and sprinted towards the front door. With my hands tied behind my back, it was going to be almost impossible to open it, but Steve reached out and caught hold of my arm before I could try. He spun round and quickly had me trapped against the wall once more. Without the use of my hands, it was impossible to wriggle out of his grasp again, but I screamed and shouted for help as loudly as I could.

'Shut her up, for Christ's sake,' Isobel said.

For a second, I thought they were going to kill me on the spot, and tensed to head butt Steve if he came any closer. It probably would have hurt me more than it hurt him, but I couldn't think of anything else to do. Isobel handed him another scarf and instructed him to gag me. The silky fabric felt soft against my cheeks, but once it had become damp with my saliva it soon became uncomfortable. Fury compounded my fear and I kicked Steve viciously on the shins. It must have hurt him, but the only consequence for me was that Isobel crouched down and tied my ankles together. Like a hobbled horse, I could stand but was no longer able to kick. Refusing to break down and cry, I stared at Isobel, hoping to unsettle her with my resolute frown, but she gazed at me with perfect composure.

'That's better,' she said, smiling. 'She was beginning to give me a headache with her din.'

36

With my arms and legs secured, Steve pushed me to the floor, grabbed me under my arms, and hauled me upstairs on my back, grumbling all the while about my weight. That was hardly fair. I hadn't asked him to drag me up the stairs and besides, I wasn't exactly well-built. Thankfully the stairs were carpeted but even so my hands scraped painfully against them with every step he took. Finally we reached the landing, where I lay gazing around helplessly while Isobel fetched an aluminium ladder and opened it into an inverted V shape. Steve positioned this carefully beneath a trapdoor in the ceiling, before dragging me towards it. I tried to protest, but from behind my gag it was impossible to make myself understood. It seemed unimaginable that he would be able to hoist me up the ladder single-handed, but he must have been stronger than he looked. By holding me under one arm, he managed to struggle upwards while I kept really still, hardly daring to breathe, scared that any movement on my part might cause the ladder to topple over, sending us both crashing to the floor. If that happened, I wouldn't even be able to put my hands out for protection

'Listen,' Steve panted, as he clambered upwards, step by painful step, 'I don't like this any more than you do, but if you go poking your nose in where it's not wanted, you have only yourself to blame if you end up in trouble. You should have kept out of affairs that aren't your concern.'

Desperate to assure him that I had learnt my lesson and would mind my own business from now on, all I could manage was a series of muffled groans which he ignored. He nearly dropped me when he reached the top of the ladder and had to manoeuvre me through the hatch, grunting with the effort of shoving me above his shoulders and into the loft.

'This is breaking my back,' he groaned.

'Well, I'm having a ball,' I thought, but of course I couldn't say anything clearly enough to be understood.

It occurred to me that he wouldn't be so careful to avoid hitting my head against the edge of the hatch if they were really planning to kill me, and that gave me courage. Once he had pushed me into the loft, he vanished through the hatch. Before I could react, the trapdoor slammed shut and I heard the bolt sliding across, followed by a series of thuds and a faint clattering as he descended the ladder and moved it away. I had been abandoned, locked in a loft, with my wrists and ankles tied, and my mouth gagged. For a moment I lay perfectly still, trying to gather my thoughts and work out what to do. My first task was to release myself from my restraints. My hands were my priority. Once they were free, it would be relatively easy to untie my ankles and remove my gag. I did my best to stretch the fabric, to allow me some room to wriggle my hands, but the ties cut into my flesh until the pain forced me to stop.

There was a small window in the roof over my head, through which a solitary star in the night sky shone down on me. Focusing on that distant point of light, I resumed working resolutely at my bonds, gritting my teeth against the pain. Hard though it was to believe that Steve and Isobel were really plotting my death, I had to accept that she had already murdered Steve's wife, allegedly in self-defence. No doubt she would justify my murder to herself along similar lines, convincing Steve that it was all my fault, for forcing them to choose between my life and their safety. Thinking about Isobel's warped morals, I was more determined than ever to free myself. But to attempt an escape, I needed the use of my hands, and Isobel had wound her scarf around my wrists so many times, it was impossible to free myself. Eventually, exhausted by my frustrating efforts, I drifted into a tearful sleep.

When I awoke, bruised and dazed, daylight was flooding into the loft through the skylight. Watching a white cloud floating past the window, I was shaken by a desperate longing to be outside, breathing in fresh air and feeling the breeze on my face. Instead, I was trapped in a loft. My head was sore from where Steve had shoved me against the wall, my wrists were smarting from the scarf restraining them, my shoulders ached from my hands being tied behind my back overnight, and my gag was chafing the corners of my mouth. The floorboards on which I was lying were hard, and the attic smelt musty and fetid. I was afraid there were rats or mice living up there. Certainly there were spiders because in the daylight I could see thick cobwebs hanging from the rafters in the roof.

I resolved to try and chew through my gag and shout for help. Possibly someone would hear me through the skylight. But after a while my jaw began to ache, and I had to stop. There was nothing to do but wait for an opportunity to escape, or hope to enlist help when Steve and Isobel moved me from the loft – if I was still alive by then. I thumped on the floor with my heels for a while, in the desperate hope that someone else might be in the house and hear me, but the effort soon tired me out.

In spite of my severe discomfort, I dozed off into a kind of stupor which was disturbed by muffled sounds. I dreamt that my alarm was going off. Returning to consciousness, I realised it was the insistent ringing of a doorbell, far away, accompanied by a distant knocking. This was followed by frantic barking, which startled me completely out of my torpor. Poppy was in the house, looking for me. Groaning as loudly as I could, I banged my feet on the floor and attempted to drum on it with my fists behind my back. My efforts were futile. The voices continued their distant murmuring for a while and then I heard a door slam and the barking ceased, as abruptly as a radio being switched off. Terrified that Steve and Isobel had silenced Poppy, I sobbed behind my gag. It was hard to believe that anyone would harm an innocent puppy, but there was no knowing what someone as crazy as Isobel might do, or the lengths Steve might go to in order to protect her. Clearly besotted with her, he seemed prepared go along with whatever insane plan she devised. Like Shakespeare's Scottish king, the pair of them had gone too far to stop at one murder. First Steve's wife, then Poppy, had been victims of their madness, and I would be next.

Apart from fearing for my life, I bitterly regretted having brought Poppy with me to London, on my misguided quest to find Adam. She should have stayed behind in Ashton Mead, with Jane and Holly. She would have missed me for a while, after my unexplained disappearance, but then she would have settled down with my friends to live out the rest of her life in tranquillity. And now she was dead. One way or another, I determined that her death would be avenged. Struggling against growing despair, I vowed there would be an opportunity for retribution once Steve carried me down from the loft. Somehow I was going to make sure he and his lunatic companion didn't escape justice. Half-delirious with thirst and grief, I envisaged breaking free of my bonds and bursting from the loft to hurl Steve off the ladder. If he landed on Isobel, so much the better. They both deserved to suffer for what they had done to Poppy. But I knew that I was raving. In order to carry out my wild plan, I would have to free my hands and feet, and that had already proved impossible.

For a while I gave in to the lure of my fantasy about shoving Steve off the ladder so forcefully that he barged into Isobel, sending them both crashing down the stairs. I knew it was a waste of time, and all my energy should be focused on my escape, but my desire for revenge was like an itch that had to be scratched. Worn out by my ordeal, I might have slept, were it not for the agonising physical pain searing into my wrists, and the torment of wondering what had happened to Poppy. As the daylight faded outside, I began to suspect my captors were planning to leave me in the loft to starve to death. The prospect was a bitter one, allowing me no chance to resist their scheming and punish them for their cruelty. Miserably I continued sporadically chewing at my gag, and wriggling my hands in an attempt to loosen the scarf that bound them.

Alternating between rage and despair, I was startled by the sudden sound of barking and voices somewhere in the house below me. Rousing myself from my exhaustion, I started banging my feet feebly on the floor once again. Without warning, the trapdoor was flung open and a face appeared. I saw enough through the gloom to realise it wasn't Steve or Isobel, before a dazzling light shone in my eyes. Temporarily blinded, after so long in darkness, I could only moan. Then, through the open hatch, I clearly heard Poppy barking. Behind my vile gag, I smiled.

37

EVERYTHING AFTER THAT WAS a blur for a while, as I was carried down from the loft and laid on a stretcher, while Poppy leapt on top of me and licked my face, until someone lifted her off me. My gag was removed and my hands and feet were gently untied. Had it not been for Poppy's wet tongue and the warmth of her body against mine, I would have thought this was a hallucination. I remembered nothing more until I woke in hospital to see my wrists bandaged and a drip attached to my arm. A nurse reassured me that I had been dehydrated but was now well on the road to recovery.

'We'll have you out of here in no time,' she said briskly, her round face creased in a smile.

'Where's Poppy? Where's my dog? Is she all right?'

'I'm afraid we can't allow dogs in here,' she said, muttering about the risk of infection. 'I've heard all about Poppy from your friends.' Her smile broadened into a grin. 'They warned me that you'd be asking about your dog. Now, there's no need to fret. Your friends asked me to assure you that your dog's in good hands, so you just rest and get better, and you'll soon be reunited with her. She's being taken care of by someone called Holly.'

I laughed, but was too tired to explain that Holly was Jane's old dog. The nurse assured me I would soon be discharged from hospital, with nothing worse than a few bruises, and welts on my wrists and ankles that were already beginning to heal. I drifted back to sleep, exhausted but relieved to know that I had been rescued, and Poppy was safe. The nurse was right. The following morning, the doctor confirmed that I could go home.

As I was collecting my few belongings, and considering whether to lash out on a taxi to the station, I was surprised to see Toby walk into the ward. As I began stammering that it was too late for visitors because I was leaving, he smiled.

'Why do you think I'm here?' he asked.

'To see me,' I replied.

'Let's put it another way,' he said. 'How are you planning to get home?'

'The same way I got here, I suppose.'

He shook his head. 'Your taxi is waiting, and we need to get going or I'll be stung for more parking charges. Do you know what this is costing me? Come on. Give me your bag and let's go.'

For a second, I was too surprised to respond.

'There's no need to thank me,' he added a little sharply.

'How did you know I was going home today?'

'Hannah found out. Don't ask me how. She has a way of finding out what's going on. I'm a bit worried she's going to turn out like Maud.' He laughed. 'Now come on, before my parking ticket runs out.'

I still felt wobbly, and was too weak to protest that there was no need to make a fuss. Muttering my thanks, I followed him out of the hospital. It was wonderful to be out of doors. The sun was shining and an invigorating breeze picked up as we hurried to the car. Revived by the fresh air, I felt lucky that my friends were so considerate. As we drove out of the hospital car park, Toby explained that he and Hannah had agreed not to tell to my mother about my terrifying experience. Hannah had called her to say that I was unable to go to London that weekend after all. My mother hadn't been very happy about it. Not unreasonably, she had complained bitterly at my not calling her myself. Hannah had done her best to mollify her by saying that we were unexpectedly very busy at the café. It was lucky my mother didn't live in the village, or she would have known the café was closed.

Although I felt guilty for hiding the truth from my mother, I was grateful for Hannah's intervention. It was far better to let my mother know what had happened when I had recovered and could play it down, than have her worrying and making a fuss over me while I was still feeling shaken. This way, I could tell her about my ordeal in my own time, if at all. Driving away from London, I seemed to be leaving the events of the past few days behind. Once my wrists had healed, there was actually no need for anyone other than my close friends to know what had happened. Of course, Barry and Richard knew all about it. I could only hope that Barry wouldn't tell Maud because, once she knew, the whole village would hear about it. But I resolved to keep the news from my mother for as long as possible. It was all over, and there was no need to upset her.

'It was all Poppy's doing,' Hannah told me once I was back in Ashton Mead.

I was sitting propped up on my sofa, with a tray of tea things on the table beside me, and Poppy lying contentedly at my feet, growling softly as I tickled her with my toes. As soon as I finished my tea, she wagged her tail and leapt onto my chest, licking my face, as Hannah refilled my cup.

'You need to keep drinking,' Hannah said solicitously. 'The hospital doctor said you were dehydrated.'

'It's true, I was, but they put me on a drip for twenty-four hours, and since I got back home I've drunk so much tea I could burst. But I won't say no to another one of your scones.'

'With cream and jam?'

I nodded happily. 'And butter. What the hell. I didn't eat for a day.'

Pushing Poppy away from my plate, which she was eyeing eagerly, I munched happily as Hannah and Toby related the story of my rescue in full. Toby had told me snatches of it in the car on the way home, but Hannah was itching to give me a detailed account of how they had found me.

'Someone came across Poppy wandering along a street in Chiswick all by herself,' Toby began.

Hannah interrupted him to tell Poppy how clever she was, and we all spent a few minutes petting her while she lay on her back, revelling in the attention.

'She was by herself,' Toby resumed his account. 'The guy who found her took her to a vet who found her chip.'

'They already knew she wasn't a stray because of her lead and collar,' Hannah interjected.

'The vet kept her overnight,' Toby went on, 'after leaving you a couple of messages. As he was unable to contact you, he decided to ring the police station in Swindon before sending Poppy to a shelter. He said Poppy was obviously so healthy, he couldn't believe she was unwanted.'

He paused in his recitation again so we could all make a fuss of Poppy.

'Most police officers would have made one attempt to contact you, if that, and Poppy would have been sent to a shelter, but by a stroke of luck Barry was on duty and overheard what had happened.'

'He wasn't prepared to give up so easily,' Hannah said.

'Barry got in touch with Hannah, and alerted her to the fact that Poppy had been found wandering around in London.'

Again Toby and Hannah suspended their story while we all petted Poppy.

'I knew something was wrong when you didn't turn up for work, and I couldn't get hold of you,' Hannah took up the story. 'We started to ask around to see if anyone knew where you were, and discovered Maud still had a spare key to your house, from before you moved in, so first thing in the morning Toby and I went to Rosecroft with Barry, but there was no sign of you. We went to collect Poppy – Barry drove us to London in a police car.' She grinned at the memory. 'If we hadn't all been so worried about you, it would have been amazing.'

Toby grunted. 'He nearly killed us jumping red lights.'

'He had his siren on,' Hannah replied. 'Anyway, we took Poppy back to where she'd been discovered and she led us to Steve's house.'

The story was interrupted again as we all made a fuss of Poppy for being so clever.

'Once we got to the house, she went crazy,' Hannah continued. 'You know how excited she gets. Well, imagine that times a hundred.'

I grabbed Poppy and held her close.

'Having met Isobel, I'll never call you crazy again,' I told her.

Toby took up the story. 'She was barking and scratching at the front door.'

'We couldn't drag her away,' Hannah said.

'Steve opened the door and Poppy dashed inside. He insisted he hadn't seen you, but Poppy refused to leave the house and kept barking and barking, straining to go upstairs. In the end we had to physically drag her away. But we both suspected Steve was lying.'

'We trusted Poppy,' Hannah explained, and I nodded, thinking that was just as well. 'Barry called for backup.

Toby and me were standing outside the house, with Poppy, who was still desperate to get back inside, when three police cars drew up. We tried to get back in the house again, but this time no one answered the bell. We had six uniformed police officers with us, as well as Barry, who insisted we had to get into the house. He said it was a matter of life and death.'

'He was right,' Toby added solemnly.

'Later on we discovered that Barry had convinced the inspector in charge of the murder investigation to rush through an emergency search warrant. Apparently she was afraid you knew too much, and as a result of your interference had quite possibly become a target for the murderer. She said you had acted with – well, never mind that. She wasn't very complimentary.'

'She probably thinks I'm an idiot,' I said cheerfully.

'Yes, well, she's not the only one,' Toby muttered. 'You should have gone to the police in the first place.'

'They would never have believed me,' I replied, stung by his criticism. 'And besides, when I went to Chiswick, I had no idea Isobel had killed Steve's wife. We all thought Isobel was dead.'

'Anyway, never mind that,' Hannah interrupted our exchange before either of us became tetchy. 'As soon as we got back in the house we let Poppy off the lead and she raced upstairs and began barking at the trapdoor to the loft. The police opened it and there you were, trussed up like a Christmas turkey.'

38

I WAS SAFE, BUT only for now.

'What about Steve and Isobel?' I asked. 'Are they still out there?'

'Don't worry,' Toby told me. 'The police picked them up at St Pancras station, trying to board a train to France. They must have slipped out through the back door while we were outside the front, waiting for the police.'

'We were only out there for a few minutes before backup arrived,' Hannah added.

'Our arrival must have put the wind up them and they panicked and ran,' Toby said.

'They left me tied up in the loft,' I said. 'If you hadn't found me –'

There was no need to complete my sentence.

'They'll get what's coming to them,' Hannah said fiercely. 'The police want you to go to Swindon to make a statement, when you feel strong enough. Barry said they'll send a police car for you, and if they don't, he'll take you there himself. He's been a real brick in all this. I don't know what we would have done without him.'

The next day, Barry picked me up, in his uniform, and drove me to Swindon in a police car. I felt like a criminal as we drove out of Ashton Mead, past several local residents.

'Don't worry about them,' Barry reassured me. 'No one's going to think you've been arrested. Everyone knows what happened.'

I thanked him, although it was hardly reassuring to know that the story of my capture was all over the village. I wondered how I was going to show my face in The Plough again.

'This is a formality,' the inspector told me kindly. 'My colleagues in London saw what had been done to you. There's no requirement for you to go into details. Isobel Jones is refusing to answer any questions, but Steven Collins has made a full confession. As well as facing charges for assault and kidnap, he's confessed to murdering his wife, and to perverting the course of justice, and framing Richard Jones for the murder.'

'No, no,' I blurted out. 'That's not what happened. He's lying to you to protect Isobel.'

I told her what I had heard.

'So to be clear,' the inspector said, 'you heard them say it was Isobel Jones who committed the murder, and Steve helped her to conceal the crime and then claimed responsibility?'

I nodded. 'That's what they both said. Isobel told me she had a fight with Steve's wife, and she was acting in self-defence. But if that was true, why did they try to cover it up?'

'And you're saying Steve was an accessory to the murder, not the perpetrator?'

'Yes, he did it to save Isobel. He would have done anything for her, even cover up the murder of his own wife. That's why he agreed to her plan to kill me. They were going to leave me to starve to death in the loft, and then put my body in the boot of their car and dump me in a quiet stretch of the river. I heard them discussing it. There's no question it was all her idea, but he seemed happy to go along with it. They were going to weigh me down with bricks so if my body was ever found, by then there would be no evidence of my having been tied up,' I added with a shudder, remembering the ravaged face of Steve's wife.

The inspector nodded. 'We found bricks in the boot of his car,' she said quietly.

In spite of everything that had happened, hearing proof of Isobel's cold-blooded plan, I was shocked. While I had been lying in the loft, she and Steve had been carefully preparing to dispose of my corpse. Whatever the reason for the fatal attack on Steve's wife, my death had been premeditated.

'Are you feeling all right?' the inspector enquired. 'You've gone very pale. Would you like a glass of water?'

'I'm fine,' I fibbed. 'I'm just glad you caught them. But don't you think they'll come after me?' I did my best to sound calm, but my voice wobbled as I asked, 'I mean, they'll want me dead, won't they? I'm the main witness against them. And Isobel's going to want her revenge.'

As long as Isobel and Steve remained in custody, they would be unable to silence me, but I didn't doubt that Isobel was crazy enough to try anything once she was at liberty. Probably she was already planning to send Steve to kill me.

The inspector reassured me. 'Bail is rarely granted for someone charged with murder. In this case, with the evidence against them, the court will consider they both pose a risk to public safety, as well as to you,' she added quietly. 'Isobel hasn't helped her case by ranting about wanting to kill Richard.'

'Richard? Why Richard?'

'It seems she expected him to protect her by confessing to killing Steve's wife.' She shook her head. 'It was really quite bizarre, listening to their conversation, once he agreed to see her. But we come across some very sick individuals in the course of our work.'

'What happened when they met?'

'Isobel basically ordered him to confess to killing Steve's wife so that she and Steve could be released. How on earth she expected Richard to comply is beyond me. Isobel is a very sick woman. But she'll stand trial and be convicted. No jury is going to believe a word she says. She's far too dangerous to ever be released.'

'What about Steve?'

'He may not have killed his wife, but he was certainly complicit in covering up the murder, and he was planning to kill you and dispose of your body. He's made a full confession, but he still insists that he was right to do what he did to protect Isobel. Those two are safely behind bars,' she assured me grimly. 'And I don't think they'll ever be free again. Thanks to you, two evil psychopaths can no longer pose a threat to anyone else who gets in their way.'

'It's thanks to Poppy, really,' I replied, and for the first time I saw the inspector's guarded features break into a smile.

'That's true' she agreed. 'If it weren't for your dog, you might well not have been discovered in time, and Steve and Isobel would probably have got away.'

And I would be dead, I thought, suppressing a shiver.

39

After my traumatic experience, Hannah insisted I take at least a fortnight off work.

'Rest for as long as you need,' she told me.

'So you're telling me you can manage without me?' I replied, with mock dismay. 'Well, I'm disappointed.'

But I was secretly relieved to be given time at home while my physical wounds began to heal. It was going to take me longer to recover from the psychological effects of my capture. Without the reassurance of knowing Isobel and Steve were behind bars, I probably would have struggled to sleep at night, even with Poppy lying across my feet watching over me. Not until I learned their application for bail had definitely been turned down did I begin to relax. It took me a while to recover my physical strength, and longer to regain the confidence to go out and face the world. After nearly two weeks, I began to feel bored and realised it was time to return to work. I couldn't hide behind my front door forever, only going out to take Poppy for a walk along the most secluded paths through the local woods. The weals on my wrists had left faint streaks which were by now barely noticeable. In time, I had been assured, they were likely to fade completely. The appearance of my minor disfigurement didn't bother me, but for a while every time I saw my scars they reminded me of my painful ordeal.

The first morning I went back to the café I was apprehensive, expecting that everyone would stare at me and whisper, but in the event no one seemed to take any notice of my return. June had arrived, and with it warm weather, and many of our customers weren't local and knew nothing about my history. The villagers who came into the café were mostly considerate, or else uninterested in my experience. Only a couple told me that they were pleased to see me back in the tea shop. Anyone listening might have assumed I had been on holiday. All the same, I was abrupt in my thanks, hoping to make it clear I had no wish to talk about what had happened to me. My ordeal was behind me now, and I was determined not to dwell on it. My memories began to fade, like my scars, until they seemed no more than the recollection of a bad dream.

My most challenging moment came when Dana Flack turned up at the café to request an interview with me. Telling her that I had no comment provoked a predictable response. She claimed that I had no business obstructing her in her pursuit of the truth, and she insisted that the public had a right to be kept fully informed. According to Dana, my remaining silent on the subject was a selfish refusal to share my news with the world at large. I couldn't think of anything worse than 'the world at large' knowing all the details of my suffering.

Dana was only doing her job, but her hectoring riled me. In the end, I told her firmly that the police had forbidden me from saying a word about it, and thankfully she believed my lie. The last thing I wanted was to see my name splashed all over the local paper, with an account of my encounter with a murderous lunatic, accompanied by all kinds of melodramatic embellishments. On reflection, I didn't blame Dana for attempting to persuade me to agree to an interview. Even without any hyperbole, the truth alone would have made a sensational story for her paper.

For several weeks after returning to work, I stayed at home in the evenings, unwilling to face anyone in a social situation, where I would be under pressure to say more than 'Would you like hot water with your tea?' and 'Cream or butter with your scones?' Hannah did her best to coax me into joining her at The Plough. She said that altering my lifestyle meant affording Isobel some kind of victory over me.

'You can't let her influence the way you live your life,' she insisted.

'I'm not letting her influence me at all.'

'Emily, don't you see that by hiding away at home, you're letting that psycho win. You're not going to do that, are you?'

Of course, Hannah was right. Having survived Isobel's aggression, it would be stupid to let my resulting anxiety ruin my life from then on. So I promised to go to the pub one evening, and I promised it would be soon. I just wasn't quite ready yet.

One warm evening, Poppy and I were hurrying along the lane on our way home from work when someone called my name. Turning, I was taken aback to see Adam standing outside The Laurels. This time, Poppy greeted him by wagging her tail cautiously. I wasn't sure what had happened to change her mind about him, and was surprised to see she had decided to accept him. But her offer of friendship came too late.

'What are you doing here?' I demanded furiously. 'How can you show your face in the village after the way you treated Hannah?'

Adam looked stunned. 'I – I'm here to see my father. I never meant to hurt Hannah –' he stammered, as he walked towards me. 'I just couldn't face her again.' He fell silent as he reached me.

'You dumped her without a word of explanation.'

He shook his head. 'No, it wasn't like that.'

'What was it like for you, then?'

'I visited Steve and my mother told me what had happened. At first I couldn't believe it. But at the same time, I knew it was true. I couldn't carry on seeing Hannah after that, as though nothing had happened. How could I face her, knowing my own mother was involved in covering up a murder? I promised my mother I would keep her vile crime a secret. The fact is, she's – she's not well, Emily. She's sick. But I couldn't stay silent, not when my father was suspected of being responsible for a crime he hadn't committed.'

'So that's why you contacted the police?'

'Yes. I told them the truth, that my father had nothing to do with it, and it was all my mother's doing. And then I panicked and –' He shrugged. 'I'm not proud of it, but the truth is I ran away and hid in a friend's house, just while I tried to work out what to do. It wasn't easy, you know, being forced to choose between my parents. But my father did nothing wrong. I couldn't let him suffer any more. It was a terrible situation to find myself in. It still is.'

Anger made me harsh. 'And what about Hannah? Didn't you care about her feelings at all, or were you too busy feeling sorry for yourself?'

'Hannah's better off without me in her life. She deserves someone decent, not the son of a vicious maniac.'

I took a deep breath. 'Listen, Adam, Hannah wants to see you, I know she does. At least you could go and talk to her and explain. You can't just abandon her without a word.'

Adam sighed. 'You're right. I let her down. Do you think she'll speak to me again? At least I could apologise to her. I don't dare hope she can forgive me.' He sighed again.

'That's between you and her. But you do need to contact her and tell her what's been going on.'

I didn't add that of all the people I had ever met, Hannah was the least likely to withhold sympathy, or hold a grudge.

'My father told me what happened to you,' he said hesitantly. 'I'm so sorry. My mother was always volatile. We all witnessed her violent rages, I mean, really violent, but we had no idea... none of us had any idea how far she would go. My father used to handle her temper, and he made sure she stayed on her medication, but without him there to keep her on track, something tipped her over the edge.'

'This must be really hard for you,' I conceded, relenting at the sight of his obvious distress.

It was easy to accuse Adam of ignoring Hannah's feelings. Wrapped up in my own suffering, I hadn't paused to consider how Isobel's psychosis would affect others. For all the public discussions about raising awareness of mental health issues, private suffering persisted. Learning that Isobel had committed one murder, and had been planning another, must have been a dreadful shock for all her family. I couldn't imagine how distraught they must be about her behaviour. With that in mind, I determined to be as kind as possible to Richard and Adam. It was easy to forget that people often hid mental and emotional pain; behind a façade of composure they might be a seething maelstrom of anguish and despair.

'I wanted to ask you a favour,' Adam said. 'Of course, I realise my family have no right to expect any help from you, and I won't be offended if you refuse. It would be perfectly reasonable if you preferred not to listen to me at all. I'd understand.'

'What do you want from me?' I asked gruffly.

It could do no harm to listen to his request, even though I was unlikely to grant it.

'It's not for me, it's for my father. He's suffered terribly, and I'm worried about him. He won't leave the house and he's convinced everyone here wants to lynch him.'

'None of this was his fault,' I replied.

'Thank you for that. Of course, I've told him he's done nothing wrong, but he thinks everyone's going to turn their backs on him. He's made up his mind to leave the village before he's hounded out.'

'That's ridiculous,' I said. 'No one blames him for what happened, and no one wants to force him to leave Ashton Mead.'

After some discussion, I agreed to call on Richard that evening and invite him to accompany me to The Plough, but only on condition that Adam came too. He agreed unwillingly. Richard looked surprised to see me on his doorstep. He seemed reluctant to speak to me, but he couldn't ignore Poppy who jumped up at him, licking his hands and growling with pleasure on seeing him again. When I explained that I was nervous about going to The Plough on my own, and hoped he would join me, he gazed at me sceptically.

'Did Adam put you up to this?' he asked.

'What if I did?' Adam said, joining us. 'Emily wants to see you, and I'm sure other people here will too.'

'No one blames you for what happened,' I assured him. 'You've been a victim of the situation just as much as me. More, in fact.'

In a way that was true. Where I had suffered a relatively brief interlude of torment, Richard had lost his wife of many years to the dark forces of insanity, or evil. Isobel had given him two sons, and had lived with him for thirty years. His whole life had been snatched away. With a sigh, Richard agreed to accompany me and Adam to the pub. There was a faint hush when we entered the bar, and then Tess's voice rang out, talking to someone at the bar.

'Are you going to pay for that pint, or what?'

As if at a signal, a mutter of voices resumed, reassured that if Tess was grumbling to a customer, everything was normal. Meanwhile, at the periphery of my vision I watched Adam crouch at Hannah's side and speak quietly to her. A moment later they left the bar together. It wasn't long before they returned, hand in hand. Hannah was beaming. Watching her face, I felt like crying. My plan to reunite them had gone horribly awry, but they had found their way back to one another in the end anyway. Passing me on her way to collect her bag, she put her hand on my shoulder.

'Thank you,' she murmured.

'What for?' I asked.

'For everything.'

I wanted to ask her what she meant, but she was already walking away, arm in arm with Adam. Our mutual confidences and congratulations would have to wait until we were back at work in the Sunshine Tea Shoppe the next morning.

Just then, Cliff approached our table to collect empty glasses. 'We're pleased to see you in here again,' he told Richard.

'Surprised, mind,' Tess added, overhearing Cliff's hearty greeting. 'We never thought he'd be back.' She lowered her voice, but everyone heard when she said, 'We all thought he'd done away with his wife.'

Cliff muttered to her, and a moment later she brought Richard a pint on the house. 'That's to welcome you to the village,' she mumbled.

Richard grinned, understanding that he had been accepted into the village community. I suspected his generosity in buying rounds had not gone unnoticed.

'What about me?' I piped up. 'I'm a newcomer to the village too. I've never been offered a drink on the house.'

'Hardly a newcomer,' Tess scoffed. 'Like it or not, you and Poppy belong here, so you might as well get used to it.'

'What Tess means is that you can pay for your own drinks, like everyone else,' an old man called out from the corner of the bar, adding that his was a pint if I was going to the bar.

'Did everyone suspect me of murder?' Richard asked sadly, gazing around at my friends.

For a moment no one answered. Then Poppy trotted over to Richard and lay down at his feet, her tail tapping on the floor.

'Not everyone,' I replied. 'Poppy always trusted you.'

Richard smiled. 'Well,' he said, leaning down to pet her, 'that's a start.'

Suddenly everyone was smiling and welcoming the latest newcomer to Ashton Mead. As for me, I was happy to be accepted as an established resident of the village that had become my home.

Acknowledgements

I would like to thank all the team at Crime and Mystery Club for having continued faith in my stories: Ion, Claire, Ellie, Hollie, Paru and Sarah. This book would never have happened without you. My thanks also go to Steven for his skilled editorial work, to Nick for his eagle-eyed proofreading, and Steve for his brilliant cover design incorporating Phillipa's lovely original artwork. Producing a book is a real team effort, and I am fortunate to have such a dedicated team of experts supporting my writing.

I am grateful to the owners of a certain little rescue dog.

As for the real Poppy, who inspired this story, I wish you a long and healthy life filled with happiness, treats, and walks in the grass.

If you enjoyed *Barking Mad*, don't miss *Barking Up the Right Tree*, the first Poppy Mystery Tale!

After losing her job and her boyfriend, Emily is devastated. As she is puzzling over what to do with the rest of her life, she is surprised to learn that her great aunt has died, leaving Emily her cottage in the picturesque Wiltshire village of Ashton Mead. But there is one condition to her inheritance: she finds herself the unwilling owner of a pet. Not knowing what to expect, Emily sets off for the village, hoping to make a new life for herself.

In Ashton Mead, she soon makes friends with Hannah who runs the Sunshine Tea Shoppe and meets other residents of the village where she decides to settle. All is going well... until Emily's ex-boyfriend turns up and against the advice of her new friends, she takes him back.

When Emily decides to investigate the mysterious disappearance of a neighbour, she unwittingly puts her own life in danger...

'Fun and heartwarming with all the mystery and tight plotting you'd expect from Leigh Russell'

VICTORIA SELMAN, *Sunday Times* bestselling author of *Truly, Darkly, Deeply*

CRIMEANDMYSTERYCLUB.CO.UK/BARKING-UP-THE-RIGHT-TREE